MARY HIGGINS CLARK

Let Me Call You Sweetheart

A NOVEL

POCKET BOOKS

New York   London   Toronto   Sydney   Tokyo   Singapore

First published in Great Britain by Simon & Schuster, 1995
First published in paperback by Pocket Books, 1996
An imprint of Simon & Schuster Ltd
A Viacom Company

Simon & Schuster Ltd
West Garden Place
Kendal Street
London W2 2AQ

Simon & Schuster of Australia Pty Ltd
Sydney

A CIP catalogue record for this book is available from the British
Library.

ISBN 0-671-85347-3

Printed and bound in Great Britain by Caledonian International
Book Manufacturing, Glasgow

ACKNOWLEDGEMENTS

No man is an island and no writer, at least not this one, writes alone. Special glowing thanks to my editors, Michael V. Korda and Chuck Adams, who are always the sine qua non of my books from conception to publication. Particularly and especially with this one and at this time, they've been wonderful.

A thousand thanks always to Eugene H. Winick, my literary agent, and Lisl Cade, my publicist. Their help is immeasurable.

A writer needs expert counsel. This book concerns plastic surgery. My thanks to Dr. Bennett C. Rothenberg of Saint Barnabas Hospital, Livingston, New Jersey, for his expert medical advice. Kudos to Kim White of the New Jersey Department of Corrections for her assistance. And once again, Ina Winick has vetted for me the psychological aspects of the story line. Thank you, Ina.

My offspring, all five of them, read the work in progress. From them I get much sound advice—legal: "Make sure you sequester the jury . . ."; or dialogue: "No one our age would say that. Put it this way . . ."—and always cheery encouragement. Thanks, kids.

Finally, my ten-year-old granddaughter, Liz, who in many ways was the role model for Robin. I would ask her, "Liz, what would you say if this were happening . . . ?" Her suggestions were "awesome."

I love you, one and all.

*For my Villa Maria Academy classmates
in this special year,
with a particularly loving tip of the hat to
Joan LaMotte Nye
June Langren Crabtree
Marjorie Lashley Quinlan
Joan Molloy Hoffman*

and in joyous memory of Dorothea Bible Davis

Heap not on this mound
    Roses that she loved so well;
Why bewilder her with roses,
    That she cannot see or smell?

Edna St. Vincent Millay,
"Epitaph"

As often as humanly possible he tried to put Suzanne out of his mind. Sometimes he achieved peace for a few hours or even managed to sleep through the night. It was the only way he could function, go about the daily business of living.

Did he still love her or only hate her? He could never be sure. She had been so beautiful, with those luminous mocking eyes, that cloud of dark hair, those lips that could smile so invitingly or pout so easily, like a child being refused a sweet.

In his mind she was always there, as she had looked in that last moment of her life, taunting him then turning her back on him.

And now, nearly eleven years later, Kerry McGrath would not let Suzanne rest. Questions and more questions! It could not be tolerated. She had to be stopped.

Let the dead bury the dead. That's the old saying, he thought, and it's still true. She would be stopped, no matter what.

1

Kerry smoothed down the skirt of her dark green suit, straightened the narrow gold chain on her neck and ran her fingers through her collar-length, dusky blond hair. Her entire afternoon had been a mad rush, leaving the courthouse at two-thirty, picking up Robin at school, driving from Hohokus through the heavy traffic of Routes 17 and 4, then over the George Washington Bridge to Manhattan, finally parking the car and arriving at the doctor's office just in time for Robin's four o'clock appointment.

Now, after all the rush, Kerry could only sit and wait to be summoned into the examining room, wishing that she'd been allowed to be with Robin while the stitches were removed. But the nurse had been adamant. "During a procedure, Dr. Smith will not permit anyone except the nurse in the room with a patient."

"But she's only ten!" Kerry had protested, then had closed her lips and reminded herself that she should be grateful that Dr. Smith was the one who had been called in after the accident. The nurses at St. Luke's-Roosevelt had assured her that he was a wonderful plastic surgeon. The emergency room doctor had even called him a miracle worker.

Reflecting back on that day, a week ago, Kerry realized she still hadn't recovered from the shock of that phone call. She'd been working late in her office at the courthouse in Hackensack, preparing for the murder case she would be prosecuting, taking advantage of the fact that Robin's father, her ex-husband, Bob Kinellen, had unexpectedly invited Robin to see New York City's Big Apple Circus, followed by dinner.

At six-thirty her phone had rung. It was Bob. There had been an accident. A van had rammed into his Jaguar while he was pulling out of the parking garage. Robin's face had been cut by flying glass. She'd been rushed to St. Luke's-Roosevelt, and a plastic surgeon had been called. Otherwise she seemed fine, although she was being examined for internal injuries.

Remembering that terrible evening, Kerry shook her head. She tried to push out of her mind the agony of the hurried drive into New York, dry sobs shaking her body, her lips forming only one word, "please," her mind racing with the rest of the prayer, *Please God, don't let her die, she's all I have. Please, she's just a baby. Don't take her from me . . .*

Robin was already in surgery when Kerry had arrived at the hospital, so she had sat in the waiting room, Bob next to her—with him but not with him. He had a wife and two other children now. Kerry could still feel the overwhelming sensation of relief she had experienced when Dr. Smith had finally appeared, and in a formal and oddly condescending manner had said, "Fortunately the lacerations did not deeply penetrate the dermis. Robin will not be scarred. I want to see her in my office in one week."

The cuts proved to be her only injuries, and Robin had bounced back from the accident, missing only two days of school. She had seemed to be somewhat proud of her bandages. It was only today, on their way into New York for the appointment, that she'd sounded frightened when she asked, "I will be okay, won't I, Mom? I mean my face won't be all messed up?"

With her wide blue eyes, oval face, high forehead and sculpted features, Robin was a beautiful child and the image of her father. Kerry had reassured her with a heartiness she hoped was truthful. Now, to distract herself, Kerry looked around the waiting room. It was tastefully furnished with several couches and chairs covered in a small floral print design. The lights were soft, the carpeting luxurious.

A woman who appeared to be in her early forties, wearing a bandage across her nose, was among those waiting to be called inside. Another, who looked somewhat anxious, was confiding to her attractive companion: "Now that I'm here, I'm glad you made me come. You look fabulous."

She does, Kerry thought as she self-consciously reached into her bag for her compact. Snapping it open, she examined herself in the mirror, deciding that today she looked every minute of her thirty-six years. She was aware that many people found her attractive, but still she remained self-conscious about her looks. She brushed the powder puff over the bridge of her nose, trying to cover the spray of detested freckles, studied her eyes and decided that whenever she was tired, as she was today, their hazel color changed from green to muddy brown. She tucked a stray strand of hair behind her ear, then with a sigh closed the compact and smoothed back the half bang that needed trimming.

Anxiously she fastened her gaze on the door that led to the examining rooms. Why was it taking so long to remove Robin's stitches? she wondered. Could there be complications?

A moment later the door opened. Kerry looked up expectantly. Instead of Robin, however, there emerged a young woman who seemed to be in her mid-twenties, a cloud of dark hair framing the petulant beauty of her face.

I wonder if she always looked like that, Kerry mused, as she studied the high cheekbones, straight nose, exquisitely shaped pouty lips, luminous eyes, arched brows.

Perhaps sensing her gaze, the young woman looked quizzically at Kerry as she passed her.

Kerry's throat tightened. I know you, she thought. But from where? She swallowed, her mouth suddenly dry. That face—I've seen her before.

Once the woman had left, Kerry went over to the receptionist and explained that she thought she might know the lady who just came out of the doctor's office. Who was she?

The name Barbara Tompkins, however, meant nothing to her. She must have been mistaken. Still, when she sat down again, an overwhelming sense of déjà vu filled her mind. The effect was so chilling, she actually shivered.

2

Kate Carpenter regarded the patients in the doctor's waiting room with something of a jaundiced eye. She had been with Dr. Charles Smith as a surgical nurse for four years, working with him on the operations he performed in the office. Quite simply, she considered him a genius.

She herself had never been tempted to have him work on her. Fiftyish, sturdily built with a pleasant face and graying hair, she described herself to her friends as a plastic surgery counterrevolutionary: "What you see is what you get."

Totally in sympathy with clients who had genuine problems,

she felt mild contempt for the men and women who came in for procedure after procedure in their relentless pursuit of physical perfection. "On the other hand," as she told her husband, "they're paying my salary."

Sometimes Kate Carpenter wondered why she stayed with Dr. Smith. He was so brusque with everyone, patients as well as staff, that he often seemed rude. He seldom praised but never missed an opportunity to sarcastically point out the smallest error. But then again, she decided, the pay and benefits were excellent, and it was a genuine thrill to watch Dr. Smith at work.

Except that lately she had noticed he was getting increasingly bad tempered. Potential new clients, directed to him because of his excellent reputation, were offended by his manner and more and more frequently were canceling scheduled procedures. The only ones he seemed to treat with flattering care were the recipients of the special "look," and that was another thing that bothered Carpenter.

And in addition to his being irascible, in these last months she had noticed that the doctor seemed to be detached, even remote. Sometimes, when she spoke to him, he looked at her blankly, as though his mind were far away.

She glanced at her watch. As she had expected, after Dr. Smith finished examining Barbara Tompkins, the latest recipient of the "look," he had gone into his private office and closed the door.

What did he do in there? she wondered. He had to realize that he was running late. That little girl, Robin, had been sitting alone in examining room 3 for half an hour, and there were other patients in the waiting room. But she had noticed that after the doctor saw one of the special patients, he always seemed to need time to himself.

"Mrs. Carpenter . . ."

Startled, the nurse looked up from her desk. Dr. Smith was staring down at her. "I think we've kept Robin Kinellen waiting long enough," he said accusingly. Behind rimless glasses, his eyes were frosty.

3

"I don't like Dr. Smith," Robin said matter-of-factly as Kerry maneuvered the car out of the parking garage on Ninth Street off Fifth Avenue.

Kerry looked at her quickly. "Why not?"

"He's scary. At home when I go to Dr. Wilson, he always makes jokes. But Dr. Smith didn't even smile. He acted like he was mad at me. He said something about how some people are given beauty while others attain it, but in neither case must it ever be wasted."

Robin had inherited her father's stunning good looks and was indeed quite beautiful. It was true that this could someday be a burden, but why would the doctor say such an odd thing to a child? Kerry wondered.

"I'm sorry I told him I hadn't finished fastening my seat belt when the van hit Daddy's car," Robin added. "That's when Dr. Smith started lecturing me."

Kerry glanced at her daughter. Robin always fastened her seat belt. That she hadn't this time meant that Bob had started the car before she had had a chance. Kerry tried to keep anger out of her voice as she said, "Daddy probably took off out of the garage in a hurry."

"He just didn't notice I hadn't had time to buckle it," Robin said defensively, picking up on the edge in her mother's voice.

Kerry felt heartsick for her daughter. Bob Kinellen had walked out on them both when Robin was a baby. Now he was married to his senior partner's daughter and was the father of a five-year-old girl and a three-year-old boy. Robin was crazy about her father, and when he was with her he made a big fuss over her. But he disappointed her so often, calling at the last minute to break a scheduled date. Because his second wife did not like to be reminded that he had another child, Robin was never invited to his home. As a result she hardly even knew her half brother and sister.

On the rare occasion when he does come through, and finally takes her out, look what happens, Kerry thought. She struggled to hide her anger, however, deciding not to pursue the subject. Instead she said, "Why don't you try to snooze till we get to Uncle Jonathan and Aunt Grace's?"

"Okay." Robin closed her eyes. "I bet they have a present for me."

4

While they waited for Kerry and Robin to arrive for dinner, Jonathan and Grace Hoover were sharing their customary late-afternoon martini in the living room of their home in Old Tappan overlooking Lake Tappan. The setting sun was sending long shadows across the tranquil water. The trees, carefully trimmed to avoid obstructing the lake view, were glowing with the brilliant leaves they would soon relinquish.

Jonathan had built the first fire of the season, and Grace had just commented that the first frost of the season was predicted for that evening.

A handsome couple in their early sixties, they had been married nearly forty years, tied by bonds and needs that went beyond affection and habit. Over that time, they seemed almost to have grown to resemble each other: both had patrician features, framed by luxuriant heads of hair, his pure white with natural waves, hers short and curly, still peppered with traces of brown.

There was, however, a distinctive difference in their bodies. Jonathan sat tall and erect in a high-backed wing chair, while Grace reclined on a sofa opposite him, an afghan over her useless legs, her bent fingers inert in her lap, a wheelchair nearby. For years a victim of rheumatoid arthritis, she had become increasingly more disabled.

Jonathan had remained devoted to her during the whole ordeal. The senior partner of a major New Jersey law firm specializing in high-profile civil suits, he had also held the position of state senator for some twenty years but had several times turned down the opportunity to run for governor. "I can do enough good or harm in the senate," was his often-quoted remark, "and anyhow, I don't think I'd win."

Anyone who knew him well didn't believe his protests. They knew Grace was the reason he had chosen to avoid the demands of gubernatorial life, and secretly they wondered if he didn't harbor some vague resentment that her condition had held him back. If he did, however, he certainly never showed it.

Now as Grace sipped her martini, she sighed. "I honestly believe this is my favorite time of year," she said, "it's so beautiful, isn't it? This kind of day makes me remember taking the train to Princeton from Bryn Mawr for the football games, watching them with you, going to the Nassau Inn for dinner . . ."

"And staying at your aunt's house and her waiting up to be sure you were safely in before she went to bed," Jonathan chuckled. "I used to pray that just once the old bat would fall asleep early, but she kept a perfect record."

Grace smiled. "The minute we would pull up in front of the house, the porch light started blinking." Then she glanced anxiously at the clock on the mantel. "Aren't they running late? I hate to think of Kerry and Robin in the thick of the commuter traffic. Especially after what happened last week."

"Kerry's a good driver," Jonathan reassured her. "Don't worry. They'll be here any minute."

"I know. It's just . . ." The sentence did not have to be completed; Jonathan understood fully. Ever since twenty-one-year-old Kerry, about to start law school, had answered their ad for a house-sitter, they'd come to think of her as a surrogate daughter. That had been fifteen years ago, and during that time Jonathan had been of frequent help to Kerry in guiding and shaping her career, most recently using his influence to have her name included on the governor's shortlist of candidates for a judgeship.

Ten minutes later the welcome sound of door chimes heralded Kerry and Robin's arrival. As Robin had predicted, there was a gift waiting for her, a book and a quiz game for her computer. After dinner she took the book into the library and curled up in a chair while the adults lingered over coffee.

With Robin out of earshot, Grace quietly asked, "Kerry, those marks on Robin's face *will* fade, won't they?"

"I asked Dr. Smith the same thing when I saw them. He not only practically guaranteed their disappearance, he made me feel as though I'd insulted him by expressing any concern about them. I have to tell you I have a hunch the good doctor has one big ego. Still, last week at the hospital, the emergency room doctor absolutely assured me that Smith is a fine plastic surgeon. In fact, he called him a miracle worker."

As she sipped the last of her coffee, Kerry thought about the woman she had seen earlier in Dr. Smith's office. She looked across the table at Jonathan and Grace. "An odd thing happened while I was waiting for Robin. There was someone in Dr. Smith's office who looked so familiar," she said. "I even asked the receptionist what her name was. I'm sure I don't know her, but I just couldn't shake the sensation that we had met before. She gave me a creepy feeling. Isn't that odd?"

"What did she look like?" Grace asked.

"A knockout in a kind of come-hither, sensually provocative way," Kerry reflected. "I think the lips gave her that look. They were kind of full and pouty. I know: Maybe she was one of Bob's old girlfriends, and I had just repressed that memory." She shrugged. "Oh well, it's going to bug me till I figure it out."

5

You've changed my life, Dr. Smith . . . That was what Barbara Tompkins had said to him as she left his office earlier today. And he knew it was true. He had changed her and, in the process, her life. From a plain, almost mousy woman who looked older than her twenty-six years, he'd transformed her into a young beauty. More than a beauty, actually. Now she had spirit. She wasn't the same insecure woman who had come to him a year ago.

At the time she had been working in a small public relations firm in Albany. "I saw what you did for one of our clients," she had said when she came into his office that first day. "I just inherited some money from my aunt. Can you make me pretty?"

He had done more than that—he had transformed her. He had made her beautiful. Now Barbara was working in Manhattan at a large, prestigious P.R. firm. She had always had brains, but combining those brains with that special kind of beauty had truly changed her life.

Dr. Smith saw his last patient for the day at six-thirty. Then he walked the three blocks down Fifth Avenue to his converted carriage house in Washington Mews.

It was his habit each day to go home, relax over a bourbon and soda while watching the evening news and then decide where he wanted to dine. He lived alone and almost never ate in.

Tonight an unaccustomed restlessness overcame him. Of all the women, Barbara Tompkins was the one most like *her*. Just seeing her was an emotional, almost cathartic experience. He had overheard Barbara chatting with Mrs. Carpenter, telling her that she was taking a client to dinner that night in the Oak Room at the Plaza Hotel.

Almost reluctantly he got up. What would happen next was inevitable. He would go to the Oak Bar, look into the Oak Room restaurant, see if there was a small table from which he could observe Barbara while he dined. With any luck she wouldn't be aware of him. But even if she was, even if she saw him, he would merely wave. She had no reason to think that he was following her.

6

After they got home from dinner with Jonathan and Grace, and long after Robin was asleep, Kerry continued to work. Her office was in the study of the house she had moved to after Bob had left them and she sold the house they had bought together. She had been able to get the new place at a good price, when the real estate market was low, and she was grateful she had—she loved it. Fifty years old, it was a roomy Cape Cod with double dormers, set on a heavily treed two-acre lot. The only time she didn't love it was when the leaves began to fall, tons and tons of them. That would begin soon, she thought with a sigh.

Tomorrow she would be cross-examining the defendant in a murder case she was prosecuting. He was a good actor. On the stand, his version of the events that led up to the death of his supervisor had seemed entirely plausible. He claimed his superior had constantly belittled him, so much so that one day he had snapped and killed her. His attorney was going for a manslaughter verdict.

It was Kerry's job to take the defendant's story apart, to show that this was a carefully planned and executed vendetta against a boss who for good reasons had passed him over for promotion. It had cost her her life. Now he has to pay, Kerry thought.

It was one o'clock before she was satisfied that she had laid out all the questions she wanted to ask, all the points she wanted to make.

Wearily she climbed the stairs to the second floor. She glanced in on a peacefully sleeping Robin, pulled the covers tighter around her, then went across the hallway to her own room.

Five minutes later, her face washed, teeth brushed, clad in her favorite nightshirt, she snuggled down into the queen-sized brass bed that she had bought in a tag sale after Bob left. She had changed all the furniture in the master bedroom. It had been impossible to live with the old things, to look at his dresser, his night table, to see the empty pillow on his side of the bed.

The shade was only partially drawn, and by the faint light from the lamp on the post by the driveway, she could see that a steady rain had begun to fall.

Well, the great weather couldn't last forever, she thought, grateful that at least it was not as cold as predicted, that the rain would not change to sleet. She closed her eyes willing her mind to stop churning, wondering why she felt so uneasy.

She woke at five, then managed to doze off until six. It was in that hour the dream came to her for the first time.

She saw herself in the waiting room of a doctor's office. There was a woman lying on the floor, her large, unfocused eyes staring into nothingness. A cloud of dark hair framed the petulant beauty of her face. A knotted cord was twisted around her neck.

Then as Kerry watched, the woman got up, removed the cord from her neck and went over to the receptionist to make an appointment.

7

During the evening it crossed Robert Kinellen's mind to call and see how Robin had made out at the doctor's, but the thought had come and gone without being acted on. His father-in-law and the law firm's senior partner, Anthony Bartlett, had taken the unusual step of appearing at the Kinellens' house after dinner to discuss strategy in the upcoming income tax evasion trial of James Forrest Weeks, the firm's most important—and controversial—client.

Weeks, a multimillion-dollar real estate developer and entrepreneur, had become something of a public figure in New York and New Jersey during the past three decades. A heavy contributor to political campaigns, a prominent donor to numerous charities, he was also the subject of constant rumors about inside deals and influence peddling, and was rumored to have connections with known mobsters.

The U.S. attorney general's office had been trying to pin something on Weeks for years, and it had been the financially rewarding job of Bartlett and Kinellen to represent him during those past investigations. Until now, the Feds had always fallen short of enough evidence for a solid indictment.

"This time Jimmy is in serious trouble," Anthony Bartlett reminded his son-in-law as they sat across from each other in the study of the Kinellen home in Englewood Cliffs. He sipped a brandy. "Which of course means we're in serious trouble with him."

In the ten years since Bob had joined the firm, he had seen it become almost an extension of Weeks Enterprises, so closely were they entwined. In fact, without Jimmy's vast business empire, they would be left with only a handful of minor clients, and with billings inadequate to maintain the firm's operations. They both knew that if Jimmy were to be found guilty, Bartlett and Kinellen as a viable law firm would be finished.

"Barney's the one I worry about," Bob said quietly. Barney Haskell was Jimmy Weeks' chief accountant and codefendant in the current case. They both knew intense pressure was being put on him to turn government witness in exchange for a plea bargain.

Anthony Bartlett nodded. "Agreed."

"And for more than one reason," Bob continued. "I told you about the accident in New York? And that Robin was treated by a plastic surgeon?"

"Yes. How is she doing?"

"She'll be all right, thank goodness. But I didn't tell you the doctor's name. It's Charles Smith."

"Charles Smith." Anthony Bartlett frowned as he considered the name. Then his eyebrows rose and he sat bolt upright. "Not the one who . . . ?"

"Exactly," Bob told him. "And my ex-wife, the assistant prosecutor, is taking our daughter on regular visits to him. Knowing Kerry, it's only a matter of time before she makes the connection."

"Oh my God," Bartlett said miserably.

8

The Bergen County prosecutor's office was located on the second floor in the west wing of the courthouse. It housed thirty-five assistant prosecutors, seventy investigators and twenty-five secretaries, as well as Franklin Green, the prosecutor.

Despite the constantly heavy workload and the serious, often macabre, nature of the business, an air of camaraderie existed within the office. Kerry loved working there. She regularly received enticing offers from law firms, asking her to come work with them, but despite the financial temptations, she had elected to stay put and now had worked her way up to the position of trial chief. In the process she had earned herself a reputation as a smart, tough and scrupulous lawyer.

Two judges who had reached the mandatory retirement age of seventy had just vacated the bench, and now there were two openings. In his capacity as a state senator, Jonathan Hoover had submitted Kerry's name for one of the seats. She did not admit even to herself how much she wanted it. The big law firms offered much more money, but a judgeship represented the kind of achievement that no money could compete with.

Kerry thought of the possible appointment this morning as she punched in the code for the lock of the outside door and, at the click, shoved the door open. Waving to the switchboard operator, she walked at a quick pace to the office set aside for the trial chief.

By the standards of the windowless cubbyholes assigned to the new assistants, her office was reasonably sized. The surface of the worn wooden desk was so completely covered with stacks of files that its condition hardly mattered. The straight-backed chairs did not match, but were serviceable. The top drawer of the file had to be yanked vigorously to get it open, but that was only a minor irritation to Kerry.

The office had cross ventilation, windows that provided both light and air. She had personalized the space with thriving green plants that edged the windowsills, and with framed pictures that Robin had taken. The effect was that of functional comfort, and Kerry was perfectly content to have it as her office.

The morning had brought the first frost of the season, prompting Kerry to grab her Burberry as she left her house. Now she hung up the coat with care. She had bought it at a sale and intended it to have a long life.

She shook off the final vestiges of last night's troubling dream as she sat at her desk. The business at hand was the trial that would be resuming in an hour.

The murdered supervisor had two teenage sons whom she had been raising alone. Who was going to take care of them now? Suppose something happened to me, Kerry thought. Where would Robin go? Surely not to her father; she would not be happy, nor welcome, in his new household. But Kerry also couldn't picture her mother and her stepfather, both now over seventy and living in Colorado, raising a ten-year-old. Pray God I stay around at least till Robin is grown, she thought as she turned her attention to the file in front of her.

At ten of nine, her phone rang. It was Frank Green, the prosecutor. "Kerry, I know you're on your way to court, but stop by for just a minute."

"Of course." And it can only be a minute, she thought. Frank knows that Judge Kafka has a fit when he's kept waiting.

She found Prosecutor Frank Green seated behind his desk. Craggy-faced with shrewd eyes, at fifty-two he'd kept the hard physique that had made him a college football star. His smile was warm but seemed odd, she thought. Did he have his teeth bonded? she wondered. If so, he's smart. They do look good, and they'll photograph well when he's nominated in June.

There was no question that Green was already preparing for the gubernatorial campaign. The media coverage accorded his office was building, and the attention he was paying to his wardrobe was obvious to everyone. An editorial had said that since the present governor had served so well for two terms and Green was his handpicked successor, it seemed very likely that he would be chosen to lead the state.

After that editorial appeared, Green became known to his staff as "Our Leader."

Kerry admired his legal skills and efficiency. He ran a tight, solid ship. Her reservation about him was that several times in these ten years he had let an assistant who had made an honest mistake hang out to dry. Green's first loyalty was to himself.

She knew her possible nomination for a judgeship had increased her stature in his eyes. "Looks like the two of us will be going on to greater things," he had told her in a rare burst of exuberance and camaraderie.

Now he said, "Come in, Kerry. I just wanted to hear personally from you about how Robin is doing. When I learned that you had asked the judge to recess the trial yesterday, I was concerned."

She briefly told him about the checkup, reassuring him that all was under control.

"Robin was with her father at the time of the accident, wasn't she?" he asked.

"Yes. Bob was driving."

"Your ex may be running out of luck. I don't think he's going to get Weeks off this time. The word is they're going to nail him, and I hope they do. He's a crook and maybe worse." He made a gesture of dismissal. "I'm glad Robin's coming along okay, and I know you are on top of things. You're cross-examining the defendant today, aren't you?"

"Yes."

"Knowing you, I'm almost sorry for him. Good luck."

9

It was almost two weeks later, and Kerry was still basking in the satisfaction of the now concluded trial. She had gotten her murder conviction. At least the sons of the murdered woman would not have to grow up knowing that their mother's killer would be walking the streets in five or six years. That would have happened if the jury had fallen for the manslaughter defense. Murder carried a mandatory thirty-year sentence, without parole.

Now, once again seated in the reception area of Dr. Smith's office, she opened her ever-present briefcase and pulled out a newspaper. This was Robin's second checkup and should be fairly routine, so she could relax. Besides, she was anxious to read the latest about the Jimmy Weeks trial.

As Frank Green had predicted, the consensus was that it would not go well for the defendant. Previous investigations for bribery, inside trading and money laundering had been dropped for lack of sufficient evidence. But this time the prosecutor was said to have an airtight case. If it ever actually got started, that is. The jury selection had been going on for several weeks, and there seemed to be no end in sight. It no doubt makes Bartlett and Kinellen happy, she thought, to have all these billable hours piling up.

Bob had introduced Kerry to Jimmy Weeks once, when she had bumped into them in a restaurant. Now she studied his picture as he sat with her ex-husband at the defense table. Take away that custom-tailored suit and phony air of sophistication, and underneath you've got a thug, she thought.

In the picture, Bob's arm was draped protectively around the back of Weeks' chair. Their heads were close together. Kerry remembered how Bob used to practice that gesture.

She scanned the article, then dropped the newspaper back into her briefcase. Shaking her head, she remembered how appalled she had been when, shortly after Robin was born, Bob had told her he had accepted a job with Bartlett and Associates.

"All their clients have one foot in jail," she had protested. "And the other foot should be there."

"And they pay their bills on time," Bob had replied. "Kerry, you stay in the prosecutor's office if you want. I have other plans."

A year later he had announced that those plans included marrying Alice Bartlett.

Ancient history, Kerry told herself now as she looked around the waiting room. Today the other occupants were an athletic-looking teenage boy with a bandage across his nose and an older woman whose deeply wrinkled skin suggested the reason for her presence.

Kerry glanced at her watch. Robin had told her that last week she had waited in the examining room for half an hour. "I wish I'd brought a book with me," she had said. This time she'd made sure she had one.

I wish to God that Dr. Smith would set realistic appointment times, Kerry thought with irritation as she glanced in the direction of the examining rooms, the door to which was just opening.

Immediately, Kerry froze, and her glance became a stare. The young woman who emerged had a face framed by a cloud of dark hair, a straight nose, pouty lips, wide-set eyes, arched brows. Kerry felt her throat constrict. It wasn't the same woman she had seen last time—but it looked like her. Could the two be related? If they were patients, surely Dr. Smith couldn't be trying to make them look alike, she thought.

And why did that face remind her so much of someone else that it had brought on a nightmare? She shook her head, unable to come up with an answer.

She looked again at the others seated in the tiny waiting room. The boy had obviously had an accident and probably had broken his nose. But was the older woman here for something as routine as a face-lift, or was she hoping to have a totally different appearance?

What would it be like to look into the mirror and find a stranger's face staring back at you? Kerry wondered. Can you just pick a look that you want? Was it that simple?

"Ms. McGrath."

Kerry turned to see Mrs. Carpenter, the nurse, beckoning to her to come to the examining rooms.

Kerry hurried to follow her. Last visit she had asked the receptionist about the woman she had seen there and been told her name was Barbara Tompkins. Now she could ask the nurse about this other woman. "That young woman who just left, she looked familiar," Kerry said. "What is her name?"

"Pamela Worth," Mrs. Carpenter said shortly. "Here we are."

She found Robin seated across the desk from the doctor, her hands folded in her lap, her posture unusually straight. Kerry saw the look of relief on her daughter's face when she turned and their eyes met.

The doctor nodded to her and with a gesture indicated that she should take the chair next to Robin. "I have gone over with Robin the follow-up care I want her to take to insure that nothing impedes the healing process. She wants to continue to play soccer, but she must promise to wear a face mask for the rest of the season. We must not risk the slightest possibility of those lacerations being reopened. I expect that by the end of six months they'll no longer be visible."

His expression became intense. "I've already explained to Robin that many people come to me seeking the kind of beauty that was freely given to her. It is her duty to safeguard it. I see from the file that you are divorced. Robin told me her father was driving the car at the time of the accident. I urge you to warn him to take better care of his daughter. She is irreplaceable."

On the way home, at Robin's request, they stopped to have dinner at Valentino's in Park Ridge. "I like the shrimp there," Robin explained. But when they were settled at a table, she looked around and said, "Daddy brought me here once. He says it's the best." Her voice was wistful.

So that's why this is the restaurant of choice, Kerry thought. Since the accident, Bob had phoned Robin only once, and that had been during school hours. The message on the answering machine was that he guessed she was in school and that must mean she was doing great. There was no suggestion she return his call. Be fair, Kerry told herself. He did check with me at the office, and he knows that Dr. Smith said she is going to be okay. But that was two weeks ago. Since then, silence.

The waiter arrived to take their orders. When they were alone again, Robin said, "Mom, I don't want to go back to Dr. Smith anymore. He's creepy."

Kerry's heart sank. It was exactly what she had been thinking. And her next thought was that she only had his word that the angry red lines on Robin's face would disappear. I've got to have someone else check her out, she thought. Trying to sound matter-of-fact, she said, "Oh, I guess Dr. Smith is all right, even if he does have the personality of a wet noodle." She was rewarded by Robin's grin.

"Even so," she continued, "he doesn't want to see you for another month, and after that, maybe not at all, so don't worry about him. It's not his fault he was born without charm."

Robin laughed. "Forget the charm. He's a major creep."

When the food arrived, they sampled each other's choices and gossiped. Robin had a passion for photography and was taking a basic course in technique. Her present assignment was to capture the autumn leaves in transition. "I showed you the great shots I got of them just as they started to turn, Mom. I know the ones I took this week with the colors at peak are terrific."

"Sight unseen?" Kerry murmured.

"Uh-huh. Now I can't wait till they get dried up and then a good storm starts scattering everything. Won't that be great?"

"Nothing like a good storm scattering everything," Kerry agreed.

They decided to skip dessert. The waiter had just returned Kerry's credit card when she heard Robin gasp. "What is it, Rob?"

"Daddy's here. He sees us." Robin jumped up.

"Wait, Rob, let him come over to you," Kerry said quietly. She turned. Accompanied by another man, Bob was following the maître d'. Kerry's eyes widened. The other man was Jimmy Weeks.

As usual, Bob looked stunning. Even a long day in court did not leave a sign of fatigue on his handsome face. Never a wrinkle or a rumple about you, Kerry thought, aware that in Bob's presence she always had the impulse to check her makeup, smooth her hair, straighten her jacket.

On the other hand, Robin looked ecstatic. Happily she returned Bob's hug. "I'm sorry I missed your call, Daddy."

Oh, Robin, Kerry thought. Then she realized that Jimmy Weeks was looking down at her. "I met you here last year," he said. "You were having dinner with a couple of judges. Glad to see you again, Mrs. Kinellen."

"I dropped that name a long time ago. It's back to McGrath.

But you do have a good memory, Mr. Weeks." Kerry's tone was impersonal. She certainly wasn't going to say she was glad to see the man.

"You bet I have a good memory." Weeks' smile made the remark seem like a joke. "It helps when you're remembering a very attractive woman."

Spare me, Kerry thought, smiling tightly. She turned from him as Bob released Robin. Now he stretched out his hand to her.

"Kerry, what a nice surprise."

"It's usually a surprise when we see you, Bob."

"Mom," Robin implored.

Kerry bit her lip. She hated herself when she jabbed at Bob in front of their daughter. She forced a smile. "We're just leaving."

When they were settled at their table and their drink orders taken, Jimmy Weeks observed, "Your ex-wife sure doesn't like you much, Bobby."

Kinellen shrugged. "Kerry should lighten up. She takes everything too seriously. We married too young. We broke up. It happens every day. I wish she'd meet someone else."

"What happened to your kid's face?"

"Flying glass in a fender bender. She'll be fine."

"Did you make sure she had a good plastic surgeon?"

"Yes, he was highly recommended. What do you feel like eating, Jimmy?"

"What's the doctor's name? Maybe he's the same one my wife went to."

Bob Kinellen seethed inwardly. He cursed the lousy luck of meeting Kerry and Robin and having Jimmy ask about the accident. "It's Charles Smith," he said finally.

"Charles Smith?" Weeks' voice was startled. "You've got to be kidding."

"I wish I were."

"Well, I hear he's retiring soon. He's got big-time health problems."

Kinellen looked startled. "How do you know that?"

Jimmy W. looked at him coldly. "I keep tabs on him. You figure out why. It shouldn't take too long."

10

That night the dream returned. Again, Kerry was standing in a doctor's office. A young woman was lying on the floor, a cord knotted around her neck, her dark hair framing a face with wide unfocused eyes, a mouth open as though gasping for breath, the tip of a pink tongue protruding.

In her dream, Kerry tried to scream, but only a moaning protest came from her lips. A moment later Robin was shaking her awake. "Mom. Mom, wake up. What's wrong?"

Kerry opened her eyes, "What. Oh my God, Rob, what a rotten nightmare. Thanks."

But when Robin had returned to her room, Kerry lay awake, pondering the dream. What was triggering it? she wondered. Why was it different from the last time?

This time there had been flowers scattered over the woman's body. Roses. *Sweetheart roses.*

She sat up suddenly. That was it! *That* was what she had been trying to remember! In Dr. Smith's office, the woman today, and the woman a couple of weeks ago, the ones who had resembled each other so closely. She knew now why they seemed so familiar. She knew who they looked like.

Suzanne Reardon, the victim in the Sweetheart Murder Case. It had been nearly eleven years ago that she had been murdered by her husband. It had gotten a lot of press attention, crime of passion and roses scattered over the beautiful victim.

The day I started in the prosecutor's office was the day the jury found the husband guilty, Kerry thought. The papers had been plastered with pictures of Suzanne. I'm sure I'm right, she told herself. I sat in at the sentencing. It made such an impression on me. But why in the name of God would two of Dr. Smith's patients be look-alikes for a murder victim?

11

Pamela Worth had been a mistake. That thought kept Dr. Charles Smith sleepless virtually all Monday night. Even the beauty of her newly sculpted face could not compensate for her graceless posture, her harsh, loud voice.

I should have known right away, he thought. And, in fact, he had known. But he hadn't been able to help himself. Her bone structure made her a ridiculously easy candidate for such a transformation. And feeling that transformation take place under his fingers had made it possible for him to relive something of the excitement of the way it had been that first time.

What would he do when it wasn't possible to operate anymore? he wondered. That time was rapidly approaching. The slight hand tremor that irritated now would become more pronounced. Irritation would yield to incapacity.

He switched on the light, not the one beside his bed, but the one that illuminated the picture on the wall opposite him. He looked at it each night before he fell asleep. She was so beautiful. But now, without his glasses, the woman in the picture became twisted and distorted, as she had looked in death.

"Suzanne," he murmured. Then, as the pain of memory engulfed him, he threw an arm over his eyes, blocking out the image. He could not bear to remember how she had looked then, robbed of her beauty, her eyes bulging, the tip of her tongue protruding over her slack lower lip and drooping jaw . . .

12

On Tuesday morning, the first thing Kerry did when she got to her office was to phone Jonathan Hoover.

As always, it was comforting to hear his voice. She got right to the point. "Jonathan, Robin had her checkup in New York yesterday, and everything seems to be fine, but I'd be a lot more comfortable with a second opinion, if another plastic surgeon concurred with Dr. Smith that there won't be any scarring. Do you know anyone who's good?"

Jonathan's voice had a smile. "Not by personal experience."

"You certainly never needed it."

"Thank you, Kerry. Let me make some inquiries. Grace and I both thought you should get a second opinion, but we didn't want to interfere. Did something happen yesterday that made you decide on this?"

"Yes and no. I have someone coming in right now. I'll tell you about it when I see you next."

"I'll get back to you with a name this afternoon."

"Thanks, Jonathan."

"You're welcome, Your Honor."

"Jonathan, don't say that. You'll jinx me."

As the phone clicked, she heard him chuckle.

Her first appointment that morning was with Corinne Banks, the assistant to whom, as trial chief, she had assigned a vehicular homicide case. It was on the court calendar for next Monday, and Corinne wanted to review some aspects of the prosecution she intended to present.

Corinne, a young black woman of twenty-seven, had the makings of a top-drawer trial lawyer, Kerry thought. A tap at the door, and Corinne came in, a large file under her arm. She was wreathed in smiles. "Guess what Joe dug up," she said happily.

Joe Palumbo was one of their best investigators.

Kerry grinned. "I can hardly wait."

"Our oh-so-innocent defendant who claimed he never was involved in another accident has a real problem. Under a phony driver's license, he has a string of serious traffic violations, including another death by auto fifteen years ago. I can't wait to nail that guy, and now I'm confident that we can." She laid down the file and opened it. "Anyhow, this is what I wanted to talk about . . ."

Twenty minutes later, after Corinne left, Kerry reached for the phone. Corinne's mention of the investigator had given her an idea.

When Joe Palumbo answered with his usual "Yup," Kerry asked, "Joe, have you got lunch plans?"

"Not a one, Kerry. Want to take me to Solari's for lunch?"

Kerry laughed. "I'd love to, but I have something else in mind. How long have you been here?"

"Twenty years."

"Were you involved with the Reardon homicide about ten years ago, the one the media called the Sweetheart Murder?"

"That was a biggie. No, I wasn't on it, but as I remember it was pretty open and shut. Our Leader made his name on that one."

Kerry knew that Palumbo was not enamored of Frank Green. "Weren't there several appeals?" she asked.

"Oh, yeah. They kept coming up with new theories. It seemed like it went on forever," Palumbo replied.

"I think the last appeal was turned down just a couple of years ago," Kerry said, "but something has come up that has me curious about that case. Anyhow, the point is, I want you to go to the files at *The Record* and dig out everything they printed on the case."

She could picture Joe good-naturedly rolling his eyes.

"For you, Kerry, sure. Anything. But why? That case is long gone."

"Ask me later."

Kerry's lunch was a sandwich and coffee at her desk. At one-thirty Palumbo came in, carrying a bulging envelope. "As requested."

Kerry looked at him affectionately. Short, graying, twenty pounds overweight and with a ready smile, Joe had a disarmingly benevolent appearance that did not reflect his ability to instinctively home in on seemingly unimportant details. She had worked with him on some of her most important cases. "I owe you one," she said.

"Forget it, but I do admit I'm curious. What's your interest in the Reardon case, Kerry?"

She hesitated. Somehow at this point it didn't seem right to talk about what Dr. Smith was doing.

Palumbo saw her reluctance to answer. "Never mind. You'll tell me when you can. See you later."

Kerry was planning to take the file home and begin to read it after dinner. But she could not resist pulling out the top clipping. I'm right, she thought. It was only a couple of years ago.

It was a small item from page 32 of *The Record*, noting that Skip Reardon's fifth appeal for a new trial had been turned down by the New Jersey Supreme Court, and that his attorney, Geoffrey Dorso, had vowed to find grounds for another appeal.

Dorso's quote was, "I'll keep trying until Skip Reardon walks out of that prison exonerated. He's an innocent man."

Of course, she thought, all lawyers say that.

13

For the second night in a row, Bob Kinellen dined with his client Jimmy Weeks. It had not been a good day in court. Jury selection still dragged along. They had used eight of their peremptory challenges. But careful as they were being in choosing this jury, it was obvious that the federal prosecutor had a strong case. It was almost certain that Haskell was going to cop a plea.

Both men were somber over dinner.

"Even if Haskell does plead, I think I can destroy him on the stand," Kinellen assured Jimmy.

"You *think* you can destroy him. That's not good enough."

"We'll see how it goes."

Weeks smiled mirthlessly. "I'm beginning to worry about you, Bob. It's about time you got yourself a backup plan."

Bob Kinellen decided to let the remark pass. He opened the menu. "I'm meeting Alice at Arnott's later. Were you planning to go?"

"Hell, no. I don't need any more of his introductions. You should know that. They've done me enough harm already."

14

Kerry and Robin sat in companionable silence in the family room. Because of the chilly evening, they had decided to have the first fire of the season, which in their case meant turning on the gas jet and then pressing the button that sent flames shooting through the artificial logs.

As Kerry explained to visitors, "I'm allergic to smoke. This fire looks real and gives off heat. In fact, it looks so real that my cleaning woman vacuumed up the fake ashes, and I had to go out and buy more."

Robin laid out her change-of-season pictures on the coffee table. "What a terrific night," she said with satisfaction, "cold and windy. I should get the rest of the pictures soon. Bare trees, lots of leaves on the ground."

Kerry was seated in her favorite roomy armchair, her feet on a hassock. She looked up. "Don't remind me of the leaves. I get tired."

"Why don't you get a leaf blower?"

"I'll give you one for Christmas."

"Funny. What are you reading, Mom?"

"Come here, Rob." Kerry held up a newspaper clipping with a picture of Suzanne Reardon. "Do you recognize that lady?"

"She was in Dr. Smith's office yesterday."

"You've got a good eye, but it's not the same person." Kerry had just begun reading the account of Suzanne Reardon's murder. Her body had been discovered at midnight by her husband, Skip Reardon, a successful contractor and self-made millionaire. He had found her lying on the floor in the foyer of their luxurious home in Alpine. She had been strangled. Sweetheart roses were scattered over her body.

I must have read about that back then, Kerry thought. It certainly must have made an impression on me, to bring on those dreams.

It was twenty minutes later when she read the clipping that made her gasp. Skip Reardon had been charged with the murder after his father-in-law, *Dr. Charles Smith,* had told the police that his daughter lived in fear of her husband's insane attacks of jealousy.

Dr. Smith was Suzanne Reardon's father! My God, Kerry thought. Is that why he's giving her face to other women? How bizarre. How many of them has he done that to? Is that why he made that speech to me and Robin about preserving beauty?

"What's the matter, Mom? You look funny," Robin said.

"Nothing. Just interested in a case." Kerry looked at the clock on the mantel. "Nine o'clock, Rob. You'd better pack it in. I'll come up in a minute to say good night."

As Robin gathered her pictures, Kerry let the papers she was holding fall into her lap. She had heard of cases in which parents could not recover from the death of a child, where they had left the child's room unchanged, the clothes still in the closet, just as the child had left them. But to "re-create" her and do it over and over? That went beyond grief, surely.

Slowly she stood up and followed Robin upstairs. After she kissed her daughter good night, she went into her own room, changed into pajamas and a robe, then went back downstairs, made a cup of cocoa and continued to read.

The case against Skip Reardon did seem open and shut. He admitted that he and Suzanne had quarreled at breakfast the morning of her death. In fact, he admitted that in the preceding days they had fought almost continually. He admitted that he had come home at six o'clock that evening and found her arranging roses in a vase. When he asked her where they came from, she had told him it was none of his business who sent them. He said he had then told her that whoever sent them was welcome to her, that he was getting out. Then he claimed he had gone back to his office, had a couple of drinks, fallen asleep on the couch and returned home at midnight, to find her body.

There had been no one, however, to corroborate what he said. The file contained part of the trial transcript, including Skip's testimony. The prosecutor had hammered at him until he became confused and seemed to be contradicting himself. He had not made a very convincing witness, to say the least.

What a terrible job his lawyer had done in preparing him to testify, Kerry thought. She didn't doubt that, with the prosecutor's strong circumstantial case, it was imperative that Reardon take the stand to deny that he had killed Suzanne. But it was obvious that Frank Green's scathing cross-examination had completely unnerved him. There's no question, she thought, Reardon had helped to dig his own grave.

The sentencing had taken place six weeks after the trial ended. Kerry had actually gone in to witness it. Now she thought back to that day. She remembered Reardon as a big, handsome redhead who looked uncomfortable in his pin-striped suit. When the judge asked him if he wanted to say anything before sentence was passed, he had once again protested his innocence.

Geoff Dorso had been with Reardon that day, serving as assistant counsel to Reardon's defense lawyer. Kerry knew him slightly. In the ten years since then, Geoff had built a solid reputation as a criminal defense lawyer, although she didn't know him firsthand. She had never argued against him in court.

She came to the newspaper clipping about the sentencing. It included a direct quote from Skip Reardon: "I am innocent of the death of my wife. I never hurt her. I never threatened her. Her father, Dr. Charles Smith, is a liar. Before God and this court, I *swear* he is a liar."

Despite the warmth from the fire, she shivered.

15

Everyone knew, or thought they knew, that Jason Arnott had family money. He had lived in Alpine for fifteen years, ever since he had bought the old Halliday house, a twenty-room mansion on a crest of land that afforded a splendid view of Palisades Interstate Park.

Jason was in his early fifties, of average height, with scant brown hair, weathered eyes and a trim figure. He traveled extensively, talked vaguely of investments in the Orient and loved beautiful things. His home, with its exquisite Persian carpets, antique furniture, fine paintings and delicate objets d'art, was a feast for the eyes. A superb host, Jason entertained lavishly and was, in return, besieged with invitations from the great, the near great and the merely rich.

Erudite and witty, Jason claimed a vague relationship with the Astors of England, although most assumed this affectation was a figment of his imagination. They knew he was colorful and a little mysterious and totally engaging.

What they didn't know was that Jason was a thief. What no one ever seemed to piece together was that after a decent interval, virtually all of the homes he visited were burglarized by someone with a seemingly infallible method of bypassing security systems. Jason's only requirement was that he be able to carry away the spoils of his escapades. Art, sculpture, jewelry and tapestries were his favorites. Only a few times in his long career had he looted the entire contents of an estate. Those episodes had involved an elaborate system of disguises and importing renegade moving men to load the van that was now in the garage of his secret dwelling in a remote area in the Catskills.

There he had yet another identity, known to his widely scattered neighbors as a recluse who had no interest in socializing. No one other than the cleaning woman and an occasional repairman was ever invited inside the doors of his country retreat, and neither cleaning woman nor repairmen had an inkling of the value of the contents.

If his house in Alpine was exquisite, the one in the Catskills was breathtaking, for it was there that Jason kept the pieces from his looting escapades that he could not bear to part with. Each piece of furniture was a treasure. A Frederic Remington occupied the wall of the dining room, directly over the Sheraton buffet, on which a Peachblow vase glistened.

Everything in Alpine had been bought with money received for stolen property Jason had sold. There was nothing housed there that would ever catch the attention of someone with a photographic memory for a stolen possession. Jason was able to say with ease and confidence, "Yes, that's quite nice, isn't it? I got it at Sotheby's in an auction last year." Or, "I went to Bucks County when the Parker estate was on the block."

The only mistake Jason had ever made came ten years ago when his Friday cleaning woman in Alpine had spilled the contents of her pocketbook. When she retrieved them, she had missed her sheet of paper containing the security pass codes for four homes in Alpine. Jason had jotted them down, replaced the paper before the woman knew it was gone and then, tempted beyond control, had burglarized the four homes: the Ellots, the

Ashtons, the Donnatellis. And the Reardons. Jason still shuddered with the memory of his narrow escape that horrific night.

But that was years ago, and Skip Reardon was securely in prison, his avenues of appeal exhausted. Tonight the party was in full swing. Jason smilingly acknowledged the gushing compliments of Alice Bartlett Kinellen.

"I hope Bob will be able to make it," Jason told her.

"Oh, he'll be along. He knows better than to disappoint me."

Alice was a beautiful Grace Kelly–type blonde. Unfortunately, she had none of that late princess' charm or warmth. Alice Kinellen was cold as ice. Also boring and possessive, Jason thought. How does Kinellen stand her?

"He's having dinner with Jimmy Weeks," Alice confided as she sipped champagne. "He's up to here with that case." She made a slashing gesture across her throat.

"Well, I hope Jimmy comes too," Jason said sincerely. "I like him." But he knew Jimmy wouldn't come. Weeks hadn't been to one of his parties in years. In fact, he had kept a wide berth of Alpine after Suzanne Reardon's murder. Eleven years ago, Jimmy Weeks had met Suzanne at a party in Jason Arnott's house.

16

I t was clear that Frank Green was irritated. The smile that he flashed so readily to show off his newly whitened teeth was nowhere in evidence as he looked across his desk at Kerry.

I suppose it's the reaction I expected, she thought. I should have known that, of all people, Frank wouldn't want to hear anyone questioning the case that made him, and especially not now, with talk of his candidacy for governor so prevalent.

After reading the newspaper file on the Sweetheart Murder Case, Kerry had gone to bed trying to decide what she should do regarding Dr. Smith. Should she confront him, ask him point-blank about his daughter, ask him why he was re-creating her in the faces of other women?

The odds were that he would throw her out of the office and deny everything. Skip Reardon had accused the doctor of lying when he gave testimony about his daughter. If he had lied, Smith certainly wouldn't admit it to Kerry now, all these years later. And even if he had lied, the biggest question of them all was, why?

By the time Kerry had finally fallen asleep, she had decided that the best place to start asking questions was with Frank Green, since he had tried the case. Now that she had filled Green in on the reason she was inquiring about the Reardon case, it was obvious that her question, "Do you think there is any possibility Dr. Smith was lying when he testified against Skip Reardon?" was not going to result in a helpful or even friendly response.

"Kerry," Green said, "Skip Reardon killed his wife. He knew she was playing around. The very day he killed her, he had called in his accountant to find out how much a divorce would cost him, and he went bananas when he was told that it would involve big bucks. He was a wealthy man, and Suzanne had given up a lucrative modeling career to become a full-time wife. He would have to pay through the nose. So questioning Dr. Smith's veracity at this point seems a waste of time and taxpayers' money."

"But there's something wrong with Dr. Smith," Kerry said slowly. "Frank, I'm not trying to make trouble, and no one more than I wants to see a murderer behind bars, but I swear to you that Smith is more than a grief-stricken father. He seems almost to be demented. You should have seen his expression when he lectured Robin and me about the necessity to preserve beauty, and how some people are given it freely and others have to attain it."

Green looked at his watch. "Kerry, you just finished a big case. You're about to take on another one. You've got a judgeship pending. It's too bad Robin was treated by Suzanne Reardon's father. If anything, he wasn't an ideal witness on the stand. There wasn't a drop of emotion in him when he talked about his daughter. In fact, he was so cold, so cut-and-dry that I was thankful that the jury even believed his testimony. Do yourself a favor and forget it."

It was clear the meeting was over. As Kerry stood up, she said, "What I am doing is having Dr. Smith's handiwork on Robin checked by another plastic surgeon, one that Jonathan found for me."

When she was back in her office, Kerry asked her secretary to hold the phone calls and sat for a long time gazing into space. She could understand Frank Green's alarm at the thought of her raising questions about his star witness in the Sweetheart Murder Case. Any suggestion that there might have been a miscarriage of justice certainly would result in negative publicity and no doubt would tarnish Frank's image as a potential governor.

Dr. Smith is probably an obsessively grieving father who is able to use his great skill to re-create his daughter, she told herself, and Skip Reardon is probably one of the countless murderers who say, "I didn't do it."

Even so, she knew that she couldn't let it rest at that. On Saturday, when she took Robin to visit the plastic surgeon Jonathan had recommended, she would ask him how many surgeons in his field would even consider giving a number of women the same face.

17

At six-thirty that evening, Geoff Dorso glanced reluctantly at the stack of messages that had come in while he was in court. Then he turned away from them. From his office windows in Newark, he had a magnificent view of the New York City skyline, a sight that after a long day on a trial was still soothing.

Geoff was a city kid. Born in Manhattan and raised there till the age of eleven, at which point the family moved to New Jersey, he felt that he had one foot on either side of the Hudson, and he liked it that way.

Thirty-eight years old, Geoff was tall and lean, with a physique that did not reflect the fact that he had a sweet tooth. His jet black hair and olive skin were evidence of his Italian ancestry. His intensely blue eyes came from his Irish-English grandmother.

Still a bachelor, Geoff looked the part. His selection of ties was hit-and-miss, and his clothes usually had a slightly rumpled look. But the stack of messages was an indication of his excellent reputation as an attorney specializing in criminal defense and of the respect he had earned in the legal community.

As he leafed through them, he pulled out the important ones and discarded the others. Suddenly he raised his eyebrows. There was a request to call Kerry McGrath. She had left two numbers, her office and her home. What's that about? he wondered. He didn't have any cases pending in Bergen County, her area of jurisdiction.

Over the years he had met Kerry at bar association dinners, and he knew she was up for a judgeship, but he didn't really know her. The call intrigued him. It was too late to get her at the office. He decided he would try her now, at home.

"I'll get it," Robin called, as the phone rang.

It's probably for you, anyhow, Kerry thought as she tested the spaghetti. I thought telephonitis didn't set in until the teen years, she mused. Then she heard Robin yelling for her to pick up.

She hurried across the kitchen to the wall phone. An unfamiliar voice said, "Kerry."

"Yes."

"Geoff Dorso here."

It had been an impulse to leave the message for him. Afterwards, Kerry was uneasy about having done it. If Frank Green heard that she was contacting Skip Reardon's attorney, she knew he would not be so gentle as he had been earlier. But the die was cast.

"Geoff, this is probably not relevant, but . . ." Her voice trailed off. Spit it out, she told herself. "Geoff, my daughter had an accident recently and was treated by Dr. Charles Smith—"

"Charles Smith," Dorso interrupted, "Suzanne Reardon's father!"

"Yes. That's the point. There is something bizarre going on with him." Now it was easier to open up. She told him about the two women who resembled Suzanne.

"You mean Smith is actually giving them his daughter's face?" Dorso exclaimed. "What the hell is that about?"

"That's what troubles me. I'm taking Robin to another plastic surgeon on Saturday. I intend to ask him about the surgical implications of reproducing a face. I'm also going to try to talk to Dr. Smith, but it occurred to me that if I could read the entire trial transcript beforehand, I'd have a better handle on him. I know I can get one through the office, it's in the warehouse somewhere, but that could take time and I don't want it getting around that I'm looking for it."

"I'll have a copy in your hands tomorrow," Dorso promised. "I'll send it to your office."

"No, better send it to me here. I'll give you the address."

"I'd like to bring it up myself and talk to you. Would tomorrow night about six or six-thirty be all right? I won't stay more than half an hour, I promise."

"I guess that would be okay."

"See you then. And thanks, Kerry." The phone clicked.

Kerry looked at the receiver. What have I gotten myself into? she wondered. She hadn't missed the excitement in Dorso's voice. I shouldn't have used the word "bizarre," she thought. I've started something I may not be able to finish.

A sound from the stove made her whirl around. Boiling water from the spaghetti pot had overflowed and was running down the sides onto the gas jets. Without looking, she knew that the al dente pasta had been transformed into a glutinous mess.

18

D r. Charles Smith did not have office hours on Wednesday afternoon. It was a time usually reserved for surgical procedures or hospital follow-up visits. Today, however, Dr. Smith had cleared his calendar completely. As he drove down East Sixty-eighth Street, toward the brownstone where the public relations firm Barbara Tompkins worked for was located, his eyes widened at his good luck. There was a parking spot open across from the entrance of her building; he would be able to sit there and watch for her to leave.

When she finally did appear in the doorway, he smiled involuntarily. She looked lovely, he decided. As he had suggested, she wore her hair full and loose around her face; the best style, he had told her, to frame her new features. She was wearing a fitted red jacket, black calf-length skirt and granny shoes. From a distance she looked smart and successful. He knew every detail of how she looked up close.

As she hailed a cab, he turned on the ignition of his twelve-year-old black Mercedes and began to follow. Even though Park Avenue was bumper-to-bumper as was usual in the rush hour, keeping up with the taxi was not a problem.

They drove south, the cab finally stopping at The Four Seasons on East Fifty-second. Barbara must be meeting someone for a drink there, he thought. The bar would be crowded now. It wouldn't be difficult for him to slip in undetected.

Shaking his head, he decided to drive home instead. The glimpse of her had been enough. Almost too much, actually. For a moment he had really believed that she was Suzanne. Now he just wanted to be alone. A sob rose in his throat. As the traffic inched slowly downtown, he repeated over and over, "I'm sorry, Suzanne. I'm sorry, Suzanne."

19

I f Jonathan Hoover happened to be in Hackensack, he usually
tried to persuade Kerry to join him for a quick lunch. "How
many bowls of cafeteria soup can any human being eat?"
was his kidding question to her.

Today, over a hamburger at Solari's, the restaurant around the
corner from the courthouse, Kerry filled him in on the Suzanne
Reardon look-alikes and her conversation with Geoff Dorso. She
also told him of her boss's less than favorable reaction to her
suggestion that she might look into the old murder case.

Jonathan was deeply concerned. "Kerry, I don't remember
much about that case except that I thought there wasn't any
question of the husband's guilt. Whatever, I think you should
stay out of it, especially considering Frank Green's involvement
—very public as I remember—in securing the conviction. Look
at the realities here. Governor Marshall is still a young man. He's
served two terms and can't run for a consecutive third, but he
loves his job. He wants Frank Green to take his place. Between

us, they've got a deal. Green is to be governor for four years, then he gets to run for the senate with Marshall's support."

"And Marshall moves back into Drumthwacket."

"Exactly. He loves living in the governor's mansion. As of now it's a foregone conclusion that Green will get the nomination. He looks good, he sounds good. He's got a great track record, the Reardon case being an important part of it. And by a remarkable coincidence, he's actually smart. He intends to stick to the way Marshall's been running the state. But if anything upsets the apple cart, he's beatable in the primary. There are a couple of other would-be candidates panting for the nomination."

"Jonathan, I was talking about simply looking into things enough to see if the chief witness in a murder case had a serious problem that might have tainted his testimony. I mean, fathers grieve when their daughters die, but Dr. Smith has gone far beyond grief."

"Kerry, Frank Green made his name by prosecuting that case. It's what got him the media attention he needed. When Dukakis ran for president, a big factor in his defeat was the commercial that suggested he released a killer who then went on a crime spree. Do you know what the media would do if it were suggested that Green sent an innocent man to prison for the rest of his life?"

"Jonathan, you're getting way ahead of me. I'm not going in with that supposition. I just feel that Smith has a big problem, and it may have affected his testimony. He was the prosecution's main witness, and if he lied, it really casts doubt in my mind as to whether Reardon is guilty."

The waiter was standing over them, holding a coffeepot. "More coffee, Senator?" he asked.

Jonathan nodded. Kerry waved her hand over her cup. "I'm fine."

Jonathan suddenly smiled. "Kerry, do you remember when you were house-sitting for us and thought the landscaper hadn't put as many shrubs and bushes in as he had in the design?"

Kerry looked uncomfortable. "I remember."

"That last day you went around, counted all of them, thought you'd proven your point, dressed him down in front of his crew. Right?"

Kerry looked down at her coffee. "Uh-huh."

"You tell me what happened."

"He wasn't satisfied with the way some of the bushes looked, called you and Grace in Florida, then took them out, intending to replace them."

"What else?"

"He was Grace's cousin's husband."

"See what I mean?" His eyes had a twinkle. Then his expression became serious. "Kerry, if you embarrass Frank Green and put his nomination in jeopardy, chances are you can kiss your judgeship good-bye. Your name will be buried in a pile on Governor Marshall's desk, and I'll be quietly asked to submit another candidate for the vacancy." He paused, then took Kerry's hand. "Give this lots of thought before you do anything. I know you'll make the right decision."

20

Promptly at six-thirty that evening the chiming of the doorbell sent Robin racing to greet Geoff Dorso. Kerry had told her he was coming and that they would be going over a case for half an hour or so. Robin had decided to eat early and promised to finish her homework in her room while Kerry was busy. In exchange she was getting an unaccustomed weeknight hour of television.

She inspected Dorso with benevolence and ushered him into the family room. "My mother will be right down," she announced. "I'm Robin."

"I'm Geoff Dorso. How does the other guy look?" Geoff asked. With a smile he indicated the still-vivid marks on her face.

Robin grinned. "I flattened him. Actually it was a fender bender with some flying glass."

"It looks as though it's healing fine."

"Dr. Smith, the plastic surgeon, says it is. Mom says you know him. I think he's creepy."

"Robin!" Kerry had just come downstairs.

"From the mouths of babes," Dorso said, smiling. "Kerry, it's good to see you."

"It's good to see you, Geoff." I hope I mean it, Kerry thought as her gaze fell on the bulging briefcase under Dorso's arm. "Robin . . ."

"I know. Homework," Robin agreed cheerfully. "I'm not the neatest person in the world," she explained to Dorso. "My last report card had 'improvement needed' checked above 'home assignments.' "

"Also, 'uses time well' had a check above it," Kerry reminded her.

"That's because when I finish an assignment in school, I forget sometimes and start to talk to one of my friends. Okay." With a wave of her hand, Robin headed for the staircase.

Geoff Dorso smiled after her. "Nice kid, Kerry, and she's a knockout. In another five or six years you'll have to barricade the door."

"A scary prospect. Geoff, coffee, a drink, a glass of wine?"

"No, thanks. I promised not to take too much of your time." He laid his briefcase on the coffee table. "Do you want to go over this in here?"

"Sure." She sat next to him on the couch as he took out two

thick volumes of bound paper. "The trial transcript," he said, "one thousand pages of it. If you really want to understand what went on, I would suggest you read it carefully. Frankly, from start to finish, I'm ashamed of the defense we mounted. I know Skip had to take the stand, but he wasn't properly prepared. The state's witnesses weren't vigorously questioned. And we only called two character witnesses for Skip when we should have called twenty."

"Why was it handled that way?" Kerry asked.

"I was the most junior counsel, having just been hired by Farrell and Strauss. Farrell had been a good defense lawyer once upon a time, no doubt about that. But when Skip Reardon hired him, he was well past his prime and pretty much burned out. He just wasn't interested in another murder case. I really think Skip would have been better off with a much less experienced attorney who had some fire in his gut."

"Couldn't you have filled the gap?"

"No, not really. I was just out of law school and didn't have much to say about anything. I had very little participation in the trial at all. I was basically a gofer for Farrell. As inexperienced as I was, though, it was obvious to me that the trial was handled badly."

"And Frank Green tore him apart on cross-examination."

"As you read, he got Skip to admit that he and Suzanne had quarreled that morning, that he'd spoken to his accountant to find out what a divorce would cost, that he'd gone back to the house at six and again quarreled with Suzanne. The coroner estimated time of death to be between six and eight o'clock, so Skip could, by his own testimony, be placed at the scene of the crime at the possible time of the murder."

"From the account I read, Skip Reardon claimed he went back to his office, had a couple of drinks and fell asleep. That's pretty thin," Kerry commented.

"It's thin but it's true. Skip had established a very successful business, mostly building quality homes, although recently he had expanded into shopping malls. Most of his time was spent in the office, taking care of the business end, but he loved to put on work clothes and spend the day with a crew. That's what he'd done that day, before coming back to work at the office. The guy was tired."

He opened the first volume. "I've flagged Smith's testimony as well as Skip's. The crux of the matter is that we are certain that there was someone else involved, and we have reason to believe it was another man. In fact, Skip was convinced that Suzanne was involved with another man, perhaps even with more than one. What precipitated the second quarrel, the one that occurred when he went home at six o'clock, was that he found her arranging a bunch of red roses—sweetheart roses, I think the press called them—that he had not sent her. The prosecution maintained that he went into a rage, strangled her, then threw the roses over her body. He, of course, swears that he didn't, that when he left, Suzanne was still blithely puttering with the flowers."

"Did anyone check the local florists to see if an order for the roses had been placed with one of them? If Skip didn't carry them home, somebody delivered them."

"Farrell did at least do that. There wasn't a florist in Bergen County who wasn't checked. Nothing turned up."

"I see."

Geoff stood up. "Kerry, I know it's a lot to ask, but I want you to read this transcript carefully. I want you to pay particular attention to Dr. Smith's testimony. Then I'd like you to consider letting me be with you when you talk to Dr. Smith about his practice of giving other women his daughter's face."

She walked with Geoff to the door. "I'll call you in the next few days," she promised.

At the door, he paused, then turned back to Kerry. "There's one more thing I wish you'd do. Come down with me to Trenton State Prison. Talk to Skip yourself. On my grandmother's grave,

I swear you'll hear the ring of truth when that poor guy tells you his story."

21

I n Trenton State Prison, Skip Reardon lay on the bunk of his cell, watching the six-thirty news. Dinnertime had come and gone with its dreary menu. As had become more and more the case, he was restless and irritable. After ten years in this place, he had managed for the most part to set himself on a middle course. In the beginning he had fluctuated between wild hope when an appeal was pending and crashing despair when it was rejected.

Now his usual state of mind was weary resignation. He knew that Geoff Dorso would never stop trying to find new grounds for an appeal, but the climate of the country was changing. On the news there were more and more reports criticizing the fact that repeated appeals from convicted criminals were tying up the courts, reports that inevitably concluded that there had to be a cutoff. If Geoff could not find grounds for an appeal, one that would actually win Skip his freedom, then that meant another twenty years in this place.

In his most despondent moments, Skip allowed himself to think back over the years before the murder, and to realize just how crazy he had been. He and Beth had practically been engaged. And then at Beth's urging he had gone alone to a party her sister and her surgeon husband were giving. At the last minute, Beth had come down with a bug, but she hadn't wanted him to miss out on the fun.

Yeah, *fun*, Skip thought ironically, remembering that night. Suzanne and her father had been there. Even now he could not forget how she looked the first time he saw her. He knew immediately she meant trouble, but like a fool he fell for her anyway.

Impatiently, Skip got up from the bunk, switched off the television and looked at the trial transcript on the shelf over the toilet. He felt as though he could recite it by heart. That's where it belongs, over the toilet, he thought bitterly. For all the good it's ever going to do me, I should tear it up and flush it.

He stretched. He used to keep his body in shape through a combination of hard work on the job site and a regular gym regimen. Now he rigidly performed a series of push-ups and sit-ups every night. The small plastic mirror attached to the wall showed his red hair streaked with gray, his face, once ruddy from outdoor work, now a pasty prison pallor.

The daydream he allowed himself was that by some miracle he was free to go back to building houses. The oppressive confinement and constant noise in this place had given him visions of middle-class homes that would be sufficiently insulated to insure privacy, that would be filled with windows to let in the outdoors. He had loose-leaf books filled with designs.

Whenever Beth came to see him, something he had tried to discourage of late, he would show the latest ones to her, and they would talk about them as though he really would one day be able to go back to the job he had loved, building homes.

Only now he had to wonder, what would the world be like, and what would people be living in when he finally got out of this terrible place?

22

Kerry could tell it was going to be another late night. She had started reading the transcript immediately after Geoff left and resumed after Robin went to bed.

At nine-thirty, Grace Hoover phoned. "Jonathan's out at a meeting. I'm propped up in bed and felt like chatting. Is this a good time for you?"

"It's always a good time when it's you, Grace." Kerry meant it. In the fifteen years she had known Grace and Jonathan, she had watched Grace's physical decline. She had gone from using a cane to crutches, finally to a wheelchair, and from being ardently involved in social activities to being almost totally housebound. She did keep up with friends and entertained with frequent catered dinner parties, but as she told Kerry, "It's just gotten to be too much effort to go out."

Kerry had never heard Grace complain. "You do what you have to," she had said wryly when Kerry candidly told her how much she admired her courage.

But after a couple of minutes of familiar chatter, it became apparent that tonight there was a purpose to Grace's call. "Kerry, you had lunch with Jonathan today, and I'm going to be honest. He's worried."

Kerry listened as Grace reiterated Jonathan's concerns, concluding with, "Kerry, after twenty years in the state senate, Jonathan has a lot of power, but not enough to make the governor appoint you to a judgeship if you embarrass his chosen successor. Incidentally," she added, "Jonathan has no idea I'm calling you."

He must have really vented to Grace, Kerry thought. I wonder what she would think if she could see what I'm doing now. Feeling evasive the entire time, Kerry did her best to assure Grace that she had no intention or desire to ruffle feathers. "But Grace, if it developed that Dr. Smith's testimony was false, I think that Frank Green would be admired and respected if he recommended to the court that Reardon be given a new trial. I don't think that the public would hold it against him that he had in good faith relied on the doctor's testimony. He had no reason to doubt him.

"And don't forget," she added, "I'm far from being convinced that justice was denied in the Reardon case. It's just that by coincidence I've stumbled on this one thing, and I can't live with myself if I don't follow through on it."

When the conversation ended, Kerry returned to the transcript. By the time she finally laid it down, she had filled pages with notes and questions.

The sweetheart roses: Was Skip Reardon lying when he said he didn't bring or send them? If he was telling the truth, if he didn't send them, then who *did*?

Dolly Bowles, the baby-sitter who had been on duty in the house across the street from the Reardon home the night of the murder: She claimed she saw a car in front of the Reardons' house at nine o'clock that night. But neighbors were having a party at the time, and a number of their guests had parked in the street. Dolly had made a particularly poor witness in court. Frank Green had brought out the fact that she had reported "suspicious-looking" people in the neighborhood on six separate occasions that year. In each instance, the suspect turned out to be a legitimate deliveryman. The result was that Dolly came through as a totally unreliable witness. Kerry was sure the jury had disregarded her testimony.

Skip Reardon had never been in trouble with the law and was

considered a very solid citizen, yet only two character witnesses had been called: Why?

There had been a series of burglaries in Alpine around the time of Suzanne Reardon's death. Skip Reardon claimed that some of the jewelry he had seen Suzanne wearing was missing, that the master bedroom had been ransacked. But a tray full of valuable jewelry was found on the dresser, and the prosecution called in a part-time housekeeper the Reardons had employed who flatly testified that Suzanne always left the bedroom in a chaotic state. "She'd try on three or four outfits, then drop them on the floor if she decided against them. Powder spilled on the dressing table, wet towels on the floor. I often felt like quitting."

As she undressed for bed that night, Kerry mentally reviewed what she had read, and noted that there were two things she had to do: make an appointment to talk with Dr. Smith, and visit Skip Reardon at the State Prison in Trenton.

23

In the nine years since the divorce, Kerry had dated on and off, but there had never been anyone special. Her closest friend was Margaret Mann, her roommate at Boston College. Marg was blond and petite, and in college she and Kerry had been dubbed the long and the short of it. Now an investment banker with an apartment on West Eighty-sixth Street, Margaret was confidante, pal and buddy. On occasional Friday evenings, Kerry would have a sitter in for Robin and drive to Manhattan. She and Margaret would have dinner and catch a Broadway show or a movie or just linger over dessert for hours and talk.

The Friday night after Geoff Dorso left the transcript, Kerry arrived at Margaret's apartment and gratefully sank onto the couch in front of a platter of cheese and grapes.

Margaret handed her a glass of wine. "Bottoms up. You look great."

Kerry was wearing a new hunter green suit with a long jacket and calf-length skirt. She looked down at it and shrugged.

75

"Thanks. I finally got a chance to buy some new clothes and I've been sporting them all week."

Margaret laughed. "Remember how your mother used to put on her lipstick and say, 'You never know where romance may linger'? She was right, wasn't she?"

"I guess so. She and Sam have been married fifteen years now, and whenever they come East or Robin and I visit them in Colorado, they're holding hands."

Margaret grinned. "We should be so lucky." Then her expression became serious. "How's Robin? Her face is healing well, I hope."

"Seems to be fine. I'm taking her to see another plastic surgeon tomorrow. Just for a consultation."

Margaret hesitated, then said, "I was trying to find a way to suggest that. At the office I was talking about the accident and mentioned Dr. Smith's name. One of the traders, Stuart Grant, picked up on it right away. He said his wife consulted Smith. She wanted to do something about the bags under her eyes, but she never went back after the first visit. She thought there was something wrong with him."

Kerry straightened up. "What did she mean?"

"Her name is Susan, but the doctor kept slipping and calling her Suzanne. Then he told her he could do her eyes, but he'd rather do her whole face, that she had the makings of a great beauty and was wasting her life not taking advantage of it."

"How long ago was that?"

"Three or four years, I guess. Oh, and something else. Smith apparently also rambled on to Susan about how beauty brings responsibility, and that some people abuse it and invite jealousy and violence." She stopped, then asked, "Kerry, what's the matter? You have a funny look on your face."

"Marg, this is important. Are you sure that Smith talked about women inviting jealousy and violence?"

"I'm sure that's what Stuart told me."

"Do you have Stuart's phone number? I want to talk to his wife."

"In the office. They live in Greenwich, but I happen to know that the number's unlisted, so it will have to wait till Monday. What's this about, anyhow?"

"I'll tell you about it over dinner," she said distractedly. It seemed to Kerry that the trial transcript was on a Rolodex in her mind. Dr. Smith swore that his daughter was in fear for her life because of Skip Reardon's *unfounded* jealousy. Had he been lying? Had Suzanne given Skip reason to be jealous? And if so, of whom?

24

At eight o'clock Saturday morning, Kerry received a phone call from Geoff Dorso. "I beeped in to the office and got your message," he told her. "I'm going to Trenton to see Skip this afternoon. Can you make it?" He explained that in order to register for the three o'clock visit, they would have to be at the prison by 1:45.

Almost as a reflex, Kerry heard herself say, "I'm sure I can make it. I'll have to make arrangements for Robin, but I'll meet you there."

Two hours later, Kerry and an impatient Robin were in Livingston, New Jersey, in the office of Dr. Ben Roth, a noted plastic surgeon.

"I'm going to miss the soccer game," Robin fretted.

"You'll be a little late, that's all," Kerry soothed. "Don't worry."

"Very late," Robin protested. "Why couldn't he see me this afternoon after the game?"

"Perhaps if you'd sent the doctor your schedule, he could have worked around it," Kerry teased.

"Oh, Mom."

"You can bring Robin in now, Ms. McGrath," the receptionist announced.

Dr. Roth, in his mid-thirties, warm and affable, was a welcome change from Dr. Smith. He examined Robin's face carefully. "The lacerations probably looked pretty bad right after the accident, but they were what we call superficial. They didn't deeply penetrate the dermis. You haven't got any problems."

Robin looked relieved. "Great. Thanks, Doctor. Let's go, Mom."

"Wait in the reception area, Robin. I'll be out in just a moment. I want to talk to the doctor." Kerry's voice carried what Robin called "the tone." It meant "and I don't want to hear any arguments."

"Okay," Robin said with an exaggerated sigh as she departed.

"I know you have patients waiting, so I won't be long, Doctor, but there is something I must ask you," Kerry said.

"I have time. What is it, Ms. McGrath?"

Kerry reduced to a few brief sentences a description of what she had seen in Dr. Smith's office. "So I guess I have two questions," she concluded. "Can you remake just any face to look like someone else, or does some fundamental factor, like a similar bone structure, have to be present? And knowing that it is possible to remake some faces so that they look alike, is this something that plastic surgeons do, I mean deliberately remake someone to look like someone else?"

It was twenty minutes later when Kerry rejoined Robin and they rushed to the soccer field. Unlike Kerry, Robin was not a natural athlete, and Kerry had spent long hours working with her, because her heart was set on being a good player. Now, as she watched Robin confidently kick the ball past the goalie, Kerry was still reflecting on Dr. Roth's flat statement: "It's a fact that some surgeons give everyone the same nose or chin or eyes, but I find it extremely unusual that any surgeon would in essence clone the faces of his patients."

At eleven-thirty she caught Robin's eye and waved good-bye. Robin would go home from the game with her best friend, Cassie, and would spend the afternoon at her house.

A few minutes later, Kerry was on the road to Trenton.

She had visited the state prison several times and always found the grim aspect of barbed wire and guard towers a sobering sight. This was not a place she looked forward to seeing again.

25

Kerry found Geoff waiting for her in the area where visitors were registered. "I'm really glad you made it," he said. They talked little while they waited for their scheduled meeting. Geoff seemed to understand that she did not want his input at this time.

Promptly at three o'clock a guard approached them and told them to follow him.

Kerry did not know what she expected Skip Reardon to look like now. It had been ten years since she had sat in at his sentencing. The impression she had retained of him was of a tall, good-looking, broad-shouldered young man with fiery red hair. But more than his appearance, it was his statement that had been burned into her mind: *Dr. Charles Smith is a liar. Before God and this court, I swear he is a liar!*

"What have you told Skip Reardon about me?" she asked Geoff as they waited for the prisoner to be escorted into the visiting area.

"Only that you've unofficially taken some interest in his case and wanted to meet him. I promise you, Kerry, I said 'unofficially.'"

"That's fine. I trust you."

"Here he is now."

Skip Reardon appeared, dressed in prison denims and an open-necked prison-issue shirt. There were streaks of gray through the red hair, but except for the lines around his eyes he still looked very much as Kerry recalled him. A smile brightened his face as Geoff introduced him.

A hopeful smile, Kerry realized, and with a sinking heart wondered if she shouldn't have been more cautious, perhaps waiting until she knew more about the case, instead of agreeing so readily to this visit.

Geoff got right to the point. "Skip, as I told you, Ms. McGrath wants to ask you some questions."

"I understand. And, listen, I'll answer them no matter what they are." He spoke earnestly, although with a hint of resignation. "You've heard that old saying, I have nothing to hide."

Kerry smiled, then went straight to the question that was to her the crux of this meeting. "In his testimony, Dr. Smith swore that his daughter, your wife, was afraid of you and that you had threatened her. You have maintained that he was lying, but what purpose would he have in lying about that?"

Reardon's hands were folded on the table in front of him. "Ms. McGrath, if I had any explanation for Dr. Smith's actions, maybe I wouldn't be here now. Suzanne and I were married four years, and during that time I never saw that much of Smith. She'd go into New York and have dinner with him occasionally, or he'd come out to the house, but usually when I was away on a business trip. At that time my construction business was booming. I was building all over the state and investing in land in

Pennsylvania for future development. I'd be gone a couple of days at a time on a fairly regular basis. Whenever I was with Dr. Smith, he seemed not to have much to say, but he never acted as though he didn't like me. And he certainly didn't act as though he thought his daughter's life was in danger."

"When you were with both him and Suzanne, what did you notice about his attitude toward her?"

Reardon looked at Dorso. "You're the guy with the fancy words, Geoff. What's a good way to put it? Wait a minute. I can tell you. When I was in parochial school, the nuns got mad at us for talking in church and told us we should have reverence for a holy place and holy objects. Well that's the way he treated her. Smith showed 'reverence' for Suzanne."

What an odd word to use about a father's attitude toward his daughter, Kerry thought.

"And he was also protective of her," Reardon added. "One night the three of us were driving somewhere for dinner and he noticed that Suzanne hadn't put on her seat belt. So he launched into a lecture about her responsibility to take care of herself. He actually got fairly agitated about it, maybe even a little angry."

It sounds like the same way he lectured Robin and me, Kerry thought. Almost reluctantly she admitted to herself that Skip Reardon certainly gave the appearance of being candid and honest.

"How did she act toward him?"

"Respectful, mostly. Although toward the end—before she was killed—the last few times I was with them, she seemed to be kind of irritated at him."

Kerry then ventured into other aspects of the case, asking him about his sworn testimony that just prior to the murder, he had noticed Suzanne wearing expensive pieces of jewelry that he had not given her.

"Ms. McGrath, I wish you'd talk to my mother. She could tell you. She has a picture of Suzanne that was run in one of the community papers, taken at a charity affair. It shows her with an old-fashioned diamond pin on the lapel of her suit. The picture was taken only a couple of weeks before she was murdered. I swear to you that that pin and a couple of other pieces of expensive jewelry, none of which I gave her, were in her jewelry box that morning. I remember it specifically because it was one of the things we argued about. Those pieces were there that morning and they weren't there the next day."

"You mean someone took them?"

Reardon seemed uncomfortable. "I don't know if someone took them or if she gave them back to someone, but I tell you there was jewelry missing the next morning. I tried to tell all this to the cops, to get them to look into it, but it was obvious from the beginning that they didn't believe me. They thought that I was trying to make it look like she had been robbed and killed by an intruder.

"Something else," he continued. "My dad was in World War II and was in Germany for two years after the war. He brought back a miniature picture frame that he gave to my mother when they became engaged. My mother gave that frame to Suzanne and me when we were married. Suzanne put my favorite picture of her in it and kept it on the night table in our room. When my mother and I sorted Suzanne's things out before I was arrested, Mom noticed it was missing. But I know it was there that last morning."

"Are you trying to say that the night Suzanne died, someone came in and stole some jewelry and a picture frame?" Kerry asked.

"I'm telling you what I know was missing. I don't know where it went, and of course I'm not sure it had anything to do with Suzanne's murder. I just know that suddenly those things weren't there and that the police wouldn't look into it."

Kerry looked up from her notes and peered directly into the eyes of the man facing her.

"Skip, what was your relationship with your wife?"

Reardon sighed. "When I met her, I fell like a ton of bricks. She was gorgeous. She was smart. She was funny. She was the kind of woman who makes a guy feel ten feet tall. After we were married . . ." He paused. "It was all heat and no warmth, Ms. McGrath. I was raised to think you're supposed to make a go of marriage, that divorce was a last resort. And, of course, there were some good times. But was I ever happy or content? No, I wasn't. But then I was so busy building up my company that I just spent more and more time at work and in that way was able to avoid dealing with it.

"As for Suzanne, she seemed to have everything she wanted. The money was rolling in. I built her the house she said she had dreamed of having. She was over at the club every day, playing golf or tennis. She spent two years with a decorator, furnishing the house the way she wanted it. There's a guy who lives in Alpine, Jason Arnott, who really knows antiques. He took Suzanne to auctions and told her what to buy. She developed a taste for designer clothes. She was like a kid who wanted every day to be Christmas. With the way I was working, she had plenty of free time to come and go as she pleased. She loved to be at affairs that got press coverage, so that her picture would be in the paper. For a long time I thought she was happy, but as I look back on it, I'm sure she stayed with me because she hadn't found any better setup."

"Until . . ." Geoff prompted.

"Until someone she met became important," Reardon continued. "That was when I noticed jewelry I hadn't seen before. Some pieces were antiques, others very modern. She claimed her father gave them to her, but I could tell she was lying. Her father has all her jewelry now, including everything I gave her."

When the guard indicated their time was up, Reardon stood and looked squarely at Kerry. "Ms. McGrath, I shouldn't be here. Somewhere out there the guy who killed Suzanne is walking around. And somewhere there has to be something that will prove it."

Geoff and Kerry walked to the parking lot together. "I bet you didn't have time for any lunch," he said. "Why don't we grab something fast?"

"I can't, I've got to get back. Geoff, I have to tell you that from what I heard today, I can't see a single reason for Dr. Smith to lie about Skip Reardon. Reardon says that they had what amounts to a reasonably cordial relationship. You heard him say that he didn't believe Suzanne when she told him that her father had given her some pieces of jewelry. If he started getting jealous about those pieces, well . . ." She did not finish the sentence.

26

On Sunday morning, Robin served at the ten o'clock mass. When Kerry watched the processional move down the aisle from the vestry, she always was reminded of how, as a child, she had wanted to be a server and was told it wasn't possible, that only boys were allowed.

Things change, she mused. I never thought I'd see my daughter on the altar, I never thought I'd be divorced, I never thought that someday I'd be a judge. *Might be* a judge, she corrected herself. She knew Jonathan was right. Embarrassing Frank Green right now was tantamount to embarrassing the governor. It could be a fatal blow to her appointment. Yesterday's visit to Skip Reardon might have been a serious mistake. Why mess up her life again? She had done it once.

She knew that she had worked her way through the emotional gamut with Bob Kinellen, first loving him, then being heartbroken when he left her, then angry at him and contemptuous of herself that she had not seen him for the opportunist he was. Now her chief reaction to him was indifference, except where

Robin was concerned. Even so, observing couples in church, whether her own age, younger, older—it didn't matter—seeing them always caused a pang of sadness. If only Bob had been the person I believed he was, she thought. If only he were the person *he* thinks he *is*. By now they would have been married eleven years. By now surely she would have had other children. She'd always wanted three.

As she watched Robin carry the ewer of water and the lavabo bowl to the altar in preparation for the consecration, her daughter looked up and met Kerry's gaze. Her brief smile caught at Kerry's heart. What am I complaining about? she asked herself. No matter what happens, I have her. And as unions go, it may have been far from perfect, but at least something good came of it. No one else except Bob Kinellen and I could have had exactly this wonderful child, she reasoned.

As she watched, her mind jumped back to another parent and child, to Dr. Smith and Suzanne. She had been the unique result of his and his former wife's genes. In his testimony, Dr. Smith had stated that after their divorce his wife moved to California and remarried, and he had permitted Suzanne to be adopted by the second husband, thinking that was in her best interests.

"But after her mother died, she came to me," he had said. "She needed me."

Skip Reardon had said that Dr. Smith's attitude toward his daughter bordered on reverence. When she heard that, a question that took Kerry's breath away had raced through her mind. Dr. Smith had transformed other women to look like his daughter. But no one had ever asked whether or not he had ever operated on Suzanne.

Kerry and Robin had just finished lunch when Bob called, suggesting he take Robin out to dinner that night. He explained that Alice had taken the children to Florida for a week, and he was driving to the Catskills to look at a ski lodge they might buy. Would Robin want to accompany him? he asked. "I still owe her dinner, and I promise I'll have her back by nine."

Robin's enthusiastically affirmative response resulted in Bob picking her up an hour later.

The unexpected free afternoon gave Kerry a chance to spend more time going over the Reardon trial transcript. Just reading the testimony gave her a certain amount of insight, but she knew that there was a big difference between reading a cold transcript and watching the witnesses as they testified. She hadn't seen their faces, heard their voices or watched their physical reactions to questions. She knew that the jury's evaluation of the demeanor of the witnesses had undoubtedly played a big part in reaching their verdict. That jury had watched and evaluated Dr. Smith. And it was obvious that they had believed him.

27

Geoff Dorso loved football and was an ardent Giants fan. It was not the reason he had bought a condominium in the Meadowlands, but as he admitted, it certainly was convenient. Nevertheless, on Sunday afternoon, sitting in Giant Stadium, his mind was less on today's very close game with the Dallas Cowboys than on yesterday's visit to Skip Reardon, and Kerry McGrath's reaction to both Skip and the trial transcript.

He had given the transcript to her on Thursday. Had she read it yet? he wondered. He had hoped that she would bring it up while they were waiting to see Skip, but she hadn't mentioned it. He tried to tell himself that it was her training to be skeptical, that her seemingly negative attitude after the visit to Skip didn't have to mean that she was washing her hands of the case.

When the Giants squeaked through with a last-second field goal as the fourth quarter of the game ended, Geoff shared in the lusty cheering but declined the suggestion of his friends that he join them for a couple of beers. Instead he went home and called Kerry.

He was elated when she admitted that she had read the transcript and that she had a number of questions. "I'd like to get together again," he said. Then a thought struck him. She can only say no, he reasoned, as he asked, "By any chance would you be free for dinner tonight?"

28

Dolly Bowles had been sixty when she moved in with her daughter in Alpine. That had been twelve years ago, when she was first widowed. She had not wanted to impose, but the truth was she had always been nervous about being alone and really didn't think she could go on living in the big house she and her husband had shared.

And, in fact, there was a basis, psychological at least, for her nervousness. Years ago, when she was still a child, she had opened the door for a deliveryman who turned out to be a burglar. She still had nightmares about the way he had tied up both her and her mother and had ransacked the house. As a result, she now tended to be suspicious of any and all strangers, and several times had irritated her son-in-law by pushing the panic button on the alarm system when she had been alone in the house and had heard strange noises or seen a man on the street she didn't recognize.

Her daughter Dorothy and her son-in-law Lou traveled frequently. Their children had still been at home when Dolly moved in with them, and she had been a help in taking care of them. But for the last several years they had been off on their own, and Dolly had had almost nothing to do. She had tried to pitch in around the house, but the live-in housekeeper wanted no part of her help.

Left with so much time on her hands, Dolly had become the neighborhood baby-sitter, a situation that worked out wonderfully. She genuinely enjoyed young children and would happily read to them or play games by the hour. She was beloved by just about everyone. The only time people got annoyed was when she made one of her all-too-frequent calls to the police to report suspicious-looking persons. And she hadn't done that in the last ten years, not since she was a witness at the Reardon murder trial. She shuddered every time she thought of that. The prosecutor had made such a fool of her. Dorothy and Lou had been mortified. "Mother, I begged you not to talk to the police," Dorothy had snapped at the time.

But Dolly had felt she had to. She had known Skip Reardon and liked him and just felt she had to try to help him. Besides, she really had seen that car, as had Michael, the five-year-old little boy with all the learning problems she had been minding that night. He had seen the car too, but Skip's lawyer had told her not to discuss it.

"That would only hurt our case," Mr. Farrell had said. "All we want you to do is to tell what you saw, that a dark sedan was parked in front of the Reardon house at nine and drove away a few minutes later."

She was sure she had made out one of the numbers and one of

the letters, a 3 and an L. But then the prosecutor had held up a license plate at the back of the courtroom and she hadn't been able to read it. And he had gotten her to admit that she was very fond of Skip Reardon because he had dug out her car one night when she got stuck in a snowdrift.

Dolly knew that just because Skip had been nice to her didn't mean that he couldn't be a murderer, but in her heart she felt that he was innocent, and she prayed for him every night. Sometimes, even now, when she was baby-sitting across the street from the Reardon house, she would look out and think about the night Suzanne was murdered. And she would think about little Michael—his family had moved away several years ago— who would be fifteen now, and how he had pointed to the strange black car and said, "Poppa's car."

Dolly could not know that at the same time on that Sunday evening that she sat looking out the window at what used to be the Reardon house, some ten miles away, at Villa Cesare in Hillsdale, Geoff Dorso and Kerry McGrath were talking about her.

29

By tacit agreement, Kerry and Geoff refrained from any discussion of the Reardon case until coffee was served. During the earlier part of the meal, Geoff talked about spending his youngest years in New York. "I thought of my New

Jersey cousins as living in the sticks," he said. "Then after we moved out ourselves and I grew up here, I decided to stay."

He told Kerry that he had four younger sisters.

"I envy you," she said. "I'm an only child, and I used to love to visit my friends' houses where there was a big family. I always thought it would be nice to have some siblings floating around. My father died when I was nineteen and my mother remarried when I was twenty-one and moved to Colorado. I see her twice a year."

Geoff's eyes softened. "That doesn't give you much family support," he said.

"No, I guess not, but Jonathan and Grace Hoover have helped to fill the gap. They've been wonderful to me, almost like parents."

They talked about law school, agreeing that the first year was a horror they would hate to have to endure again. "What made you decide to be a defense lawyer?" Kerry asked.

"I think it went back to when I was a kid. A woman in our apartment building, Anna Owens, was one of the nicest people I ever knew. I remember when I was about eight and ran through the lobby to catch the elevator, I slammed into her and knocked her over. Anyone else would have had a screaming fit, but she just picked herself up and said, 'Geoff, the elevator will come back, you know.' Then she laughed. She could tell how upset I was."

"That didn't make you become a defense lawyer." Kerry smiled.

"No. But three months later when her husband walked out on her, she followed him to his new girlfriend's apartment and shot him. I honestly believe it was temporary insanity, which was the defense her lawyer tried, but she went to prison for twenty years anyway. I guess the key phrase is 'mitigating circumstances.' When I believe those are present, or when I believe the defendant is innocent, as with Skip Reardon, I take the case." He paused. "And what made you become a prosecutor?"

"The victim and the family of the victim," she said simply. "Based on your theory I could have shot Bob Kinellen and pled mitigating circumstances."

Dorso's eyes flashed with mild irritation, then became amused. "Somehow I don't see you shooting anybody, Kerry."

"I don't either, unless . . ." Kerry hesitated, then continued, "Unless Robin were in danger. Then I'd do whatever it took to save her. I'm sure of that."

Over dinner, Kerry found herself talking about her father's death. "I was in my sophomore year at Boston College. He had been a Pan Am captain and later went into the corporate end and was made an executive vice president. From the time I was three years old, he took my mother and me all over. To me, he was the greatest man in the world." She gulped. "And then one weekend when I was home from college, he said he wasn't feeling right. But he didn't bother going to the doctor because he'd just had his annual physical. He said he'd be fine in the morning. But the next morning, he didn't wake up."

"And your mother remarried two years later?" Geoff asked softly.

"Yes, right before I graduated from college. Sam was a widower and a friend of Dad's. He'd been about to retire to Vail when Dad died. He has a lovely place there. It's been good for both of them."

"What would your father have thought of Bob Kinellen?"

Kerry laughed. "You're very perceptive, Geoff Dorso. I think he would have been underwhelmed."

Over coffee they finally discussed the Reardon case. Kerry began by saying frankly, "I sat in on the sentencing ten years ago, and the look on his face and what he said were imprinted in my memory. I've heard a lot of guilty people swear they were innocent—after all, what have they got to lose?—but there was something about his statement that got to me."

"Because he was telling the truth."

Kerry looked directly at him. "I warn you, Geoff, I intend to play devil's advocate, and while reading that transcript raises a lot of questions for me, it certainly doesn't convince me that Reardon is an innocent man. Neither did yesterday's visit. Either he's lying or Dr. Smith is lying. Skip Reardon has a very good reason to lie. Smith doesn't. I still think it's damaging that the very day Suzanne died, Reardon had discussed divorce and apparently flipped when he learned what it might cost him."

"Kerry, Skip Reardon was a self-made man. He pulled himself out of poverty and had become very successful. Suzanne had already cost him a fortune. You heard him. She was a big-time shopaholic, buying whatever struck her fancy." He paused. "No. Being angry and being vocal about it is one thing. But there's a hell of a difference between blowing off steam and murder. If anything, even though a divorce was going to be expensive, he was actually relieved that his sham marriage was going to be over, so he could get on with his life."

They talked about the sweetheart roses. "I absolutely believe Skip neither brought nor sent them," Geoff said as he sipped espresso. "So if we accept that, we then have the factor of another person."

As Geoff was paying the bill, they both agreed that Dr. Smith's testimony was the linchpin that had convicted Skip Reardon. "Ask yourself this," Geoff urged. "Dr. Smith claimed that Suzanne was afraid of Skip and his jealous rages. But if she were so afraid of him, how could she stand there and calmly arrange flowers another man had sent her, and not only arrange them, but flaunt them, at least according to Skip. Does that make sense?"

"*If* Skip was telling the truth, but we don't know that for an absolute fact, do we?" Kerry said.

"Well, I for one *do* believe him," Geoff said with passion. "Besides, no one testified in corroboration of Dr. Smith's testimony. The Reardons were a popular couple. Surely if he were abusive to her, someone would have come forward to say so."

"Perhaps so," Kerry conceded, "but then why were there no

defense fact witnesses to say that he wasn't insanely jealous? Why were there only two character witnesses called to help counter Dr. Smith's testimony? No, Geoff, I'm afraid that based on the information the jury was given, they had no reason not to trust Dr. Smith and believe him. Besides, aren't we in general conditioned to trust a physician?"

They were quiet on the drive home. As Geoff walked Kerry to her door, he reached for her key. "My mother said you should always open the door for the lady. I hope that's not too sexist."

"No, it isn't. Not for me at least. But maybe I'm just old-fashioned." The sky above them was blue-black and brilliant with stars. A sharp wind was blowing, and Kerry shivered from the chill.

Geoff noticed and quickly turned the key, then pushed open the door. "You're not dressed warmly enough for the night air. You'd better get inside."

As she moved through the entrance, he stayed on the porch, making no move to indicate that he expected her to invite him in. Instead he said, "Before I leave, I have to ask, where do we go from here?"

"I'm going in to see Dr. Smith as soon as he'll give me an appointment. But it's better that I go alone."

"Then we'll talk in the next few days," Geoff said. He smiled briefly and started down the porch steps. Kerry closed the door and walked into the living room but did not immediately turn on the light. She realized she was still savoring the moment when Geoff had taken the key from her hand and opened the door for her. Then she went to the window and watched as he backed his car out of the driveway and disappeared down the street.

Daddy is such fun, Robin thought as she contentedly sat next to him in the Jaguar. They had inspected the ski lodge Bob Kinellen was thinking about buying. She thought it was cool, but he said it was a disappointment. "I want one where we can ski to the door," he had said, and then he'd laughed. "We'll just keep looking."

Robin had brought her camera, and her father waited while she took two rolls of film. Even though there was only a little snow on the peaks, she thought the light on the mountains was fantastic. She caught the last rays of the setting sun, and then they started back. Her father said he knew a great place where they could get terrific shrimp.

Robin knew that Mom was mad at Daddy because he hadn't talked to her after the accident, but he *had* left a message. And it was true, she didn't get to see him much, but when they were together, he was great.

At six-thirty they stopped at the restaurant. Over shrimp and scallops, they talked. He promised that this year for sure they would go skiing, just the two of them. "Sometime when Mom's on a date." He winked.

"Oh, Mom doesn't date much," she told him. "I kind of liked someone who took her out a couple of times during the summer, but she said he was boring."

"What did he do?"

"He was an engineer, I think."

"Well, when Mommy's a judge, she'll probably end up dating another judge. She'll be surrounded by them."

"A lawyer came to the house the other night," Robin said. "He was nice. But I think it was just business."

Bob Kinellen had been only partially involved in the conversation. Now he became attentive. "What was his name?"

"Geoff Dorso. He brought over a big file for Mommy to read."

When her father suddenly became very quiet, Robin had the guilty feeling that maybe she had said too much, that maybe he was mad at her.

When they got back in the car, she slept the rest of the way, and when her father dropped her off at nine-thirty, she was glad to be home.

30

The senate and assembly of the State of New Jersey were having a busy fall. The twice-weekly sessions were almost one hundred percent attended, and for a good reason: The upcoming gubernatorial election, although still a year away, created a behind-the-scenes electricity that crackled through the atmosphere of both chambers.

The fact that Governor Marshall seemed intent on backing Prosecutor Frank Green as his successor did not sit well with a number of his party's other eager would-be candidates. Jonathan Hoover knew full well that any crack in Green's potential ability to be elected would be welcomed by other contenders. They would seize on it and create as much of a distraction as possible. If it got loud enough, it could easily shake loose Green's hold on the nomination. Right now it was far from a lock.

As president of the senate, Hoover had enormous power in party politics. One of the reasons he had been elected five times to four-year terms was his ability to take the long-range view when making decisions or when casting votes. His constituents appreciated that.

On days that the senate met, he sometimes stayed in Trenton and had dinner with friends. Tonight he would be dining with the governor.

Following the afternoon session, Jonathan returned to his private office, asked his secretary to take messages and closed the door. For the next hour he sat at his desk, his hands folded under his chin. It was the posture Grace called "Jonathan at prayer."

When he finally got up, he walked over to the window to stare at the darkening sky. He had made an important decision. Kerry McGrath's probing into the Reardon murder case had created a real problem. It was exactly the kind of thing the media would run with, trying to make it into something sensational. Even if in the end it came to nothing, which Jonathan fully expected, it would create a negative perception of Frank Green and would effectively derail his candidacy.

Of course, Kerry might just drop the whole thing before it got that far—he certainly hoped she would, for everyone's sake. Still, Jonathan knew it was his duty to warn the governor about her investigation so far and to suggest that, for the present, her name should not be submitted to the senate for approval of her judgeship. He knew it would be embarrassing to the governor to have one of his potential appointees effectively working against him.

31

On Monday morning Kerry found a package in her office, and inside was a Royal Doulton china figurine, the one called "Autumn Breezes." There was a note with it:

Dear Ms. McGrath,

Mom's house is sold and we've cleared out all our stuff. We're moving to Pennsylvania to live with our aunt and uncle.

Mom always kept this on her dresser. It had been her mother's. She said it made her happy to see it.

You've made us so happy by making sure that the guy who killed Mom pays for his crime that we want you to have it. It's our way of saying thanks.

The letter was signed by Chris and Ken, the teenage sons of the supervisor who had been murdered by her assistant.

Kerry blinked back tears as she held the lovely object. She called in her secretary and dictated a brief letter:

By law, I'm not allowed to accept any gifts, but, Chris and Ken, I promise you, if it were different, this would be one I'd cherish. Please keep it for me and for your mom.

As she signed the letter she thought about the obvious bond between these brothers, and between them and their mother. What would become of Robin if something happened to me? she wondered. Then she shook her head. There's nothing to be gained in being morbid, she thought. Besides, there was another, more pressing, parent/child situation to investigate.

It was time to pay a visit to Dr. Charles Smith. When she called his office, the answering service picked up. "They won't be in until eleven today. May I take a message?"

Shortly before noon, Kerry received a return call from Mrs. Carpenter.

"I'd like to have an appointment to speak with the doctor as soon as possible," Kerry said. "It's important."

"What is this in reference to, Ms. McGrath?"

Kerry decided to gamble. "Tell the doctor it's in reference to Suzanne."

She waited nearly five minutes, then heard Dr. Smith's cold, precise voice. "What do you want, Ms. McGrath?" he asked.

"I want to talk to you about your testimony at Skip Reardon's trial, Doctor, and I'd appreciate doing it as soon as possible."

By the time she hung up, he had agreed to meet with her in his office at seven-thirty the next morning. She mused that it meant she would have to leave home by six-thirty. And that meant she would have to arrange for a neighbor to phone Robin to make sure she didn't fall back asleep after Kerry had gone.

Otherwise, Robin would be fine. She always walked to school with two of her girlfriends, and Kerry was sure that she was old enough to get herself a bowl of cereal.

Next she phoned her friend Margaret at her office and got Stuart Grant's home phone number. "I talked to Stuart about you and your questions about that plastic surgeon, and he said his wife will be home all morning," Margaret told her.

Susan Grant answered on the first ring. She repeated exactly what Margaret had reported. "I swear, Kerry, it was frightening. I just wanted to have a tuck around the eyes. But Dr. Smith was so intense. He kept calling me Suzanne, and I know that if I had let him have his way, I wouldn't have looked like myself anymore."

Just before lunch, Kerry asked Joe Palumbo to stop by her office. "I have a little extracurricular situation I need your help with," she told him when he slumped in a chair in front of her desk. "The Reardon case."

Joe's quizzical expression demanded an answer. She told him about the Suzanne Reardon look-alikes and Dr. Charles Smith. Hesitantly she admitted that she had also visited Reardon in prison and that, while everything she was doing was strictly unofficial, she was beginning to have her doubts about the way the case was handled.

Palumbo whistled.

"And, Joe, I'd appreciate it if we could keep this just between us. Frank Green is not happy about my interest in the case."

"I wonder why," Palumbo murmured.

"The point is that Green himself told me the other day that Dr. Smith was an unemotional witness. Strange for a father of a murder victim, wouldn't you say? On the stand, Dr. Smith testified that he and his wife had separated when Suzanne was a baby and that a few years later he allowed her to be adopted by her stepfather, a man named Wayne Stevens, and that she grew up in Oakland, California. I'd like you to locate Stevens. I'd be very interested in learning from him what kind of girl Suzanne was growing up, and especially I want to see a picture of her taken when she was a teenager."

She had pulled out several pages of the Reardon trial transcript. Now she shoved them across the desk to Palumbo. "Here's the testimony of a baby-sitter who was across the street the night of the murder and who claims she saw a strange car in front of the Reardon house around nine o'clock that night. She lives—or lived—with her daughter and son-in-law in Alpine. Check her out for me, okay?"

Palumbo's eyes reflected keen interest. "It will be a pleasure,

Kerry. You're doing me a favor. I'd love to see Our Leader be the one on the hot seat for a change."

"Look, Joe, Frank Green's a good guy," Kerry protested. "I'm not interested in upsetting things for him. I just feel that there were some questions left open in the case, and frankly, meeting Dr. Smith and seeing his look-alike patients has spooked me. If there's a chance that the wrong man is in jail, I feel it's my duty to explore it. But I'll do it only if I am convinced."

"I fully understand," Palumbo said. "And don't get me wrong. In most ways I agree with you that Green is an okay guy. It's just that I prefer someone who doesn't run for cover every time someone in this office is taking heat."

32

When Dr. Charles Smith hung up the phone after talking to Kerry McGrath, he realized that the faint tremor that came and went in his right hand was beginning again. He closed his left hand over it, but even so, he could feel the vibrations in his fingertips.

He knew that Mrs. Carpenter had looked at him curiously when she told him about the McGrath woman's phone call. The mention of Suzanne had meant nothing to Carpenter, which no doubt had made her wonder what this mysterious call was all about.

Now he opened Robin Kinellen's file and studied it. He remembered that her parents were divorced, but he had not studied the personal data Kerry McGrath had submitted along with Robin's medical history. It said that she was an assistant prosecutor, Bergen County. He paused for a moment. He didn't remember ever having seen her at the trial . . .

There was a tap at the door. Mrs. Carpenter stuck her head in the office to remind him that he had a patient waiting in examinating room 1.

"I'm aware of that," he said brusquely, waving her away. He turned back to Robin's file. She had come in for checkups on the eleventh and the twenty-third. Barbara Tompkins had been in for a checkup on the eleventh and Pamela Worth on the twenty-third. Unfortunate timing, he thought. Kerry McGrath had probably seen both of them, and it had somehow triggered whatever memory she had of Suzanne.

For long minutes he sat at the desk. What did her call really mean? What interest had she in the case? Nothing could have changed. The facts were still the same. Skip Reardon was still in prison, and that's where he would remain. Smith knew that his testimony had helped to put him there. And I won't change one word of it, he thought bitterly. Not one word.

33

Sandwiched between his two attorneys, Robert Kinellen and Anthony Bartlett, Jimmy Weeks sat in federal district court as the seemingly endless process of selecting a jury for his income tax evasion trial dragged on.

After three weeks, only six jurors had been found acceptable to both prosecution and defense. The woman being questioned now was the kind he most dreaded. Prim and self-righteous, a pillar-of-the-community type. President of the Westdale Women's Club, she had stated; her husband the CEO of an engineering firm; two sons at Yale.

Jimmy studied her as the questioning went on and her attitude became more and more condescending. Sure she was satisfactory to the prosecution, no question about that. But he knew from the disdainful glance she swept in his direction that she considered him dirt.

When the judge was finished questioning the woman, Jimmy Weeks leaned over to Kinellen and said, "Accept her."

"Are you out of your mind?" Bob snapped incredulously.

"Bobby, trust me." Jimmy lowered his voice. "This will be a freebie." Then Jimmy glanced angrily down the defense table to where an impassive Barney Haskell sat watching the proceedings with his lawyer. If Haskell cut a deal with the prosecution and became their witness, Kinellen claimed he could destroy Barney on the stand.

Maybe. And maybe not. Jimmy Weeks wasn't so sure, and he was a man who always liked a sure thing. He had at least one juror in his pocket. Now he probably had two.

So far, there had only been the mention of Kinellen's ex-wife looking into the Reardon murder case, Weeks mused, but if anything actually went forward with it, he knew it could prove awkward for him. Especially if Haskell got wind of it. It might occur to him that he had another way to sweeten any deal he was trying to make with the prosecution.

34

Late that afternoon, Geoff Dorso's secretary buzzed him on the intercom. "Miss Taylor is here," she said. "I told her I was sure you couldn't see her without an appointment. She said it will only take a few minutes and that it's important."

For Beth Taylor to just show up without calling first, it had to be important. "It's okay," Geoff said. "Send her in."

His pulse quickened as he waited. He prayed that she wasn't there to tell him that something had happened to Skip Reardon's mother. Mrs. Reardon had had a heart attack shortly after Skip's conviction and another one five years ago. She had managed to bounce back from both, declaring that there was no way on earth that she was going to die while her son was still in prison for a crime he didn't commit.

She wrote Skip every day—cheery, happy letters, full of plans for his future. On a recent visit to the prison, Geoff had listened as Skip read him an excerpt from one he had received that day: "At mass this morning, I reminded God that while all things come to him who waits, we've waited long enough. And you know, Skip, the most wonderful feeling came over me. It was almost as though I was hearing in my mind a voice saying, 'not much longer.'"

Skip had laughed wryly. "You know, Geoff, when I read this, I almost believed it."

When his secretary escorted Beth into his office, Geoff came around his desk and kissed her affectionately. Whenever he saw her, the same thought always flashed immediately into his mind: What a different life Skip would have had if he had married Beth Taylor and never met Suzanne.

Beth was Skip's age, almost forty now, about five feet six, comfortable size 12, with short, wavy brown hair, lively brown eyes and a face that radiated intelligence and warmth. She had been a teacher when she and Skip were dating fifteen years ago. Since then she had earned her master's degree and now worked as a guidance counselor in a nearby school.

By her expression today it was obvious she was deeply troubled. Indicating a comfortable seating area at the end of the room, Geoff said, "I know they made a fresh pot of coffee half an hour ago. How about it?"

Her smile came and went. "I'd like that."

He studied her expression as they made casual chatter and he poured them both some coffee. She looked worried rather than grief-stricken. He was now sure nothing had happened to Mrs. Reardon. Then another possibility occurred to him. Good God, has Beth met someone she's interested in and doesn't know how to tell Skip? He knew that such a thing might happen—perhaps even *should* happen—but he knew that it would be rough on Skip.

As soon as they were settled, Beth came directly to the point. "Geoff, I talked to Skip on the phone last night. He sounds so terribly depressed. I'm really worried. You know how much talk there is about cutting off repeated appeals from convicted murderers. Skip has practically been kept alive on the hope that someday one of the appeals will be upheld. If he ever gives up that hope completely—I know him, he'll want to die. He told me about that assistant prosecutor visiting him. He's sure she doesn't believe him."

"Do you think he's becoming suicidal?" Geoff asked quickly. "If so, we have to do something about it. As a model prisoner, he's getting more privileges. I should warn the warden."

"No, no! Don't even think about reporting that!" Beth cried. "I don't mean he'd do anything to himself now. He knows he'd be killing his mother too. I just . . ." She threw out her hands in a helpless gesture. "Geoff," she burst out, "is there any hope I can give him? Or maybe I'm asking if you realistically believe you'll find grounds to file a new appeal."

If this were a week ago, Geoff thought, I'd have had to tell her that I've gone over every inch of this case and I can't find even a suggestion of new grounds. Kerry McGrath's call, however, had made the difference.

Careful not to sound overly encouraging, he told Beth about the two women Kerry McGrath had seen in Dr. Smith's office and of Kerry's growing interest in the case. As he watched the radiant hope grow on Beth's face, he prayed that he was not leading her and Skip down a path that would ultimately prove to be another dead end.

Beth's eyes were filling with tears. "Then Kerry McGrath still is looking into the case?"

"Very definitely. She's quite something, Beth." As Geoff heard himself saying those words, he was visualizing Kerry; the way she tucked a lock of blond hair behind her ear as she was concentrating, the wistful look in her eyes when she talked about her father, her trim, slender body, her rueful, self-deprecating smile when Bob Kinellen's name came up, the joyful pride that emanated from her when she talked about her daughter.

He was hearing her slightly husky voice and seeing the almost shy smile she gave him when he had taken the key and opened the door for her. It was obvious to him that after her father's death, no one had ever taken care of Kerry.

"Geoff, if there are grounds for an appeal, do you think we made a mistake last time by not telling about me?"

Beth's question yanked him back to the present. She was referring to one aspect of the case that had never come out in court. Just prior to Suzanne Reardon's death, Skip and Beth had started to see each other again. A few weeks earlier, they had bumped into each other, and Skip had insisted on taking her to lunch. They had ended up talking for hours, and he had confessed to her how unhappy he was and how much he regretted their breakup. "I made a stupid mistake," he had told her, "but for what it's worth, it's not going to last much longer. I've been married to Suzanne for four years, and for at least three of them I've been wondering how I ever let you go."

On the night Suzanne died, Beth and Skip were scheduled to have dinner together. She had had to cancel at the last minute, however, and it was then that Skip had gone home to find Suzanne arranging the roses.

At the time of the trial, Geoff had agreed with Skip's chief counsel, Tim Farrell, that to put Beth on the stand was a double-edged sword. The prosecution no doubt would try to make it seem that in addition to avoiding the expense of a divorce, Skip Reardon had another compelling reason for killing his wife.

On the other hand, Beth's testimony might have been effective in dispelling Dr. Smith's contention that Skip was insanely jealous of Suzanne.

Until Kerry had told him about Dr. Smith, and about the look-alikes, Geoff had been sure that they had made the right decision. Now he was less sure. He looked squarely at Beth. "I didn't tell Kerry about you yet. But now I want her to meet you, and to hear your story. If we have any chance at all for a new and successful appeal, all the cards have to be on the table."

35

When she was ready to leave the house for her early morning appointment with Dr. Smith, Kerry shook awake a protesting Robin. "Come on, Rob," she urged. "You're always telling me I treat you like a baby."

"You do," Robin mumbled.

"All right. I'm giving you a chance to prove your independence. I want you to get up now and get dressed. Otherwise you'll fall asleep again. Mrs. Weiser will phone at seven to be sure you didn't let yourself fall back asleep. I left cereal and juice out. Make certain the door is locked when you leave for school."

Robin yawned and closed her eyes.

"Rob, please."

"Okay." With a sigh Robin swung her legs over the side of the bed. Her hair fell forward over her face as she rubbed her eyes.

Kerry smoothed it back. "Can I trust you?"

Robin looked up with a slow, sleepy smile. "Uh-huh."

"Okay." Kerry kissed the top of her head. "Now remember, same rules as any other time. Don't open the door for anyone.

I'll set the alarm. You deactivate it only when you're ready to leave, then reset it. Don't take a ride from anyone unless you're with Cassie and Courtney and it's one of their parents."

"I know. I know." Robin sighed dramatically.

Kerry grinned. "I know I've given you the same spiel a thousand times. See you tonight. Alison will be here at three."

Alison was the high school student who stayed with Robin after school until Kerry came home. Kerry had thought about having her come over this morning to see Robin off but had acceded to her daughter's vigorous protest that she wasn't a baby and could get herself off to school.

"See you, Mom."

Robin listened to Kerry's steps going down the stairs, then went over to the window to watch the car pull out of the driveway.

The room was chilly. By seven o'clock, when she usually got up, the house was toasty warm. Just for a minute, Robin thought as she slipped back into bed. I'll just lie here for a minute more.

At seven o'clock, after the phone had rung six times, she sat up and answered it. "Oh, thanks, Mrs. Weiser. Yes, I'm sure I'm up."

I am now, she thought as she hurried out of bed.

36

Despite the early hour, the traffic into Manhattan was heavy. But at least it was moving at a reasonable clip, Kerry thought. Nevertheless it took her a full hour to drive from New Jersey, down what was left of the West Side Highway and across town to Dr. Smith's Fifth Avenue office. She was three minutes late.

The doctor let her in himself. Even the minimal courtesy he had shown on Robin's two visits was lacking this morning. He did not greet her except to say, "I can give you twenty minutes, Ms. McGrath, and not a second more." He led her to his private office.

If that's the way we're going to play it, Kerry thought, then fine. When she was seated across his desk from him, she said, "Dr. Smith, after seeing two women emerge from this office who startlingly resembled your murdered daughter, Suzanne, I became curious enough about the circumstances of her death to take time this last week to read the transcript of Skip Reardon's trial."

She did not miss the look of hatred that came over Dr. Smith's face when she mentioned Reardon's name. His eyes narrowed, his mouth tightened, deep furrows appeared on his forehead and in vertical slashes down his cheeks.

She looked directly at him. "Dr. Smith, I want you to know

how terribly sorry I am that you lost your daughter. You were a divorced parent. I'm a divorced parent. Like you, I have an only child, a daughter. Knowing the agony I was in when I received the call that Robin had been in an accident, I can only imagine how you felt when you were told about Suzanne."

Smith looked at her steadily, his fingers locked together. Kerry had the feeling that there was an impenetrable barrier between them. If so, the rest of their conversation was entirely predictable. He would hear her out, make some sort of statement about love and loss, and then usher her to the door. How could she break through that barrier?

She leaned forward. "Dr. Smith, your testimony is the reason Skip Reardon is in prison. You said he was insanely jealous, that your daughter was afraid of him. He swears that he never threatened Suzanne."

"He's lying." The voice was flat, unemotional. "He truly was insanely jealous of her. As you said, she was my only child. I doted on her. I had become successful enough to give her the kinds of things I could never give her as a child. It was my pleasure from time to time to buy her a piece of fine jewelry. Yet, even when I spoke to Reardon, he refused to believe that they had been gifts from me. He kept accusing her of seeing other men."

Is it possible? Kerry wondered. "But if Suzanne was in fear for her life, why did she stay with Skip Reardon?" she asked.

The morning sun was flooding the room in such a way that it shone on Smith's rimless glasses, making it so that Kerry could no longer see his eyes. Could they possibly be as flat as his expressionless voice? she thought to herself. "Because unlike her mother, my former wife, Suzanne had a sense of deep commitment to her marriage," he responded after a pause. "The grave mistake of her life was to fall in love with Reardon. An even graver mistake was not to take his threats seriously."

Kerry realized she was getting nowhere. It was time to ask the question that had occurred to her earlier, but that possibly held implications she wasn't sure she was prepared to face. "Dr. Smith, did you ever perform any surgical procedures of any kind on your daughter?"

It was immediately clear that her question outraged him. "Ms. McGrath, I happen to belong to the school of physicians who would never, except in dire emergency, treat a family member. Beyond that, the question is insulting. Suzanne was a natural beauty."

"You've made at least two women resemble her to a startling degree. Why?"

Dr. Smith looked at his watch. "I'll answer this final question, and then you will have to excuse me, Ms. McGrath. I don't know how much you know about plastic surgery. Fifty years ago, by today's standards, it was quite primitive. After people had nose jobs, they had to live with flaring nostrils. Reconstructive work on victims born with deformities such as a harelip was often a crude procedure. It is now very sophisticated, and the results are most satisfying. We've learned a great deal. Plastic surgery is no longer for only the rich and famous. It is for anyone, whether he or she needs it, or simply wants it."

He took off his glasses and rubbed his forehead as though he had a headache. "Parents bring in teenagers, boys as well as girls, who are so conscious of a perceived defect that they simply can't function. Yesterday I operated on a fifteen-year-old boy whose ears stuck out so much that they were the only thing one saw when looking at him. When the bandages come off, all his other quite pleasing features, which had been obscured by this offending problem, will be what people see when they look at him.

"I operate on women who look in the mirror and see sagging skin or baggy eyes, women who had been beautiful girls in their youth. I raise and clamp the forehead under the hairline, I tighten the skin and pull it up behind the ears. I take twenty years off their appearance, but more than that, I transform their self-deprecation into self-worth."

His voice rose. "I could show you before-and-after pictures of accident victims whom I have helped. You ask me why several of my patients resemble my daughter. I'll tell you why. Because in these ten years, a few plain and unhappy young women came into this office and I was able to give them her kind of beauty."

Kerry knew he was about to tell her to leave. Hurriedly, she asked, "Then why several years ago did you tell a potential patient, Susan Grant, that beauty sometimes is abused, and the result is jealousy and violence? Weren't you talking about Suzanne? Isn't it a fact that Skip Reardon may have had a reason to be jealous? Perhaps you did buy her all the jewelry Skip couldn't account for, but he swears he did not send Suzanne those roses she received on the day of her death."

Dr. Smith stood up. "Ms. McGrath, I should think in your business you ought to know that murderers almost inevitably plead innocence. And now, this discussion is over."

There was nothing Kerry could do except follow him from the room. As she walked behind him, she noticed that he was holding his right hand rigidly against his side. Was that a tremor in his hand? Yes, it was.

At the door he said, "Ms. McGrath, you must understand that the sound of Skip Reardon's name sickens me. Please call Mrs. Carpenter and give her the name of another physician to whom she can forward Robin's file. I do not want to hear from you or see you or your daughter again."

He was so close to her that Kerry stepped back involuntarily. There was something genuinely frightening about the man. His eyes, filled with anger and hatred, seemed to be burning through her. If he had a gun in his hand right now, I swear he'd use it, she thought to herself.

37

After she locked the door and started down the steps, Robin noticed the small dark car parked across the street. Strange cars weren't common on this street, especially at this hour, but she didn't know why this one gave her an especially funny feeling.

It was cold. She shifted her books to her left arm and zipped her jacket the rest of the way to her neck, then quickened her steps. She was meeting Cassie and Courtney at the corner a block away and knew they probably were already waiting. She was a couple of minutes late.

The street was quiet. Now that the leaves were almost gone, the trees had a bare, unfriendly look. Robin wished she had remembered to wear gloves.

When she reached the sidewalk, she glanced across the street. The driver's window in the strange car was opening slowly, stopping after it had been lowered only a few inches. She stared at it as hard as she could, hoping to see a familiar face inside, but the bright morning sun reflected in such a way that she could see nothing. Then she saw a hand reach out, pointing something at her. Suddenly panicked, Robin began to run. With a roar, the car came rushing across the road, seemingly aimed right toward her. Just as she thought it was going to come up the curb and hit her, it swerved into a U-turn and then raced down the block.

Sobbing, Robin ran across the lawn of their neighbor's house and frantically rang the doorbell.

38

When Joe Palumbo finished his investigation of a break-in in Cresskill, he realized that it was only nine-thirty. Since he was a scant few minutes away from Alpine, it seemed like a perfect opportunity to look up Dolly Bowles, the baby-sitter who had testified at the Reardon murder trial. Fortunately, he also happened to have her phone number with him.

Dolly initially sounded a little guarded when Palumbo explained that he was an investigator with the Bergen County prosecutor's office. But after he told her that one of the assistant prosecutors, Kerry McGrath, very much wanted to hear about the car Dolly had seen in front of the Reardon house the night of the murder, she announced that she had been following the trial Kerry McGrath recently had prosecuted and was so glad that the man who shot his supervisor had been convicted. She told Palumbo about the time she and her mother had been tied up in their home by an intruder.

"So," she finished, "if you and Kerry McGrath want to talk to me, that's fine."

"Well, actually," Joe told her somewhat lamely, "I'd like to come over and talk to you right now. Maybe Kerry will talk to you later."

There was a pause. Palumbo could not know that, in her mind, Dolly was seeing again the derisive expression on the face of Prosecutor Green when he cross-examined her at the trial.

Finally she spoke. "I think," she said, with dignity, "that I would be more comfortable discussing that night with Kerry McGrath. I think it's best we wait until she is available."

39

It was 9:45 before Kerry got to the courthouse, much later than she normally arrived. Anticipating the possibility of receiving a bit of flack about it, she had phoned to say she had an errand and was going to be late. Frank Green was always at his desk promptly at seven o'clock. It was something they joked about, but it was obvious he believed that his entire staff should be on board with him. Kerry knew he would have a fit if he learned that her errand was to see Dr. Charles Smith.

When she punched in the code that admitted her to the prosecutor's office, the switchboard operator looked up and said, "Kerry, go right into Mr. Green's office. He's expecting you."

Oh boy, Kerry thought.

As soon as she walked into Green's office, she could see he was not angry. She knew him well enough to be able to read his mood. As usual he came directly to the point. "Kerry, Robin is fine. She's with your neighbor, Mrs. Weiser. Emphatically, she is all right."

Kerry felt her throat tighten. "Then what's wrong?"

"We're not sure and maybe nothing. According to Robin, you left the house at six-thirty." There was a glint of curiosity in Green's eyes.

"Yes, I did."

"When Robin was leaving the house later, she said she noticed a strange car parked across the street. When she reached the sidewalk, the window on the driver's door opened slightly, and she was able to see a hand holding some kind of object. She couldn't tell what it was, and she wasn't able to see the driver's face. Then the car started up and veered across the street so suddenly she thought it would come up on the sidewalk and hit her, but it quickly went into a U-turn and took off. Robin ran to your neighbor's house."

Kerry sank into a chair. "She's there now?"

"Yes. You can call her, or go home if that would reassure you. My concern is, does Robin have an overactive imagination, or is it possible someone was trying to frighten her and ultimately frighten you?"

"Why would anyone want to frighten Robin or me?"

"It's happened before in this office after a high-profile case. You've just completed a case that got a lot of media attention. The guy you convicted of murder was clearly an out-and-out sleaze and still has relatives and friends."

"Yes, but all of them I met seemed to be pretty decent people," Kerry said. "And to answer your first question, Robin is a level-headed kid. She wouldn't imagine something like this." She hesitated. "It's the first time I let her get herself out in the morning, and I was bombarding her with warnings about what to do and not do."

"Call her from here," Green directed.

Robin answered Mrs. Weiser's telephone on the first ring. "I knew you'd call, Mom. I'm okay now. I want to go to school. Mrs. Weiser said she'd drive me. And Mom, I've still got to go out this afternoon. It's Halloween."

Kerry thought quickly. Robin was better off in school than sitting at home all day, thinking about the incident. "All right, but I'll be there at school to pick you up at quarter of three. I don't want you walking home." And I'll be right with you when you trick-or-treat, she thought. "Now let me talk to Mrs. Weiser, Rob," she said.

When she hung up, she said, "Frank, is it all right if I leave early today?"

His smile was genuine. "Of course it is. Kerry, I don't have to tell you to question Robin carefully. We have to know if there's any chance someone really was watching for her."

As Kerry was leaving, he added, "But isn't Robin a bit young to see herself off to school?"

Kerry knew he was fishing to find out what had been so important that she had left Robin alone at home at six-thirty.

"Yes, she is," she agreed. "It won't happen again."

Later that morning, Joe Palumbo stopped by Kerry's office and told her about his call to Dolly Bowles. "She doesn't want to talk to me, Kerry, but I'd still like to go with you when you see her."

"Let me phone her now."

Her six-word greeting, "Hello, Mrs. Bowles, I'm Kerry McGrath," led to being on the receiving end of a ten-minute monologue.

Palumbo crossed his legs and leaned back in the chair as with some amusement he watched Kerry try to interject a word or question. Then he was irritated when, after Kerry finally got an opportunity to say that she would like to bring her investigator, Mr. Palumbo, with her, it was obvious the answer was no.

Finally she hung up. "Dolly Bowles is not a happy camper about the way she was treated by this office ten years ago. That was the gist of the conversation. The rest is that her daughter and son-in-law don't want her talking about the murder or what she saw anymore, and they're coming back from a trip tomorrow. If I want to see her, it's got to be about five o'clock today. That's going to take some juggling. I told her I'd let her know."

"Can you get out of here in time?" Joe asked.

"I have a few appointments I'm canceling anyhow." She told Palumbo about Robin and the incident this morning.

The investigator rose to his feet and tried to close the jacket that always strained over his generous middle. "I'll meet you at your place at five," he suggested. "While you're with Mrs. Bowles, let me take Robin for a hamburger. I'd like to talk to her about this morning." He saw the look of disapproval on Kerry's face and hastened to speak before she could protest. "Kerry, you're smart, but you're not going to be objective about this. Don't do my job for me."

Kerry studied Joe thoughtfully. His appearance was always a little disheveled, and his paperwork was usually somewhat disorganized, but he was just about the best there was at his job. Kerry had seen him question young children so skillfully that they didn't realize every word they said was being analyzed. It would be very helpful to have Joe's spin on this. "Okay," she agreed.

40

On Tuesday afternoon, Jason Arnott drove from Alpine to the remote area near Ellenville in the Catskills where his sprawling country home, hidden by the surrounding mountain range, concealed his priceless stolen treasures.

He knew the house was an addiction, an extension of the sometimes uncontrollable drive that made him steal the beautiful things he saw in the homes of his acquaintances. For it was beauty, after all, that made him do those things. He loved beauty, loved the look of it, the feel. Sometimes the urge to hold something, to caress it, was so strong it was almost overwhelming. It was a gift, and as such, both a blessing and a curse. Someday it would get him in trouble. As it almost had already. It made him impatient when visitors admired carpets or furniture or paintings or objets d'art in his Alpine home. Often he amused himself by contemplating how shocked they would be if he were to blurt out, "This place is ordinary by my standards."

But, of course, he never would say that, for he had no desire to share his private collection with anyone. That was his alone. And must be kept that way.

Today is Halloween, he thought dismissively as he drove swiftly up Route 17. He was glad to get away. He had no desire to be victimized by children endlessly ringing his doorbell. He was tired.

Over the weekend he had stayed at a hotel in Bethesda, Maryland, and used the time to burglarize a Chevy Chase home at which he had attended a party a few months earlier. At that gathering, the hostess, Myra Hamilton, had rattled on about her son's upcoming wedding, which would take place on October 28th in Chicago, effectively announcing to one and all that the house would be empty on that date.

The Hamilton house was not large, but it was exquisite, filled with precious items the Hamiltons had collected over the years. Jason had salivated over a Fabergé desk seal in sapphire blue with a gold egg-shaped handle. That and a delicate three-by-five-foot Aubusson with a central rosace that they used as a wall hanging were the two things he most wanted to wrest from them.

Now both objects were in the trunk of his car, on their way to his retreat. Unconsciously, Jason frowned. He was not experiencing his usual sensation of triumph at having achieved his goal. A vague, indefinable worry was nagging at him. Mentally he reviewed the modus operandi of entering the Hamilton home, going over it step by step.

The alarm had been on but easy to disengage. Clearly the house was empty, as he had anticipated. For a moment, he had been tempted to go through the place quickly, looking for anything of great value he might have missed noticing at the party. Instead he stuck to his original plan, taking only those things he had scoped out earlier.

He had barely inched his way into the traffic on Route 240 when two police cars, sirens screaming and lights flashing, raced past him and turned left onto the street he had just exited. It was obvious to him that they were on their way to the Hamilton home. Which, of course, meant that he had somehow triggered a silent alarm that operated independently of the master system.

What other kind of security did the Hamiltons have? he wondered. It was so easy to conceal cameras now. He had been wearing the stocking mask he always put on when entering one of the houses he had chosen to honor with his attention, but at one point this night he had pulled it up to examine a bronze figurine, a foolish thing to do—it had proved to be of no real value.

One chance in a million that a camera caught my face, Jason reassured himself. He would dismiss his misgivings and go on with his life, albeit a bit more cautiously for a while.

The afternoon sun was almost lost behind the mountains when he pulled into his driveway. At last he felt a measure of buoyancy. The nearest neighbor was several miles away. Maddie, the weekly cleaning woman—large, stolid, unimaginative and unquestioning woman that she was—would have been in yesterday. Everything would be shining.

He knew she didn't recognize the difference between an Aubusson and a ten-dollar-a-yard carpet remnant, but she was one of those rare creatures who took pride in her work and was satisfied only with perfection. In ten years, she had never so much as chipped a cup.

Jason smiled to himself, thinking of Maddie's reaction when she found the Aubusson hanging in the foyer and the Fabergé desk seal in the master bedroom. *Hasn't he got enough stuff to dust?* she would wonder and go on with her chores.

He parked the car at the side door and, with the rush of anticipation that always surged over him when he came here, entered the house and reached for the light switch. Once again, the sight of so many beautiful things made his lips and hands moist with pleasure. A few minutes later, after his overnight case, a small bag of groceries and his new treasures were safely inside, he locked the door and drew the bolt. His evening had begun.

His first task was to carry the Fabergé seal upstairs and place it on the antique dressing table. Once it was in place, he stood back to admire it, then leaned over to compare it with the miniature frame that had been on his night table for the past ten years.

The frame represented one of the few times he had been fooled.

It was a decent Fabergé copy, but certainly not the real thing. That fact seemed so obvious now. The blue enamel looked muddy when compared to the deep color of the desk seal. The gold border encrusted with pearls was nothing like authentic Fabergé workmanship. But from inside that frame, Suzanne's face smiled back at him.

He didn't like to think about that night, almost eleven years ago. He had gone in through the open window of the sitting room of the master bedroom suite. He knew the house was supposed to be empty. That very day, Suzanne had told him about her dinner engagement for the evening, and the fact that Skip would not be home. He had the security code, but when he got there, he saw that the window was wide open. When he entered the upstairs floor, it was dark. In the bedroom he spotted the miniature frame he had seen earlier; it was on top of the night table. From across the room it looked authentic. He was just examining it closely when he heard a raised voice. Suzanne! Panicking, he had dropped the frame in his pocket and hidden in a closet.

Jason looked down at the frame now. Over the years he had sometimes wondered what perverse reason kept him from removing Suzanne's picture from it, or from throwing the whole thing away. The frame was, after all, only a copy.

But as he stared at it this night, he understood for the first time why he had left the picture and frame intact. It was because it made it easier for him to blot out the memory of how gruesome and distorted Suzanne's features had been when he made his escape.

41

"Well, we've got our jury impaneled and it's a good one," Bob Kinellen told his client with a heartiness he did not feel.

Jimmy Weeks looked at him sourly. "Bobby, with a few exceptions, I think that jury stinks."

"Trust me."

Anthony Bartlett backed up his son-in-law. "Bob's right, Jimmy. Trust him." Then Bartlett's eyes strayed to the opposite end of the defense table where Barney Haskell was sitting, his expression morose, his hands supporting his head. He saw that Bob was looking at Haskell too, and he knew what Bob was thinking.

Haskell's a diabetic. He won't want to risk years in prison. He's got dates and facts and figures that we'll have a hell of a time contradicting . . . He knew all about Suzanne.

The opening arguments would begin the next morning. When he left the courthouse, Jimmy Weeks went directly to his car. As the chauffeur held the door open, he slid into the backseat without his usual grunted good-bye.

Kinellen and Bartlett watched the car pull away. "I'm going back to the office," Kinellen told his father-in-law. "I've got work to do."

Bartlett nodded. "I would say so." There was an impersonal tone to his voice. "See you in the morning, Bob."

Sure you will, Kinellen thought as he walked to the parking garage. You're distancing yourself from me so that if my hands get dirty, you're not part of it.

He knew that Bartlett had millions salted away. Even if Weeks was convicted and the law firm went under, he would be all right. Maybe he would get to spend more time in Palm Beach with his wife, Alice Senior.

I'm taking all the risks, Bob Kinellen thought as he handed his ticket to the cashier. I'm the one who risks going down. There had to be a reason Jimmy insisted on leaving the Wagner woman on the jury. What was it?

42

Geoff Dorso phoned Kerry just as she was about to leave the office. "I saw Dr. Smith this morning," she told him hurriedly, "and I'm seeing Dolly Bowles around five. I can't talk now. I've got to meet Robin at school."

"Kerry, I'm anxious to know what happened with Dr. Smith, and what you learn from Dolly Bowles. Can we have dinner?"

"I don't want to go out tonight, but if you don't mind a salad and pasta . . ."

"I'm Italian, remember?"

"About seven-thirty?"

"I'll be there."

When she picked up Robin at school, it was clear to Kerry that her daughter's mind was much more on Halloween trick-or-treating than on the early-morning incident. In fact, Robin seemed to be embarrassed about it. Taking her cue from her daughter, Kerry dropped the subject, for now at least.

When they reached home, she gave Robin's teenage sitter the afternoon off. This is the way other mothers live, she thought as, with several of them, she trailed a cluster of trick-or-treating children. She and Robin arrived back at their place just in time to let Joe Palumbo in.

He was carrying a bulging briefcase, which he tapped with a satisfied smile. "The records of the office investigation of the Reardon case," he told her. "It'll have Dolly Bowles' original statement. Let's see how it compares with what she has to say to you now."

He looked at Robin, who was wearing a witch's costume. "That's some outfit, Rob."

"It was between this and being a corpse," Robin told him.

Kerry did not realize she had winced until she caught the look of understanding in Palumbo's eyes.

"I'd better be on my way," she said hurriedly.

During the twenty-minute drive to Alpine, Kerry realized her nerves were on edge. She had finally gotten Robin to talk briefly about the incident that morning. By then, Robin was trying to play the whole thing down. Kerry wanted to believe that Robin had exaggerated what had happened. She wanted to conclude that someone had stopped to check an address and then realized he was on the wrong block. But Kerry knew her daughter would not have exaggerated or imagined the incident.

. . .

It was obvious to Kerry that Dolly Bowles had been watching for her. As soon as she was parked in the driveway of the massive Tudor house, the door was yanked open.

Dolly was a small woman with thinning gray hair and a narrow, inquisitive face. She was already talking when Kerry reached her, ". . . just like your picture in *The Record*. I was so sorry I was busy baby-sitting and couldn't make it to the trial of that awful man who killed his supervisor."

She led Kerry into a cavernous foyer and indicated a small sitting room to the left. "Let's go in here. That living room is too big for my taste. I tell my daughter my voice echoes in it, but she loves it 'cause it's great for parties. Dorothy loves to throw parties. When they're home, that is. Now that Lou is retired, they never settle down; they're here and there, hither and yon. Why they need to pay a full-time housekeeper is beyond me. I say, why not have someone come in once a week? Save the money. Of course, I don't really like to be alone overnight, and I suppose that has something to do with it. On the other hand . . ."

Oh my God, Kerry thought, she's a sweet woman, but I'm just not in the mood for this. She chose a straight-backed chair, while Mrs. Bowles settled on the chintz-covered couch. "Mrs. Bowles, I don't want to take too much of your time and I have someone minding my daughter, so I can't stay too long . . ."

"You have a daughter. How nice. How old is she?"

"Ten. Mrs. Bowles, what I'd like to know—"

"You don't look old enough to have a ten-year-old daughter."

"Thank you. I can assure you I feel old enough." Kerry felt as though she had driven into a ditch and might never get out. "Mrs. Bowles, let's talk about the night Suzanne Reardon died."

Fifteen minutes later, after she had heard all about Dolly baby-sitting across the street from the Reardons, and how Michael, the little boy she was minding that night, had serious developmental problems, she managed to isolate one nugget of information.

"You say that you are positive that the car you saw parked in front of the Reardons did not belong to one of the guests at the neighbors' party. Why are you so sure of that?"

"Because I talked to those people myself. They were entertaining three other couples. They told me who the guests were. They're all from Alpine, and after Mr. Green made me feel like such a fool on the stand, I called each of them myself. And you know what? None of those guests was driving Poppa's car."

"*Poppa's car!*" Kerry exclaimed incredulously.

"That's what Michael called it. You see, he had a real problem with colors. You'd point to a car and ask him what color it was, and he wouldn't know. But no matter how many cars were around, he could pick out one that was familiar, or one that looked just like a familiar car. When he said 'Poppa's car' that night, he had to have been pointing at the black Mercedes four-door sedan. You see, he called his grandfather Poppa and loved to ride with him in his car—his black Mercedes four-door sedan. It was dark, but the torch light at the end of the Reardons' driveway was on so he could see it clearly."

"Mrs. Bowles, you testified that you had seen the car."

"Yes, although it wasn't there at seven-thirty when I got to Michael's house, and when he pointed it out it was pulling away, so I didn't get a good look at it. Still, I had an impression of a 3 and an L on the license plate." Dolly Bowles leaned forward intensely, and behind the round glasses her eyes widened. "Ms. McGrath, I tried to tell Skip Reardon's defense attorney about this. His name was Farrer—no, Farrell. He told me that hearsay evidence usually isn't admissible and, even if it were, hearsay evidence from a developmentally disabled child would only dilute my testimony that I'd seen the car. But he was wrong. I don't see why I couldn't have told the jury that Michael became all excited when he thought he had seen his grandfather's car. I think that would have helped."

Her voice lost its faint quaver. "Ms. McGrath, at a couple of minutes past nine o'clock that night, a black Mercedes four-door sedan drove away from the Reardon home. I know that for a fact. Absolutely."

43

Jonathan Hoover was not enjoying his predinner martini this evening. Usually he savored this time of day, sipping the smooth gin diluted with precisely three drops of vermouth and enhanced with two olives, sitting in his wing chair by the fire, conversing with Grace about the day.

Tonight, added to his own concerns, it was obvious that something was troubling Grace. If the pain was worse than usual he knew she would never admit it. They never discussed her health. Long ago he had learned not to ask more than a perfunctory, "How do you feel, dear?"

The answer was inevitably, "Not bad at all."

The increasing rheumatic assault on her body did not prevent Grace from dressing with her innate elegance. Nowadays she always wore long loose sleeves to cover her swollen wrists and in the evening, even when they were alone, chose flowing hostess gowns that concealed the steadily progressing deformity of her legs and feet.

Propped up as she was, in a half-lying position on the couch, the curvature in her spine was not apparent, and her luminous gray eyes were beautiful against the alabaster white of her complexion. Only her hands, the fingers gnarled and twisted, were visible indicators of her devastating illness.

Because Grace always stayed in bed till midmorning, and Jonathan was an early riser, the evening was their time to visit and gossip. Now Grace gave him a wry smile. "I feel as though I'm looking in a mirror, Jon. You're upset about something too, and I bet it's the same thing that was bothering you earlier, so let me go first. I spoke to Kerry."

Jonathan raised his eyebrows. "And?"

"I'm afraid she has no intention of letting go of the Reardon case."

"What did she tell you?"

"It's what she *didn't* tell me. She was evasive. She listened to me, then said that she had reason to believe that Dr. Smith's testimony was false. She did acknowledge that she had no concrete reason to believe that Reardon wasn't the murderer, but she felt it was her obligation to explore the possibility that there might have been a miscarriage of justice."

Jonathan's face flushed to a deep, angry red. "Grace, there's a point where Kerry's sense of justice approaches the ludicrous. Last night I was able to persuade the governor to delay submitting to the senate the names of candidates for appointment to the bench. He agreed."

"Jonathan!"

"It was the only thing I could do short of asking him to withhold Kerry's appointment for the present. I had no choice. Grace, Prescott Marshall has been an outstanding governor. You know that. Working with him, I've been able to lead the senate in getting necessary reforms into law, in revising the tax structure, in attracting business to the state, in welfare reform that doesn't mean depriving the poor while searching out the welfare cheats. I want Marshall back in four years. I'm no great fan of Frank Green, but as governor he'll be a good benchwarmer and won't undo what Marshall and I have accomplished. On the other hand, if Green fails, and if the other party gets in, then everything we've accomplished will be taken apart."

Suddenly the intensity the anger had inspired drained from his face and he looked to Grace only very tired and every minute of his sixty-two years.

"I'll invite Kerry and Robin to dinner Sunday," Grace said. "That will give you another chance to talk sense to her. I don't think anyone's future should be sacrificed for that Reardon man."

"I'm going to call her tonight," Jonathan told her.

44

Geoff Dorso rang the doorbell at exactly seven-thirty and once again was greeted by Robin. She was still wearing her witch's costume and makeup. Her eyebrows were thick with charcoal. Pasty white powder covered her skin except where the lacerations streaked her chin and cheek. A wig of tangled black hair flapped around her shoulders.

Geoff jumped back. "You scared me."

"Great," Robin said enthusiastically. "Thanks for being on time. I'm due at a party. It's starting right now, and there's a prize for the scariest costume. I need to be going."

"You'll win in a landslide," Geoff told her as he stepped into the foyer. Then he sniffed. "Something smells good."

"Mom's making garlic bread," Robin explained, then called, "Mom, Mr. Dorso's here."

The kitchen was at the back of the house. Geoff smiled as the door swung open and Kerry emerged, drying her hands on a towel. She was dressed in green slacks and a green cowl-neck sweater. Geoff couldn't help but notice how the overhead light accentuated the gold streaks in her hair and the spray of freckles across her nose.

She looks about twenty-three, he thought, then realized that her warm smile did not disguise the concern in her eyes.

"Geoff, good to see you. Go inside and be comfortable. I have to walk Robin down the block to a party."

"Why not let me do that?" Geoff suggested. "I've still got my coat on."

"I guess that would be okay," Kerry said slowly, assessing the situation, "but be sure to see her inside the door, won't you? I mean, don't just leave her at the driveway."

"Mom," Robin protested, "I'm not scared anymore. Honest."

"Well, I am."

What's that about? Geoff wondered. He said, "Kerry, all of my sisters are younger than I am. Until they went to college, I was forever dropping them off and picking them up, and God help me if I didn't see them safely inside wherever they were going. Get your broom, Robin. I assume you have one."

As they walked along the quiet street, Robin told him about the car that had frightened her. "Mom acts cool about everything, but I can tell she's freaking out," she confided. "She worries about me too much. I'm sort of sorry I told her about it."

Geoff stopped short and looked down at her. "Robin, listen to me. It's a lot worse *not* to tell your mother when something like that happens. Promise me you won't make that mistake."

"I won't. I already promised Mom." The exaggerated painted lips separated in a mischievous smile. "I'm real good at keeping promises except when it comes to getting up on time. I hate getting up."

"So do I," Geoff agreed fervently.

Five minutes later, when he was sitting on a counter stool in the kitchen watching Kerry make a salad, Geoff decided to try a direct approach. "Robin told me about this morning," he said. "Is there a reason to worry?"

Kerry was tearing freshly washed lettuce into the salad bowl. "One of our investigators, Joe Palumbo, talked to Robin this afternoon. He's concerned. He thinks that a car doing a reckless U-turn a few feet from where you're walking could make anybody jumpy, but Robin was so specific about the window opening and then a hand appearing with something pointing at her . . . Joe suggested that somebody might have taken her picture."

Geoff heard the tremor in Kerry's voice.

"But why?"

"I don't know. Frank Green feels that it might be connected to that case I just prosecuted. I don't agree. I could have nightmares wondering if some nut may have seen Robin and developed a fixation. That's another possibility." She began to tear the lettuce with savage force. "The point is, what can I do about it? How do I protect her?"

"It's pretty tough to carry that worry alone," Geoff said quietly.

"You mean because I'm divorced? Because there was no man here to take care of her? You've seen her face. That happened when she was with her father. Her seat belt wasn't fastened, and he's the kind of driver who floors the accelerator and then makes sudden stops. I don't care whether it's macho stuff or just the fact that Bob Kinellen is a risk taker, in his case, Robin and I are better off alone."

She ripped the final piece of lettuce, then said apologetically,

"I'm sorry. I guess you picked the wrong night for pasta in this house, Geoff. I'm not much company. But then that doesn't matter. What is important are my meetings with Dr. Smith and Dolly Bowles."

Over salad and garlic bread she told him about her encounter with Dr. Smith. "He hates Skip Reardon," she said. "It's a different kind of hatred."

Noting the look of confusion on Geoff's face, she added, "What I mean is that typically when I deal with relatives of victims, most of them despise the murderer and want him to be punished. What they're expressing is anger so entwined with grief that both emotions are flying out of them. Parents will frequently show you baby pictures and graduation pictures of the murdered daughter, then tell you the kind of girl she was and if she won a spelling bee in the eighth grade. Then they break down and cry, their grief is so overwhelming, and one of them, usually the father, will tell you he wants five minutes alone with the killer, or he'll say that he'd like to pull the switch himself. But I didn't get any of that from Smith. From him I got only hatred."

"What does that say to you?" Geoff asked.

"It says that either Skip Reardon is a lying murderer or we need to find out whether Smith's intense animosity to Skip Reardon preceded Suzanne's death. As part of the latter consideration, we also need to know exactly what Smith's relationship with Suzanne was. Don't forget, by his own testimony, he didn't lay eyes on her from the time she was an infant till she was nearly twenty. Then one day she just appeared in his office and introduced herself. From her pictures you can see she was a remarkably attractive woman."

She stood up. "Think about that while I put together the pasta. Then I want to tell you about Dolly Bowles and 'Poppa's car.'"

Geoff was almost unaware of how delicious the linguine with clam sauce tasted as he listened to Kerry's report of her visit to Dolly Bowles. "The thing is," she concluded, "from what Dolly tells me, both our office and your people brushed aside even the possibility that little Michael might have been a very reliable witness."

"Tim Farrell interviewed Dolly Bowles himself," Geoff recalled. "I kind of remember a reference to a learning-disabled five-year-old seeing a car, but I passed over it."

"It's a long shot," Kerry said, "but Joe Palumbo, the investigator I told you about who spoke to Robin, brought the Reardon file with him this afternoon. I want to go through it to see what names might have come up—of men Suzanne was possibly getting cozy with. It shouldn't be too hard to check with the Motor Vehicle Division to see if any of those named owned a black Mercedes sedan eleven years ago. Of course, it's possible the car was registered in someone else's name, or even rented, in which case we won't get anywhere."

She looked at the clock over the kitchen stove. "Plenty of time," she said.

Geoff knew she was talking about getting Robin. "What time is the party over?"

"Nine. There usually aren't weeknight parties, but Halloween really is the kids' special night, isn't it? Now how about espresso or regular coffee? I keep meaning to buy a cappuccino machine but never seem to find the time."

"Espresso is fine. And while we're having it, I'm going to tell you about Skip Reardon and Beth Taylor."

When he finished giving her the background of Beth's relationship with Skip, Kerry said slowly, "I can see why Tim Farrell was afraid to use Taylor as a witness, but if Skip Reardon was in love with her at the time of the murder, it tends to take some of the credibility away from Dr. Smith's testimony."

"Exactly. Skip's whole attitude about seeing Suzanne arranging flowers given to her by another man can be summed up in two words: 'Good riddance.' "

The wall phone rang and Geoff looked at his watch. "You said nine o'clock for Robin, didn't you? I'll get her while you're on the phone."

"Thanks." Kerry reached for the receiver. "Hello."

She listened, then said warmly, "Oh, Jonathan, I was going to call you."

Geoff got up, and with a "see you" motion of his hand, went into the foyer and reached in the closet for his coat.

As they walked back home, Robin said she had had a good time at the party even though she had not won first prize for her costume. "Cassie's cousin was there," she explained. "She had on a dorky skeleton outfit, but her mother had sewed soup bones all over it. I guess that made it special. Anyhow, thanks for walking me, Mr. Dorso."

"You win some, you lose some, Robin. And why don't you call me Geoff?"

The moment Kerry opened the door for them, Geoff could see that something was terribly wrong. It was an obvious effort for her to keep an attentive smile on her face as she listened to Robin's enthusiastic description of the party.

Finally Kerry said, "Okay, Robin, it's after nine and you promised . . ."

"I know. Off to bed and no dragging my heels." Robin kissed Kerry quickly. "Love you, Mom. Good night, Geoff." She bounced up the stairs.

Geoff watched as Kerry's mouth began to quiver. He took her arm, led her into the kitchen and closed the door. "What's the matter?"

She tried to keep her voice steady. "The governor was supposed to be submitting three names to the senate tomorrow for approval of judicial appointments. Mine was to be one of them. Jonathan has asked the governor to postpone the action for now, because of me."

"Senator Hoover did that to you!" Geoff exclaimed. "I thought he was your big buddy." Then he stared at her. "Wait a minute. Does this have something to do with the Reardon case and Frank Green?"

He didn't need her nod to know he was right. "Kerry, that's lousy. I'm so sorry. But you said 'postponed,' not 'withdrawn.' "

"Jonathan would never withdraw my nomination. I know that." Now Kerry's voice was becoming steadier. "But I also know that I can't expect him to go out on a limb for me. I told Jonathan about seeing Dr. Smith and Dolly Bowles today."

"What was his reaction?

"He wasn't impressed. He feels that by reopening this case I am needlessly bringing into question both the capability and the credibility of Frank Green, and that I'm leaving myself open to criticism for wasting taxpayers' money on a case that was decided ten years ago. He pointed out that five appeals courts have confirmed Reardon's guilt."

She shook her head, as though trying to clear her mind. Then she turned away from Geoff. "I'm sorry to have wasted your time this way, Geoff, but I guess I've decided that Jonathan is right. A murderer is in prison, put there by a jury of his peers, and the courts have been consistent in upholding his conviction. Why do I think I know something they don't?"

Kerry turned back and looked at him. "The killer is in prison, and I'm just going to have to let this drop," she said with as much conviction as she could muster.

Geoff's face tightened in suppressed anger and frustration. "Very well, then. Good-bye, Your Honor," he said. "Thanks for the pasta."

45

In the laboratory of FBI headquarters in Quantico, four agents watched the computer screen freeze on the profile of the thief who had broken into the Hamilton home in Chevy Chase over the weekend.

He had pulled the stocking mask up so that he could have a better look at a figurine. At first, the image taken by the hidden camera had seemed impossibly blurry, but after some electronic enhancement, a few details of the face were visible. Probably not enough to make a real difference, thought Si Morgan, the senior agent. It's still pretty difficult to see much more than his nose and the outline of his mouth. Nonetheless, it was all they had, and it might just jog someone's memory.

"Get a couple of hundred of these run off and see that they're circulated to the families in every break-in that matches the profile of the Hamilton case. It's not much, but at least we now have a chance of getting that bastard."

Morgan's face turned grim. "And I only hope that when we get him we can match his thumbprint to the one we found the night Congressman Peale's mother lost her life because she'd canceled her plans to go away for the weekend."

46

It was still early morning as Wayne Stevens sat reading the newspaper in the family room of his comfortable Spanish-style house in Oakland, California. Retired two years from his modestly successful insurance business, he looked the part of a contented man. Even in repose, his face maintained a genial expression. Regular exercise kept his body trim. His two married daughters and their families both lived less than half an hour away. He had been married to his third wife, Catherine, for eight years now, and in that time had come to realize that his first two marriages had left much to be desired.

That was why when the phone rang he had no premonition that the caller was about to evoke unpleasant memories.

The voice had a distinct East Coast accent. "Mr. Stevens, I'm Joe Palumbo, an investigator for the Bergen County, New Jersey, prosecutor's office. Your stepdaughter was Suzanne Reardon, was she not?"

"Suzanne Reardon? I don't know anyone by that name. Wait a minute," he said. "You're not talking about Susie, are you?"

"Is that what you called Suzanne?"

"I had a stepdaughter we called Susie, but her name was Sue

Ellen, not Suzanne." Then he realized the inspector had used the past tense: "was." "Has something happened to her?"

Three thousand miles away, Joe Palumbo gripped the phone. "You don't know that Suzanne, or Susie as you call her, was murdered ten years ago?" He pushed the button that would record the conversation.

"Dear God." Wayne Stevens' voice fell to a whisper. "No, of course I didn't know it. I send a note to her every Christmas in care of her father, Dr. Charles Smith, but I've heard nothing from her in years."

"When did you last see her?"

"Eighteen years ago, shortly after my second wife, Jean, her mother, died. Susie was always a troubled, unhappy and, frankly, *difficult* girl. I was a widower when her mother and I married. I had two young daughters and I adopted Susie. Jean and I raised the three together. Then, after Jean died, Susie received the proceeds of an insurance policy and announced that she was moving to New York. She was nineteen then. A few months later I received a rather vicious note from her saying she'd always been unhappy living here and wanted nothing to do with any of us. She said that she was going to live with her real father. Well, I phoned Dr. Smith immediately, but he was extremely rude. He told me that it had been a grave mistake to allow me to adopt his daughter."

"So Suzanne, I mean Susie, never spoke to you herself?" Joe asked quickly.

"Never. There seemed to be nothing to do but let it go. I hoped in time she'd come around. What happened to her?"

"Ten years ago her husband was convicted of killing her in a jealous rage."

Images ran through Wayne Stevens' head. Susie as a whiny toddler, a plump, scowling teenager who turned to golf and tennis for recreation but seemed to take no pleasure in her own prowess in either sport. Susie listening to the jangle announcing phone calls that were never for her, glowering at her stepsisters when their dates came to pick them up, slamming doors as she stomped upstairs. "Jealous because she was involved with another man?" he asked slowly.

"Yes." Joe Palumbo heard the bewilderment in the other man's voice and knew that Kerry's instinct was right when she had asked him to delve into Suzanne's background. "Mr. Stevens, would you please describe your stepdaughter's physical appearance?"

"Sue was . . ." Stevens hesitated. "She was not a pretty girl," he said quietly.

"Do you have pictures of her you could send me?" Palumbo asked. "I mean, those that were taken closest to the time she left to come East."

"Of course. But if this happened over ten years ago, why are you bringing it up now?"

"Because one of our assistant prosecutors thinks there's more to the case than came out at the trial."

And boy, was Kerry's hunch right! Joe thought as he hung up the phone after having secured Wayne Stevens' promise to send the pictures of Susie by overnight mail.

47

K erry was barely settled in her office Wednesday morning
when her secretary told her that Frank Green wanted to
see her.

He did not waste words. "What happened, Kerry? I understand that the governor has postponed presenting the nomina-
tions for judgeship. The indication was that he was having a
problem with your inclusion. Is something wrong? Is there anything I can do?"

Well, yes, as a matter of fact there is, Frank, Kerry thought.
You can tell the governor that you welcome any inquiry that
might reveal a gross miscarriage of justice, even if you're left with
egg on your face. You could be a stand-up guy, Frank.

Instead she said, "Oh, I'm sure it will all go through soon."

"You're not on the outs with Senator Hoover, are you?"

"He's one of my closest friends."

As she turned to go, the prosecutor said, "Kerry, it stinks to
be twisting in the wind, waiting for these appointments. Hey,
I've got my own nomination coming up. Right? I get nightmares
hoping it doesn't get screwed up somewhere."

She nodded and left him.

Back in her office, she tried desperately to keep her mind on
the trial schedule. The grand jury had just indicted a suspect in a
bungled gas station holdup. The charge was attempted murder

and armed robbery. The attendant had been shot and was still in intensive care. If he didn't make it, the charge would be upgraded to murder.

Yesterday the appeals court had overturned the guilty verdict of a woman convicted of manslaughter. That had been another high-profile case, but the appeals court decision that the defense had been incompetent at least did not reflect badly on the prosecutor.

They had planned that Robin would hold the Bible when she was sworn in. Jonathan and Grace had insisted that they would buy her judicial robes, a couple of everyday ones and a special one for ceremonial occasions. Margaret kept reminding her that, as her best friend, she would be allowed to hold the robe Kerry would wear that day and assist her in putting it on. "I, Kerry McGrath, do solemnly swear that I will . . .

Tears stung her eyes as she heard Jonathan's impatient voice again. *Kerry, five appeals courts have found Reardon guilty. What's the matter with you?* Well, he was right. Later this morning, she would call him and tell him that she had dropped the whole matter.

She became aware that someone had knocked on her door several times. Impatiently she brushed the backs of her hands across her eyes and called, "Come in."

It was Joe Palumbo. "You're one smart lady, Kerry."

"I'm not so sure. What's up?"

"You said it occurred to you to wonder if Dr. Smith ever did any work on his daughter."

"He all but denied it, Joe. I told you that."

"I know you did, and you also had me check on Suzanne's background. Well, listen to this."

With a flourish, Joe laid a tape recorder on the desk. "This is most of my call to Mr. Wayne Stevens, Suzanne Reardon's stepfather." He pressed the button.

As Kerry listened, she felt a new wave of confusion and conflicting emotions sweep over her. Smith's a liar, she thought as she remembered his outrage at even the suggestion that he had performed any surgical procedure on his daughter. *He's a liar and he's a good actor.*

When the recorded conversation was finished, Palumbo smiled in anticipation. "What next, Kerry?"

"I don't know," she said slowly.

"You don't know? Smith's lying."

"We don't know that yet. Let's wait for those pictures from Stevens before we get too excited. Lots of teenagers suddenly blossom after they get a good haircut and a makeover at a salon."

Palumbo looked at her in disbelief. "Sure they do. And pigs have wings."

48

Deidre Reardon had heard the discouragement in her son's voice when she spoke to him on Sunday and Tuesday, which was why she decided on Wednesday to make the long trip by bus and train and another bus to the Trenton prison to see him.

A small woman who had passed on to her son her fiery red hair, warm blue eyes and Celtic complexion, Deidre Reardon now looked every day of her age, which would soon be seventy. Her compact body hinted of frailness, and her step had lost much of its bounce. Her health had forced her to give up her job as a saleswoman at A&S, and now she supplemented her social security check by doing some clerical work at the parish office.

The money she had saved during the years when Skip was doing so well and was so generous to her was gone now, most of it spent on the court costs of the unsuccessful appeals.

She arrived at the prison in midafternoon. Because it was a weekday, they could only communicate by telephone, with a window between them. From the minute Skip was brought in and she saw the look on his face, Deidre knew that the one thing she feared had happened. Skip had given up hope.

Usually when he was very discouraged, she tried to get his mind off himself with gossip about the neighborhood and the parish, the kind of gossip that someone would enjoy who was away but expected to come home soon and wanted to be kept up on events.

Today she knew such small talk was useless. "Skip, what's the matter?" she asked.

"Mom, Geoff called last night. That prosecutor who came down to see me. She's not going to follow up. She's pretty much washed her hands of me. I made Geoff be honest and not snow me."

"What was her name, Skip?" Deidre asked, trying to keep her voice matter-of-fact. She knew her son well enough to avoid offering platitudes now.

"McGrath. Kerry McGrath. Apparently, she's going to be made a judge soon. With my luck they'll put her on the appeals court so if ever Geoff does find another reason to file an appeal, she'll be there to kick it out."

"Doesn't it take a long time for judges to be put on the appeals court?" Deidre asked.

"What does it matter? We don't have anything *but* time, do we, Mom?" Then Skip told her that he had refused Beth's call today. "Mom, Beth has to get on with her life. She never will if all her life is tied up with worrying about me."

"Skip, Beth loves you."

"Let her love someone else. I did, didn't I?"

"Oh, Skip." Deidre Reardon felt the shortness of breath that always preceded the numbness in her arm and the stabbing pain in her chest. The doctor had warned that she was going to need another bypass operation if the angioplasty next week didn't work. She hadn't told Skip about that yet. She wouldn't now either.

Deidre bit back tears as she saw the hurt in her son's eyes. He had always been such a good kid. She had never had a hint of trouble with him when he was growing up. Even as a baby, when he was tired, he hadn't gotten crabby. One of her favorite stories about him was of the day he had toddled from the living room of the apartment into the bedroom and pulled his security blanket through the bars of the crib, wrapped himself up in it and gone to sleep on the floor under the crib.

She had left him alone in the living room while she started supper, and when she couldn't find him, she had gone racing through the tiny apartment, shouting his name, terrified that somehow he had gotten out, maybe was lost. Deidre had that same feeling now. In a different way, Skip was getting lost.

Involuntarily she reached out her hand and touched the glass. She wanted to put her arms around him, that fine, good man who was her son. She wanted to tell him not to worry, that it would be all right, just as she had years ago when something had hurt him. Now she knew what she had to say.

"Skip, I don't want to hear you talk like this. You can't decide that Beth isn't going to love you anymore, because she is. And I'm going to see that Kerry McGrath woman. There has to be a reason why she came to see you in the first place. Prosecutors don't just drop in on convicted people. I'm going to find out why she took an interest in you, and why she's turning her back on you now. But you've got to cooperate; don't you dare let me down by talking like this."

Their visiting time was up much too quickly. Deidre managed

not to cry until after the guard had led Skip away. Then she dabbed her eyes fiercely. Her mouth set in a determined line, she stood up, waited for the stab of chest pain to pass and walked briskly out.

49

It feels like November, Barbara Tompkins thought as she walked the ten blocks from her office on Sixty-eighth Street and Madison Avenue to her apartment on Sixty-first and Third Avenue. She should have worn a heavier coat. But what did a few blocks of discomfort matter when she felt so good?

There wasn't a day that she didn't rejoice in the miracle that Dr. Smith had performed for her. It seemed impossible that less than two years ago, she had been stuck in a drudge P.R. job in Albany, assigned to getting mentions in magazines for small cosmetics clients.

Nancy Pierce had been one of the few clients she had enjoyed. Nancy always joked about being the Plain Jane with a total inferiority complex because she worked with gorgeous models. Then Nancy took an extended vacation and came back looking like a million dollars. Openly, even proudly, she told the world she had had aesthetic surgery.

"Listen," she had said. "My sister has the face of Miss America, but she's always fighting her weight. She says inside her there's a thin gal trying to fight her way out. I always said to myself that inside me there was a very pretty gal trying to fight her way out. My sister went to the Golden Door. I went to Dr. Smith."

Looking at her, at her new ease and confidence, Barbara had promised herself, "If I ever get money, I'll go to that doctor too." And then, dear old Great Aunt Betty had been gathered to her reward at age eighty-seven and left $35,000 to Barbara, with the instruction that she kick up her heels and have fun with it.

Barbara remembered that first visit to Dr. Smith. He had come into the room where she was sitting on the edge of the examining table. His manner was cold, almost frightening. "What do you want?" he had barked.

"I want to know if you can make me pretty," Barbara had told him, somewhat tentatively. Then, gathering courage, she'd corrected herself. "Very pretty."

Wordlessly, he had stood in front of her, turned a spotlight on her, held her chin in his hand, run his fingers over the contours of her face, probed her cheekbones and her forehead and studied her for several long minutes.

Then he had stepped back. "Why?"

She told him about the pretty woman struggling to get out of the shell. She told him about how she knew that she shouldn't care so much, and then burst out, "But I *do* care."

Unexpectedly he had smiled, a narrow, mirthless, but nevertheless genuine smile. "If you didn't care, I wouldn't be bothered," he had told her.

The procedure he prescribed had been incredibly involved. The operations gave her a chin and reduced her ears, and took the dark circles from under her eyes and the heavy lids from over them, so that they became wide and luminous. The surgery made her lips full and provocative and removed the acne scars from her cheeks and narrowed her nose and raised her eyebrows. There had even been a process to sculpt her body.

Then the doctor sent her to a salon to have her hair changed from mousy tan to charcoal brown, a color that enhanced the creamy complexion he had achieved through acid peeling. Another expert at the salon taught her about the subtleties of applying makeup.

Finally, the doctor told her to invest the last of her windfall in clothes and sent her with a personal shopper to the Seventh Avenue designer workrooms. Under the shopper's guidance, she accumulated the first sophisticated wardrobe she had ever owned.

Dr. Smith urged her to relocate to New York City, told her where to look for an apartment and even took personal interest by inspecting the apartment she had found. Then he insisted that she come in every three months for checkups.

It had been a dizzying year since she had moved to Manhattan and started the job at Price and Vellone. Dizzying but exciting. Barbara was having a wonderful time.

But as she walked the last block to her apartment, she glanced nervously over her shoulder. Last night, she had had dinner with some clients in The Mark Hotel. When they were leaving, she had noticed Dr. Smith seated alone at a small table off to the side.

Last week she had caught a glimpse of him in the Oak Room at the Plaza.

She had dismissed it at the time, but the night last month when she met clients at The Four Seasons, she had had the impression that someone was watching her from a car across the street when she hailed a taxi.

Barbara felt a surge of relief as the doorman greeted her and opened the door. Then once again she looked over her shoulder.

A black Mercedes was stopped in traffic directly in front of the apartment building. There was no mistaking the driver, even though his face was turned partly away as though he were looking across the street.

Dr. Smith.

"You okay, Miss Tompkins?" the doorman asked. "You look like you don't feel so great."

"No. Thank you. I'm fine." Barbara walked quickly into the foyer. As she waited for the elevator, she thought, he *is* following me. But what can I do about it?

50

Although Kerry had fixed Robin one of their favorite meals—baked chicken breasts, baked potatoes, green beans, green salad and biscuits—they ate in near silence.

From the moment Kerry arrived home and Alison, the high school baby-sitter, had whispered, "I think Robin's upset," Kerry had bided her time.

As she prepared dinner, Robin sat at the counter doing her homework. Kerry had waited for a time to talk to her, for some sign, but Robin seemed extraordinarily busy with her assignments.

Kerry even made certain to ask, "Are you sure you're finished, Rob?" before she put their dinner on the table.

After she began to eat, Robin visibly relaxed. "Did you finish your lunch today?" Kerry asked, finally breaking the silence, trying to sound casual. "You seem hungry."

"Sure, Mom. Most of it."

"I see."

Kerry thought, she is so like me. If she's hurt, she handles it herself. Such a private person.

Then Robin said, "I like Geoff. He's neat."

Geoff. Kerry dropped her eyes and concentrated on cutting chicken. She didn't want to think about his derisive, dismissive comment when he left the other night. *Good-bye, Your Honor*.

"Uh-huh," she responded, hoping that she was conveying the fact that Geoff was unimportant in their lives.

"When is he coming back?" Robin asked.

Now it was Kerry's turn to be evasive. "Oh, I don't know. He really just came because of a case he's been working on."

Robin looked troubled. "I guess I shouldn't have told Daddy about that."

"What do you mean?"

"Well, he was saying that when you're a judge, you'll probably meet a lot of judges and end up marrying one of them. I didn't mean to talk about you to him, but I said a lawyer I liked had come to the house on business the other night, and Daddy asked who it was."

"And you told him it was Geoff Dorso. There's nothing wrong with that."

"I don't know. Daddy seemed to get upset with me. We'd been having fun, then he got quiet and told me to finish my shrimp. That it was time to get home."

"Rob, Daddy doesn't care who I go out with, and certainly Geoff Dorso has no connection to him or any of his clients. Daddy is involved in a very tough case right now. Maybe you had kept his mind off it for a while, and then when dinner was almost over, he started thinking about it again."

"Do you really think so?" Robin asked hopefully as her eyes brightened.

"I really think so," Kerry said firmly. "You've seen me when I'm in a fog because I'm on a trial."

Robin began to laugh. "Oh boy, have I!"

. . .

At nine o'clock, Kerry looked in on Robin, who was propped up in bed reading. "Lights out," she said firmly as she went over to tuck her in.

"Okay," she said reluctantly. As Robin snuggled down under the covers, she said, "Mom, I was thinking. Just because Geoff came here on business doesn't mean we can't ask him back, does it? He likes you. I can tell."

"Oh, Rob, he's just one of those guys who likes people, but certainly he's not interested in me especially."

"Cassie and Courtney saw him when he picked me up. They think he's cute."

I think he is too, Kerry thought as she turned out the light.

She went downstairs, planning to tackle the chore of balancing her checkbook. But when she got to her desk, she gazed for a long minute at the Reardon file Joe Palumbo had given her yesterday. Then she shook her head. Forget it, she told herself. Stay out of it.

But it wouldn't hurt just to take a look at it, she reasoned. She picked it up, carried it to her favorite chair, laid the file on the hassock at her feet, opened it and reached for the first batch of papers.

The record showed that the call had come in at 12:20 A.M. Skip Reardon had dialed the operator and shouted at her to connect him to the Alpine police. "My wife is dead, my wife is dead," he had repeated over and over. The police reported they had found him kneeling beside her, crying. He told the police that as soon as he came into the house he had known she was dead and had not touched her. The vase that the sweetheart roses had been in was overturned. The roses were scattered over the body.

The next morning, when his mother was with him, Skip Reardon had claimed he was sure a diamond pin was missing. He said he remembered it in particular because it was one of the pieces he had not given her, that he was certain another man must have given her. He also swore that a miniature frame with Suzanne's picture that had been in the bedroom that morning was gone.

At eleven o'clock, Kerry got to Dolly Bowles' statement. It was essentially the same story she had narrated when Kerry visited her.

Kerry's eyes narrowed when she saw that a Jason Arnott had been questioned in the course of the investigation. Skip Reardon had mentioned him to her. In his statement, Arnott described himself as an antiques expert who for a commission would accompany women to auctions at places like Sotheby's and Christie's and advise them in their efforts in bidding on certain objects.

He said that he enjoyed entertaining and that Suzanne often came to his cocktail parties and dinners, sometimes accompanied by Skip, but usually alone.

The investigator's note showed that he had checked with mutual friends of both Suzanne and Arnott, and that there was no suggestion of any romantic interest between them. In fact one friend commented that Suzanne was a natural flirt and joked about Arnott, calling him "Jason the neuter."

Nothing new here, Kerry decided when she had completed half the file. The investigation was thorough. Through the open window, the Public Service meter reader had heard Skip shouting at Suzanne at breakfast. "Boy, was that guy steaming," was his comment.

Sorry, Geoff, Kerry thought as she went to close the file. Her eyes were burning. She would skim through the rest of it tomorrow and return it. Then she glanced at the next report. It was the interview with a caddie at the Palisades Country Club, where Suzanne and Skip were members. A name caught her eye, and she picked up the next batch of papers, all thought of sleep suddenly gone.

The caddie's name was Michael Vitti, and he was a fountain of information about Suzanne Reardon. "Everybody loved to caddie for her. She was nice. She'd kid around with the caddies and gave big tips. She played with lots of the men. She was good, and I mean *good*. A lot of the wives got sore at her because the men all liked her."

Vitti had been asked if he thought Suzanne was involved with any of the men. "Oh, I don't know about that," he said. "I never saw her really alone with anyone. The foursomes always went back to the grill together, you know what I mean?"

But when pressed he said that just maybe there was something going on between Suzanne and Jimmy Weeks.

It was Jimmy Weeks' name that had jumped out at Kerry. According to the investigator's notes, Vitti's remark wasn't taken seriously because, although Weeks was known to be a ladies' man, on being questioned about Suzanne, he absolutely denied that he had ever seen her outside the club and said that he had been having a serious relationship with another woman at that time, and besides, he had an ironclad alibi for the entire night of the murder.

Then Kerry read the last of the caddie's interview. He admitted that Mr. Weeks treated all the women pretty much alike and called most of them things like Honey, Darlin' and Lovey.

The caddie was asked if Weeks had a special name for Suzanne.

The answer: "Well, a couple of times I heard him call her 'Sweetheart.' "

Kerry let the papers drop in her lap. Jimmy Weeks. Bob's client. Was that why his attitude changed so suddenly when Robin told him that Geoff Dorso had come to see her on business?

It was fairly widely known that Geoff Dorso represented Skip Reardon and had been trying doggedly, but unsuccessfully, for ten years to get a new trial for him.

Was Bob, as Jimmy Weeks' counsel, afraid of what a new trial might entail for his client?

A couple of times I heard him call her Sweetheart. The words haunted Kerry.

Deeply troubled, she closed the file and went up to bed. The caddie had not been called as a witness at the trial. Neither had Jimmy Weeks. Did the defense team ever interview the caddie? If not, they should have, she thought. Did they talk to Jason Arnott about any other men Suzanne might have seemed interested in at his parties?

I'll wait for the pictures to come in from Suzanne's stepfather, Kerry told herself. It's probably nothing, or at least nothing more than what I told Joe today. Maybe Suzanne just had a good makeover done when she came to New York. She did have money from her mother's insurance policy. And Dr. Smith did, in effect, deny that he ever did any procedure whatsoever on Suzanne.

Wait and see, she told herself. Good advice, since it was all she could do for the present anyway.

51

On Thursday morning, Kate Carpenter arrived at the office at quarter of nine. There were no procedures scheduled, and the first patient wasn't arriving until ten o'clock, so Dr. Smith had not come in yet.

The receptionist was at her desk, a worried look on her face. "Kate, Barbara Tompkins wants you to phone her, and she specifically asked that Dr. Smith not be told about her call. She says it's very important."

"She's not having any problems because of the surgery?" Kate asked, alarmed. "It's been over a year."

"She didn't say anything about that. I told her you'd be along very soon. She's waiting at home to hear from you."

Without stopping to take off her coat, Kate went into the closet-sized private office the accountant used, closed the door and dialed Tompkins' number.

With increasing dismay she listened as Barbara related her absolute conviction that Dr. Smith was obsessively following her. "I don't know what to do," she said. "I'm so grateful to him.

You know that, Mrs. Carpenter. But I'm beginning to be frightened."

"He's never approached you?"

"No."

"Then let me think about it and talk to a few people. I beg you not to discuss this with anyone else. Dr. Smith has a wonderful reputation. It would be terrible to have it destroyed."

"I'll never be able to repay Dr. Smith for what he did for me," Barbara Tompkins said quietly. "But please get back to me quickly."

52

At eleven o'clock, Grace Hoover phoned Kerry and invited her and Robin for Sunday dinner. "We haven't seen nearly enough of you two lately," Grace told her. "I do hope you can come. Celia will outdo herself, I promise."

Celia was the weekend housekeeper and a better cook than the Monday-to-Friday live-in. When she knew Robin was going to be coming, Celia made brownies and chocolate chip cookies to send home with her.

"Of course we'll come," Kerry said warmly. Sunday is such a family day, she thought as she hung up the phone. Most Sunday afternoons she tried to do something special with Robin, like going to a museum or a movie or occasionally to a Broadway show.

If only Dad had lived, she thought. He and Mother would be living nearby at least part of the time. And if only Bob Kinellen had been the man I thought he was.

Mentally she shook herself to shrug off that line of reflection. Robin and I are darn lucky to have Jonathan and Grace, she reminded herself. They'll always be there for us.

Janet, her secretary, came in and closed the door. "Kerry, did you make an appointment with a Mrs. Deidre Reardon and forget to tell me?"

"Deidre Reardon? No, I did not."

"She's in the waiting room and she says she's going to sit there until you see her. Shall I call security?"

My God, Kerry thought. Skip Reardon's mother! What does she want? "No. Tell her to come in, Janet."

Deidre Reardon got directly to the point. "I don't usually force my way into people's offices, Ms. McGrath, but this is too important. You went to the prison to see my son. You had to have had a reason for that. Something made you wonder if there had been a miscarriage of justice. I know there was. I know my son, and I know that he is innocent. But why after seeing Skip did you not want to help him? Especially in light of what's been uncovered about Dr. Smith."

"It's not that I didn't want to help him, Mrs. Reardon. It's that I *can't* help him. There's no new evidence. It's peculiar that Dr. Smith has given other women his daughter's face, but it's not illegal, and it might be simply his way of coping with bereavement."

Deidre Reardon's expression changed from anxiety to anger. "Ms. McGrath, Dr. Smith doesn't know the meaning of the word 'bereavement.' I didn't see much of him in the four years Suzanne and Skip were married. I didn't want to. There was something absolutely unhealthy about his attitude toward her. I remember one day, for example, there was a smudge on Suzanne's cheek. Dr. Smith went over to her and wiped it off. You'd have thought he was dusting a statue the way he studied her face to make sure he'd gotten it all. He was proud of her. I'll grant you that. But affection? *No*."

Geoff had talked about how unemotional Smith was on the stand, Kerry thought. But that doesn't prove anything.

"Mrs. Reardon, I do understand how you must be feeling—" she began.

"No, I'm sorry, you don't," Deidre Reardon interrupted. "My son is incapable of violence. He would no more have deliberately taken that cord from Suzanne's waist and pulled it around her neck and strangled her than you or I would have done such a thing. Think about the kind of person who could commit a crime like that. What kind of monster is he? Because that monster who could so viciously kill another human being was in Skip's house that night. Now think about Skip."

Tears welled in Deidre Reardon's eyes as she burst out, "Didn't some of his essence, his goodness, come through to you? Are you blind and deaf, Ms. McGrath? Does my son look or sound like a murderer to you?"

"Mrs. Reardon, I looked into this case only because of my concern over Dr. Smith's obsession with his daughter's face, not because I thought your son was innocent. That was for the courts to decide, and they have. He has had a number of appeals. There is nothing I can do."

"Ms. McGrath, I think you have a daughter, don't you?"

"Yes, I do."

"Then try to visualize her caged for ten years, facing twenty years more in that cage for a crime she didn't commit. Do you think your daughter would be capable of murder someday?"

"No, I do not."

"Neither is my son. Please, Ms. McGrath, you are in a position to help Skip. Don't abandon him. I don't know why Dr. Smith lied about Skip, but I think I've come to understand. He was jealous of him because Skip was married to Suzanne, with all that implies. Think about that."

"Mrs. Reardon, as a mother I understand how heartbroken

you are," Kerry said gently as she looked into the worn and anxious face.

Deidre Reardon got up. "I can see that you're dismissing everything I'm telling you, Ms. McGrath. Geoff said that you're going to become a judge. God help the people who stand before you pleading for justice."

Then as Kerry watched, the woman's complexion became ghastly gray.

"Mrs. Reardon, what is it?" she cried.

With shaking hands, the woman opened her purse, took out a small vial and shook a pill into her palm. She slipped it under her tongue, turned and silently left the office.

For long minutes Kerry sat staring at the closed door. Then she reached for a sheet of paper. On it, she wrote:

1. Did Doctor Smith lie about operating on Suzanne?
2. Did little Michael see a black, four-door Mercedes sedan in front of the Reardons' house when Dolly Bowles was baby-sitting him that night? What about the partial license-plate numbers Dolly claims she saw?
3. Was Jimmy Weeks involved with Suzanne, and, if so, does Bob know anything about it, and is he afraid of having it come out?

She studied the list as Deidre Reardon's honest, distressed face loomed accusingly in her mind.

53

Geoff Dorso had been trying a case in the courthouse in Newark. At the last minute he had gotten a plea bargain for his client, an eighteen-year-old kid who had been joyriding with friends in his father's car when he had crashed into a pickup truck whose driver had sustained a broken arm and leg.

But there had been no alcohol involved, and the boy was a good kid and genuinely contrite. Under the plea bargain he got a two-year suspension of his driver's license and was ordered to do one hundred hours of community service. Geoff was pleased—sending him to jail instead of college would have been a serious mistake.

Now, on Thursday afternoon, Geoff had the unusual luxury of unscheduled time, and he decided to drop in on the Jimmy Weeks trial. He wanted to hear the opening arguments. Also, he admitted to himself, he was anxious to see Bob Kinellen in action.

He took a seat in the back of the courtroom. There were plenty of media representatives present, he noticed. Jimmy Weeks had managed to avoid indictment so many times that they had taken to calling him "Teflon Jimmy," a takeoff on the Mafia mobster who had been known as "The Teflon Don," now in prison for life.

Kinellen was just starting his opening statement. He's smooth, Geoff thought. He knows how to play to the jury, knows when to sound indignant, then outraged, knows how to ridicule the charges. He is also picture-perfect in appearance and presentation, Geoff thought, trying to imagine Kerry married to this guy. Somehow he couldn't see it. Or maybe he didn't want to see it, he admitted to himself. At least, he thought, taking some comfort, she certainly didn't seem to be hung up on Kinellen.

But then, why should that matter? he asked himself, as the judge declared a recess.

In the corridor he was approached by Nick Klein, a reporter for the *Star-Ledger*. They exchanged greetings, then Geoff commented, "A lot of you guys around, aren't there?"

"Fireworks expected," Nick told him. "I have a source in the attorney general's office. Barney Haskell is trying to make a deal. What they're offering him isn't good enough. Now he's hinting he can tie Jimmy to a murder that someone else is serving time for."

"I sure wish I had a witness like that for one of my clients," Geoff commented.

54

At four o'clock, Joe Palumbo received delivery of an Express Mail package with the return address of Wayne Stevens in Oakland, California. He immediately slit it open and eagerly reached inside for the two stacks of snapshots held together with rubber bands. A note was clipped to one of them.

It read:

Dear Mr. Palumbo,

The full impact of Susie's death hit me only after I began putting these photos together for you. I am so sorry. Susie was not an easy child to raise. I think these pictures tell the story. My daughters were very attractive from the time they were infants. Susie was not. As the girls grew up, that led to intense jealousy and unhappiness on Susie's part.

Susie's mother, my wife, had great difficulty watching her step-daughters enjoy their teen years while her own child was so desperately insecure and basically friendless. I'm afraid the situation caused a great deal of friction in our home. I think I always entertained the hope that a mature and well-adjusted Susie would show up at the door one day and have a wonderful reunion with us. She had many gifts that she did not appreciate.

But for now, I hope these pictures will help.

Sincerely,
Wayne Stevens

Twenty minutes later, Joe went into Kerry's office. He dropped the snapshots on her desk. "Just in case you think Susie—sorry, I mean Suzanne—became a beauty because of a new hairdo," he commented.

At five o'clock, Kerry phoned Dr. Smith's office. He had already left for the day. Anticipating that, she next asked, "Is Mrs. Carpenter available?"

When Kate Carpenter came to the phone, Kerry said, "Mrs. Carpenter, how long have you been with Dr. Smith?"

"Four years, Ms. McGrath. Why are you asking?"

"Well, from something you said, I had an idea that you had been with him longer than that."

"No."

"Because I wanted to know if you were there when Dr. Smith either operated on his daughter, Suzanne, or had a colleague operate on her. I can tell you what she looked like. In your office I saw two patients and asked their names. Barbara Tompkins and Pamela Worth are both dead ringers for Dr. Smith's daughter, at least as she looked after extensive plastic surgery, not as she was born."

She heard the woman gasp. "I didn't know Dr. Smith had a daughter," Mrs. Carpenter said.

"She died nearly eleven years ago, murdered, as the jury decided, by her husband. He is still in prison and continues to protest his innocence. Dr. Smith was the principal witness against him."

"Ms. McGrath," Mrs. Carpenter said, "I feel terribly disloyal to the doctor, but I think it's very important that you speak to Barbara Tompkins immediately. Let me give you her number." Then the nurse explained about the frightened woman's call.

"Dr. Smith is stalking Barbara Tompkins!" Kerry said, as her mind raced with the possibilities of what such an action might mean.

"Well, following her, anyhow," Mrs. Carpenter said defensively. "I have both her numbers, home and office."

Kerry took them. "Mrs. Carpenter, I must talk to Dr. Smith and I doubt very much that he will agree to see me. Is he going to be in tomorrow?"

"Yes, but he has a very full schedule. He won't be done until sometime after four o'clock."

"I'll be there then, but don't tell him I'm coming." A question occurred to Kerry. "Does Dr. Smith own a car?"

"Oh, yes. His home is in Washington Mews. He lives in a converted carriage house and it has a garage, so it's easy for him to keep one."

"What kind of car does he drive?"

"The same one he's always driven. A four-door Mercedes sedan."

Kerry gripped the phone. "What color is it?"

"Black."

"You say 'always driven.' You mean he *always* selects a black Mercedes sedan?"

"I mean he drives the same one he's driven for at least twelve years. I know, because I've heard him talking about it to one of his patients who happens to be a Mercedes executive."

"Thank you, Mrs. Carpenter." As Kerry returned the receiver to its cradle, Joe Palumbo reappeared. "Hey, Kerry, was Skip Reardon's mother in here to see you?"

"Yes."

"Our Leader saw and recognized her. He was rushing out to a meeting with the governor. He wants to know what the hell she was doing in here asking for you."

55

When Geoff Dorso got home on Thursday night, he stood at the window of his condominium and stared at the New York skyline. All day the memory of how he had sarcastically called Kerry "Your Honor" had been plaguing him, but he resolutely had pushed it out of his mind. Alone now, and at the end of his day, he had to face it.

What a hell of a nerve I had, he thought. Kerry was decent

enough to call me and ask to read the transcript. She was decent enough to talk to Dr. Smith and Dolly Bowles. She made the trek to Trenton to meet Skip. Why shouldn't she worry about losing her judgeship, especially if she honestly doesn't believe that Skip is innocent?

I had no right to speak to her that way, and I owe her an apology, he thought, although I wouldn't blame her if she hung up on me. Face it, he told himself. You were convinced that the more she looked into the Sweetheart Murder Case, the more she would believe that Skip was innocent. But why should he be so sure? She certainly has the right to agree with the jury and with the appeals court, and it was a cheap shot to insinuate that she was being self-serving.

He shoved his hands in his pockets. It was November 2. In three weeks it would be Thanksgiving. Another Thanksgiving in prison for Skip. And in that time Mrs. Reardon would be going in for another angioplasty. Ten years of waiting for a miracle had taken its toll on her.

One thing, however, had come out of all this, he reminded himself. Kerry might not believe in Skip's innocence, but she had opened two lines of inquiry that Geoff would follow up on. Dolly Bowles' story of "Poppa's car," a black four-door Mercedes, was one, and the other was Dr. Smith's bizarre need to duplicate Suzanne's face in other women. At least they both were new angles on what had become a very familiar story.

The ringing of the phone interrupted his thoughts. He was tempted not to answer it, but years of listening to his mother jokingly say, "How can you not answer the phone, Geoff? For all you know it's news about a pot of gold," made him reach for it.

It was Deidre Reardon calling to tell him about her visit with Skip, and then with Kerry McGrath.

"Deidre, you didn't say that to Kerry?" Geoff asked. He made no effort to conceal how upset he was with what she had done.

"Yes, I did. And I'm not sorry," Mrs. Reardon told him.

"Geoff, the only thing that's keeping Skip going is hope. That woman singlehandedly put out that hope."

"Deidre, thanks to Kerry I have some new angles that I'm going to pursue. They could be very important."

"She went down to see my son, looked into his face, questioned him and decided he was a killer," Mrs. Reardon said. "I'm sorry, Geoff. I guess I'm getting old and tired and bitter. I don't regret a word of what I said to Kerry McGrath." She hung up without saying good-bye.

Geoff took a deep breath and dialed Kerry's number.

When Kerry got home and the sitter had left, Robin looked at her critically. "You look bushed, Mom."

"I am bushed, kiddo."

"Tough day?"

"You could call it that."

"Mr. Green on your back?"

"He will be. But let's not talk about it. I think I'd rather forget it for the moment. How was your day?"

"Fine. I think Andrew likes me."

"Really!" Kerry knew that Andrew was considered the coolest boy in the fifth grade. "How do you know that?"

"He told Tommy that even with my face banged up, I'm better looking than most of the dorks in our class."

Kerry grinned. "Now that's what I call a compliment."

"That's what I thought. What are we having for dinner?"

"I stopped at the supermarket. How does a cheeseburger sound?"

"Perfect."

"No, it's not, but I try. Oh well, I guess you'll never have much reason to brag about your mother's home cooking, Rob."

The phone rang and Robin grabbed it. It was for her. She tossed the receiver to Kerry. "Hang up in a minute, okay? I'll take it upstairs. It's Cassie."

When she heard Robin's exuberant "I'm on," Kerry replaced the receiver, carried the mail into the kitchen, laid it on the counter and began to sort through it. A plain white envelope with her name and address in block printing caught her eye. She slit it open, pulled out a snapshot, looked at it and went cold.

It was a color Polaroid of Robin coming down the walk outside their house. Her arms were full of books. She was dressed in the dark blue slacks she had worn on Tuesday, the day she had been frightened by the car that she thought was going to hit her.

Kerry's lips felt rubbery. She bent over slightly as though reeling from a kick in the stomach. Her breath came in short, fast gasps. Who did this? Who would take Robin's picture, drive a car at her, then mail the picture to me, she wondered, her thoughts dazed and confused.

She heard Robin clattering down the stairs. Quickly she shoved the picture in her pocket. "Mom, Cassie reminded me that I'm supposed to be watching the Discovery Channel now. The program is about what we're studying in science. That doesn't count as entertainment, does it?"

"No, of course not. Go ahead."

The phone rang again as Kerry sank into a chair. It was Geoff Dorso. She cut off his apologies. "Geoff, I just opened the mail." She told him about the picture. "Robin was right," she half whispered. "There *was* someone watching her from that car. My God, suppose he had pulled her into it. She'd have disappeared, just like those kids in upstate New York a couple of years ago. Oh my God."

Geoff heard the fear and despair in her voice. "Kerry, don't say anything else. Don't let Robin see that picture or realize that you're upset. I'm on my way. I'll be there in half an hour."

56

Dr. Smith had sensed something amiss in Kate Carpenter's attitude toward him all day. Several times he had caught her staring at him with a questioning look. Why? he wondered.

As he sat in his library that evening, in his usual chair, sipping his usual after-office cocktail, he pondered the possible reasons for her odd behavior. He was sure Carpenter had detected the slight tremor in his hand when he performed the rhinoplasty the other day, but that wouldn't explain the looks she had given him. Whatever was on her mind now was something more troubling, of that he was certain.

It had been a terrible mistake to follow Barbara Tompkins last night. When his car was caught in traffic in front of her apartment building, he had turned away as much as possible, but even so, he thought she might have seen him.

On the other hand, midtown Manhattan was a place where people did frequently catch a glimpse of people they knew. So his being there really wasn't so unusual.

But a quick, casual glimpse wasn't enough. He wanted to see Barbara again. Really see her. Talk to her. She wasn't due for a checkup for another two months. He had to see her before then. He couldn't wait that long to watch the way her eyes, now so luminous without the heavy lids that had concealed their beauty, smiled at him across the table.

She wasn't Suzanne. No one could be. But like Suzanne, the more Barbara became accustomed to her beauty, the more her personality enhanced it. He recalled the sullen, plain creature who had first appeared in his office; within a year of the operation Suzanne had capped the transformation with her total change of personality.

Smith smiled faintly, remembering Suzanne's provocative body language, the subtle moves that made every man turn to look at her. Then she had begun to tilt her head just a little, so that she gave whomever she was talking with the sense of being the only person in the universe.

She had even lowered the tone of her voice until it had a husky, intimate quality. Teasingly she would run a fingertip over the hand of the man—and it was always a man—who was chatting with her.

When he had commented on the personality transformation she had undergone, she had said, "I had two good teachers, my stepsisters. We reversed the fairy tale. They were the beauties and I was ugly Cinderella. Only instead of a fairy godmother, I have you."

Toward the end, however, his Pygmalion fantasy had begun to turn into a nightmare. The respect and the affection she had seemed to have for him had begun to fade. She seemed no longer willing to listen to his counsel. Toward the end she had gone beyond simple flirting. How many times had he warned her that she was playing with fire, that Skip Reardon would be capable of murder if he found out the way she was carrying on?

Any husband of a woman that desirable would be capable of murder, Dr. Smith thought.

With a jolt he looked down angrily at his empty glass. Now there wouldn't be another chance to reach the perfection he had achieved in Suzanne. He would have to give up surgery before a disaster occurred. It was too late. He knew he was in the beginning stages of Parkinson's.

If Barbara wasn't Suzanne, she was of all his living patients the most striking example of his genius. He reached for the phone.

Surely that wasn't stress in her voice, he thought, when she picked up the receiver and said hello.

"Barbara, my dear, is anything wrong? This is Dr. Smith."

Her gasp was audible, but then she said quickly, "Oh, no, of course not. How are you, Doctor?"

"I'm fine but I think you might be able to do me a favor. I'm stopping in at Lenox Hill Hospital for a moment to see an old friend who is terminal, and I know I'll be feeling a bit down. Would you have mercy on me and join me for dinner? I could stop by for you at about seven-thirty."

"I, I don't know . . ."

"Please, Barbara." He tried to sound playful. "You did say that you owed me your new life. Why not spare me two hours of it?"

"Of course."

"Wonderful. Seven-thirty then."

"All right, Doctor."

When Smith hung up, he raised his eyebrows. Was that a note of resignation in Barbara's voice? he wondered. She almost sounded as though he had *forced* her into meeting him.

If so, it was one more way in which she was beginning to resemble Suzanne.

57

Jason Arnott could not shake the feeling that something was wrong. He had spent the day in New York with fifty-two-year-old Vera Shelby Todd, trailing after her as she took him on her endless hunt for Persian carpets.

Vera had phoned him that morning and asked if he could be available for the day. A Rhode Island Shelby, she lived in one of the handsome manor houses in Tuxedo Park and was used to getting her way. After her first husband died, she had married Stuart Todd but decided to keep the Tuxedo Park place. Now, using Todd's seemingly unlimited checkbook, Vera frequently availed herself of Jason's infallible eye for rare finds and bargains.

Jason had first met Vera not in New Jersey, but at a gala the Shelbys gave in Newport. Her cousins had introduced them, and when Vera realized how relatively close he lived to her Tuxedo Park home, she had begun inviting him to her parties and eagerly accepting invitations to his gatherings as well.

It always amused Jason that Vera had told him every detail of the police investigation into the Newport robbery he had committed years ago.

"My cousin Judith was so upset," she had confided. "She couldn't understand why someone would take the Picasso and the Gainsborough and pass up the Van Eyck. So she brought in some art expert, and he said that she had a discriminating criminal: The Van Eyck is a fake. Judith was furious, but for the rest of us who had had to listen to her bragging about her peerless knowledge of the great masters, it's become a family joke."

Today, after having exhaustively examined ludicrously expensive rugs ranging from Turkomans to Safavids, with Vera finding none of them to be exactly what she had in mind, Jason was wild to get home and away from her.

But first, at her insistence they had a late lunch at The Four Seasons, and that pleasant interlude perked Jason up considerably. At least until, as she finished her espresso, Vera had said, "Oh, did I forget to tell you? You remember how five years ago my cousin Judith's place in Rhode Island was burglarized?"

Jason had pursed his lips. "Yes, of course I do. Terrible experience."

Vera nodded. "I should say. But yesterday Judith got a photograph from the FBI. There was a recent burglary in Chevy Chase, and a hidden camera caught the robber. The FBI thinks it may be the same person who broke into Judith's house and dozens of others."

Jason had felt every nerve in his body tingle. He had only met Judith Shelby a few times and hadn't seen her at all in almost five years. Obviously she hadn't recognized him. Yet.

"Was it a clear picture?" he asked casually.

Vera laughed. "No, not at all. I mean from what Judith says, it's in profile and the lighting is bad and a stocking mask was pushed up on the guy's forehead but was still covering his head. She said she could just about make out something of the nose and mouth. She threw it out."

Jason stifled a spontaneous sigh of relief, although he knew he had nothing to celebrate. If the photo went out to the Shelbys, it probably also went out to dozens of others whose homes he had broken into.

"But I think Judith is finally over her Van Eyck incident," Vera continued. "According to the information with the photograph, that man is considered dangerous. He's wanted for questioning in the murder of Congressman Peale's mother. She apparently stumbled in on him during a robbery at her house. Judith almost went home early the night her place was burglarized. Just think what might have happened if she'd found him there."

Nervously, Jason pursed his lips. They had tied him to the Peale death!

When they left The Four Seasons, they shared a taxi to the garage on West Fifty-seventh Street where both had parked. After an effusive good-bye and Vera's strident promise, "We'll just keep looking. The perfect rug for me is out there somewhere," Jason was at last on his way home to Alpine.

How indistinct was the picture the hidden camera had taken of him? he wondered as he drove in the steadily moving afternoon traffic up the Henry Hudson Parkway. Would someone look at it and find that it reminded him, or her, of Jason Arnott?

Should he cut and run? he asked himself as he crossed the George Washington Bridge and turned onto the Palisades Parkway. No one knew about the place in the Catskills. He owned it under an assumed name. Under other alternate identities, he had plenty of money in negotiable securities. He even had a fake passport. Maybe he should leave the country immediately.

On the other hand, if the picture was as indistinguishable as Judith Shelby found it, even if some people saw a resemblance to him, they would find it patently absurd to tie him to a theft.

By the time Jason exited onto the road into Alpine, he had made up his mind. With the exception of this photograph, he was almost sure he had left no tracks, no fingerprints. He had been extremely careful, and his caution had paid off. He simply couldn't give up his wonderful lifestyle just because of what might happen. He had never been a fearful man. If he had been, he certainly wouldn't have lived this life for so many years.

No, he would not panic. He would just sit tight. But no more jobs for a long time, he promised himself. He didn't need the money, and this was a warning.

He got home at quarter of four and went through the mail. One envelope caught his eye and he slit it open, pulled out the contents—a single sheet of paper—studied it, and burst out laughing.

Surely no one would link him to that vaguely comical figure with the stocking mask pushed up and the grainy caricature of a profile literally inches away from the copy of the Rodin figurine.

"Vive le junk," Jason exclaimed. He settled in the den for a nap. Vera's constant stream of talk had exhausted him. When he awoke, it was just time for the six o'clock news. He reached for the remote control and turned on the set.

The lead story was that Jimmy Weeks' codefendant, Barney Haskell, was rumored to be cutting a deal with the attorney general.

Nothing like the deal I could cut, Jason thought. It was a comforting reminder. But of course it would never happen.

58

Robin turned off the science program just as the doorbell rang. She was delighted to hear Geoff Dorso's voice in the foyer and came running out to greet him. She could see that both his face and her mother's were serious. Maybe they had a fight, she thought, and want to make up.

Throughout the meal, Robin noticed that her mother was un-usually quiet, while Geoff was funny, telling stories about his sisters.

Geoff is so nice, Robin thought. He reminded her of Jimmy Stewart in that movie she watched with her mother every Christ-mas, *It's a Wonderful Life.* He had the same sort of shy, warm smile and hesitant voice, and the kind of hair that looked as though it wouldn't ever really stay in place.

But Robin noticed that her mother seemed to be only half listening to Geoff's stories. It was obvious something was up between them and that they needed to talk—without her in the room. So she decided to make the big sacrifice and work on her science project upstairs in her room.

After she had helped clear the table, she announced her plans and caught the look of relief in her mother's eyes. She does want to talk to Geoff alone, Robin thought happily. Maybe this is a good sign.

Geoff listened at the bottom of the stairs. When he heard the click of Robin's bedroom door closing, he went back into the kitchen. "Let's see the picture."

Kerry reached into her pocket, drew it out and handed it to him.

Geoff studied it carefully. "It looks to me as though Robin had it straight when she told what had happened," he said. "That car must have been parked directly across the street. Someone caught her coming head-on from the house."

"Then she was right about the car racing toward her," Kerry said. "Suppose it hadn't swerved into a U-turn? But Geoff, why?"

"I don't know, Kerry. But I do know that this has to be treated seriously. What are you thinking of doing about it?"

"Showing this to Frank Green in the morning. Getting a check to see if any sex offenders have moved into the area. Driving Robin to school on my way to work. Not letting her walk home with the other kids but having the sitter pick her up.

Notifying the school so that they're aware that someone may be after her."

"What about telling Robin?"

"I'm not sure. Not yet anyhow."

"Did you let Bob Kinellen know yet?"

"Good Lord, it never occurred to me. Of course Bob has to know about this."

"I'd want to know if it were my child," Geoff agreed. "Look, why don't you give him a call and let me pour us another coffee."

Bob was not at home. Alice was coldly civil to Kerry. "He's still at the office," she said. "He practically lives there these days. Is there a message I can give him?"

Only that his oldest child is in danger, Kerry thought, and she doesn't have the advantage of a live-in couple to be there to protect her when her mother is working. "I'll call Bob at the office. Good-bye, Alice."

Bob Kinellen picked up the phone on the first ring. He paled as he listened to Kerry's recounting of what had happened to Robin. He had no doubt who had taken the picture. It had Jimmy Weeks' signature all over it. That was the way he worked. Start a war of nerves, then step it up. Next week there would be another picture, taken from long range. Never a threat. No notes. Just a picture. A get-the-message-or-else situation.

It wasn't an effort for Kinellen to sound concerned and to agree with Kerry that it would be better if Robin were driven to and from school for a while.

When he hung up, he slammed his fist on the desk. Jimmy was spinning out of control. They both knew that it was all over if Haskell completed his deal with the U.S. attorney.

Weeks figured that Kerry would probably call me about the picture, Bob thought. It's his way of telling me to warn her away from the Reardon case. And it's his way of telling me I'd better find a way to get him off on this tax evasion charge or else. But what Weeks doesn't know, he told himself, is that Kerry doesn't get scared off. In fact, if she perceived that picture as a warning to her, it would be like waving a red flag in front of a bull.

But Kerry doesn't understand that when Jimmy Weeks turns on someone, it's all over for that person, he thought.

Bob's mind jumped back to the day nearly eleven years ago when Kerry, three months pregnant, had looked at him with eyes that were both astonished and furious. "You're quitting the prosecutor's office to go with that law firm? Are you crazy? All their clients have one foot in jail. And the other foot should be there," she'd said.

They had had a heated argument that ended with Kerry's contemptuous warning, "Just remember this, Bob. There's an old saying: Lie down with dogs and you'll get up with fleas."

59

Dr. Smith took Barbara Tompkins to Le Cirque, a very chic, very expensive restaurant in midtown Manhattan. "Some women enjoy quiet little out-of-the-way places, but I suspect you enjoy the high-profile spots where one can see and be seen," he said to the beautiful young woman.

He had picked her up at her apartment and did not miss the fact that she had been ready to leave immediately. Her coat was on a chair in the small foyer, her purse on the table beside it. She did not offer him an aperitif.

She doesn't want to be alone with me, he had thought.

But at the restaurant, with so many people around them and the attentive maître d' hovering nearby, Barbara visibly relaxed. "It's a lot different from Albany," she said. "I'm still like a kid having a daily birthday."

He was stunned for a moment by her words. So similar to Suzanne, who had compared herself to a kid with an ever-present Christmas tree and gifts always waiting to be opened. But from being an enchanted child, Suzanne had changed into an ungrateful adult. I asked so little of her, he thought. Shouldn't an artist be allowed to take pleasure in his creation? Why should the creation be wasted among leering dregs of humanity while the artist suffers for a glimpse of it?

Warmth filled him as he noticed that in this room filled with attractive, elegant women, sidelong glances rested on Barbara. He pointed that out to her.

She shook her head slightly as though dismissing the suggestion.

"It's true," Smith persisted. His eyes became cold. "Don't take it for granted, Suzanne. That would be insulting to me."

It was only later, after the quiet meal was over and he had seen her back to her apartment, that he asked himself if he had called her Suzanne. And if so, how many times had he slipped?

He sighed and leaned back, closing his eyes. As the cab jostled downtown, Charles Smith reflected how easy it had been to drive past Suzanne's house when he was starved for a glimpse of her. When she wasn't out playing golf, she invariably sat in front of the television and never bothered to draw the drapes over the large picture window in her recreation room.

He would see her curled up in her favorite chair, or sometimes he would be forced to witness her sitting side by side on the couch with Skip Reardon, shoulders touching, legs stretched out on the cocktail table, in the casual intimacy he could not share.

Barbara wasn't married. From what he could tell there wasn't anyone special in her life. Tonight he had asked her to call him

Charles. He thought about the bracelet Suzanne had been wearing when she died. Should he give it to Barbara? Would it endear him to her?

He had given Suzanne several pieces of jewelry. Fine jewelry. But then she had started accepting other pieces from other men, and demanding that he lie for her.

Smith felt the glow from being with Barbara ooze away. A moment later he realized that for the second time the cabbie's impatient voice was saying, "Hey, mister, you asleep? You're home."

60

Geoff did not stay long after Kerry had called Kinellen. "Bob agrees with me," she told him as she sipped the coffee.

"No other suggestions?"

"No, of course not. Sort of his usual, 'You handle it, Kerry. Anything you decide is fine.' "

She put down the cup. "I'm not being fair. Bob honestly did seem concerned, and I don't know what else he could suggest."

They were sitting in the kitchen. She had turned off the overhead light, thinking they would carry their coffee into the living room. Now the only illumination in the room came from the dim light in a wall fixture.

Geoff studied the grave face across the table from him, aware of the hint of sadness in Kerry's hazel eyes, the determination in the set of her generous mouth and finely sculpted chin, the vulnerability in her overall posture. He wanted to put his arms around her, to tell her to lean on him.

But he knew she didn't want that. Kerry McGrath did not expect or want to lean on anyone. He tried again to apologize for his dismissive remark to her the other night, suggesting that she was being self-serving, and for Deidre Reardon's intrusive visit to her office. "I had a hell of a nerve," he said. "I know that if you believed in your heart that Skip Reardon was innocent, you of all people would not hesitate in trying to help him. You're a stand-up guy, McGrath."

Am I? Kerry wondered. It was not the moment to share with Geoff the information she had found in the prosecutor's file about Jimmy Weeks. She would tell him, but first she wanted to see Dr. Smith again. He had angrily denied that he had touched Suzanne surgically, but he had never said that he hadn't sent her to someone else. That meant that technically he wasn't a liar.

As Geoff left a few minutes later, they stood for a moment in the foyer. "I like being with you," he told her, "and that has nothing to do with the Reardon case. How about our going out to dinner on Saturday night and bringing Robin with us?"

"She'd like that."

As Geoff opened the door he leaned down and brushed her cheek with his lips. "I know it's unnecessary to tell you to double lock the door and to turn on the alarm, but I will suggest you don't do any heavy thinking about that picture after you go to bed."

When he was gone, Kerry went upstairs to check on Robin. She was working on her science report and did not hear her mother come in. From the doorway Kerry studied her child. Robin's back was to her, her long dark brown hair spilling over her shoulders, her head bent in concentration, her legs wrapped around the rungs of the chair.

She is the innocent victim of whoever took that picture, Kerry thought. Robin is like me. Independent. She's going to hate having to be driven to and picked up from school, hate not being able to walk over to Cassie's by herself.

And then in her mind she heard again Deidre Reardon's pleading voice begging her to ask herself how she would like to see her child caged for ten years for a crime she didn't commit.

61

The plea bargaining was not going well for Barney Haskell. At 7:00 A.M. on Friday morning he met attorney Mark Young in his handsome law office in Summit, half an hour and a world away from the federal courthouse in downtown Newark.

Young, head of Barney's defense team, was about the same age he was, fifty-five, but there the resemblance ended, Barney thought sourly. Young was smoothly elegant even at this early hour, dressed in his lawyer's pin-striped suit that seemed to fit like a second skin. But Barney knew that when the jacket came off, those impressive shoulders disappeared. Recently the *Star-Ledger* had done a write-up on the high-profile lawyer, including the fact that he wore one-thousand-dollar suits.

Barney bought his suits off the rack. Jimmy Weeks had never paid him enough to allow him to do otherwise. Now he was facing years in prison if he stuck with Jimmy. So far the Feds were hanging tough. They would only talk reduced sentence, not a free ride, if he handed Jimmy over to them. They thought they could convict Weeks without Barney.

Maybe. But maybe not, Barney thought. He figured they were bluffing. He had seen Jimmy's lawyers get him off before. Kinellen and Bartlett were good, and they had always managed to get him through those past investigations without any real damage.

This time, though, judging from the U.S. attorney's opening statement, the Feds had plenty of hard evidence. Still, they had to be scared that Jimmy would pull another rabbit out of his hat.

Barney rubbed his hand over his fleshy cheek. He knew he had the innocent look of a dumb bank clerk, an aspect that had always been helpful. People tended not to notice or remember him. Even the guys closest to Weeks never paid much attention to him. They thought of him as a gofer. None of them had realized he was the one who converted the under-the-table cash into investments and took care of bank accounts all over the world.

"We can get you into the witness protection program," Young was saying. "But only after you've served a minimum of five years."

"Too much," Barney grunted.

"Look, you've been hinting you can tie Jimmy to a murder," Young said as he examined a ragged edge on his thumbnail. "Barney, I've milked that as far as I can. You've got to either put up or shut up. They'd love to hang a murder on Weeks. That way they'll never have to deal with him again. If he's in for life, his organization probably would collapse. That's what they're gunning for."

"I can tie him to one. Then they'll have to prove he did it. Isn't there talk that the U.S. attorney on this case is thinking about running for governor against Frank Green?"

"If each gets his party's nomination," Young commented as he reached in his desk drawer for a nail file. "Barney, I'm afraid you'll have to stop talking in circles. You'd better trust me with whatever it is you're hinting about. Otherwise I won't be able to help you make an intelligent choice."

A frown momentarily crossed Barney's cherubic face. Then his forehead cleared and he said, "All right. I'll tell you. Remember the Sweetheart Murder Case, the one involving that sexy young wife who was found dead with roses scattered all over her? It was ten years ago, but it was the case that Frank Green made his name on."

Young nodded. "I remember. He got a conviction on the husband. Actually it wasn't that hard, but the case got a lot of publicity and sold a lot of newspapers." His eyes narrowed. "What about it? You're not saying Weeks was connected to that case, are you?"

"You remember how the husband claimed he didn't give his wife those roses, that they must have been sent by some man she was involved with?" At Young's nod, Haskell continued, "Jimmy Weeks sent those roses to Suzanne Reardon. I should know. I delivered them to her house at twenty of six the night she died. There was a card with them that he wrote himself. I'll show you what was on it. Give me a piece of paper."

Young shoved the telephone message pad at him. Barney reached for his pen. A moment later he handed back the pad. "Jimmy called Suzanne 'Sweetheart,' " he explained. "He had made a date with her for that night. He filled out the card like this."

Young examined the paper Barney pushed back to him. It held six notes of music in the key of C, with five words written underneath: "I'm in love with you." It was signed "J."

Young hummed the notes, then looked at Jimmy. "The opening phrase of the song 'Let Me Call You Sweetheart,' " he said.

"Uh-huh. Followed by the rest of the first line of the song, 'I'm in love with you.' "

"Where is this card?"

"That's the point. Nobody mentioned it being in the house

when the body was found. And the roses were scattered over her body. I only delivered them, then I kept going. I was on my way to Pennsylvania for Jimmy. But afterwards I heard the others talking. Jimmy was crazy about that woman, and it drove him nuts that she was always playing up to other guys. When he sent her those flowers he had already given her an ultimatum that she had to get a divorce—and stay away from other men."

"What was her reaction?"

"Oh, she liked to make him jealous. It seemed to make her feel good. I know one of our guys tried to warn her that Jimmy could be dangerous, but she just laughed. My guess is that that night she went too far. Throwing those roses over her body is just the kind of thing Jimmy would do."

"And the card was missing?"

Barney shrugged. "You didn't hear nothing about it at the trial. I was ordered to keep my mouth shut about her. I do know that she kept Jimmy waiting or stood him up that night. A couple of the guys told me he exploded and said he'd kill her. You know Jimmy's temper. And there was one other thing. Jimmy had bought her some expensive jewelry. I know, because I paid for it and kept a copy of the receipts. There was a lot of talk about jewelry at the trial, stuff the husband claimed he hadn't given her, but anything they found, the father swore he gave her."

Young tore the sheet of paper Barney had used off the pad, folded it and put it in his breast pocket. "Barney, I think you're going to be able to enjoy a wonderful new life in Ohio. You realize that you've not only delivered the U.S. attorney a chance to nail Jimmy for murder but also to annihilate Frank Green for prosecuting an innocent man."

They smiled across the desk at each other. "Tell them I don't want to live in Ohio," Barney joked.

They left the office together and walked down the corridor to the bank of elevators. When one arrived and the doors started to part, Barney sensed immediately that something was wrong.

There was no light on inside it. Gut instinct made him turn to run.

He was too late. He died immediately, moments before Mark Young felt the first bullet shred the lapel of his thousand-dollar suit.

62

Kerry heard about the double homicide on WCBS Radio as she was driving to work. The bodies were discovered by Mark Young's private secretary. The report stated that Young and his client Barney Haskell had been scheduled to meet in the parking lot at 7:00 A.M., and it was surmised that Young had disengaged the alarm system when he opened the downstairs door of the small building. The security guard did not come on duty until eight o'clock.

The outside door was unlocked when the secretary arrived at 7:45, but she thought Young had simply forgotten to relock it, as she reported he often had in the past. Then she had taken the elevator upstairs and made the discovery.

The report concluded with a statement from Mike Murkowski, the prosecutor of Essex County. He said it appeared both men had been robbed. They might have been followed into the building by potential muggers and then lost their lives when they tried to resist. Barney Haskell had been shot in the back of his head and neck.

The CBS reporter asked if the fact that Barney Haskell reportedly had been in the process of plea bargaining in the Jimmy Weeks case, and was rumored to be about to connect Weeks to a murder, was being considered as a possible motive for the double slaying. The prosecutor's sharp answer was, "No comment."

It sounds like a mob hit, Kerry thought as she snapped off the radio. And Bob represents Jimmy Weeks. Wow, what a mess!

As she had expected, there was a message from Frank Green waiting on her desk. It was very short. "See me." She tossed off her coat and went across the main hall to his private office.

He did not waste words. "What was Reardon's mother doing coming in here and demanding to see you?"

Kerry chose her words carefully. "She came because I went down to the prison to see Skip Reardon and he received from me the correct impression that I didn't see anything new that would be grounds for an appeal."

She could see the lines around Green's mouth relax, but it was clear he was angry. "I could have told you that. Kerry, ten years ago if I had thought there was one *shred* of evidence to suggest Skip Reardon's innocence, I'd have run it into the ground. There wasn't. Do you know what kind of hay the media would make of this if they thought my office was investigating that case now? They'd love to portray Skip Reardon as a victim. It sells papers —and it's the kind of negative publicity they love to print about political candidates."

His eyes narrowed, and he thudded his fingers on the desk for emphasis. "I'm damn sorry you weren't in the office when we were investigating that murder. I'm damn sorry you didn't see that beautiful woman strangled so viciously that her eyes had almost popped out. Skip Reardon had shouted at her so loudly in the morning that the meter reader who overheard them wasn't sure whether he should call the cops before something happened. That was his statement under oath on the stand. I happen to think you'll make a good judge, Kerry, if you get the chance, but a good judge exercises judgment. And right now I think yours is lousy."

If you get the chance.

Was that a warning? she wondered. "Frank, I'm sorry if I've upset you. If you don't mind, let's move on to something else." She took Robin's picture from the pocket of her jacket and handed it to him. "This came in a plain white envelope in yesterday's mail. Robin is wearing the outfit she had on Tuesday morning when she said she saw that unfamiliar car parked across the street and thought someone might be after her. She was right."

The anger vanished from Green's face. "Let's talk about protecting her."

He agreed with Kerry's plan to notify the school, and to drop Robin off and have her picked up. "I'll find out if we have any convicted sex offenders recently released or moved into the area. I still think that sleaze you convicted last week may have friends who want to get back at you. We'll request that the Hohokus police keep an eye on your house. Do you have a fire extinguisher?"

"A sprinkler system."

"Get a couple of extinguishers just in case."

"You mean in case of a firebomb?"

"It's been known to happen. I don't want to frighten you, but precautions have to be taken."

It was only as she turned to leave that he mentioned the murder in Summit.

"Jimmy Weeks worked fast, but your ex is still going to have a hell of a time getting him off, even *without* Haskell's plea bargain."

"Frank, you talk as though it's a foregone conclusion that this was a hit!"

"Everybody knows it was, Kerry. The wonder is that Jimmy waited this long to get Haskell. Be glad you got rid of Weeks' mouthpiece when you did."

63

Bob Kinellen did not hear the news about Barney Haskell and Mark Young until he entered the courthouse at ten of nine and the media pounced on him. As soon as he heard what had happened, he realized that he had been expecting it.

How could Haskell have been so stupid as to think Jimmy would let him live to testify against him?

He managed to appear appropriately shocked, and to sound convincing when, in answer to a question, he said that Haskell's death would in no way change Mr. Weeks' defense strategy. "James Forrest Weeks is innocent of all charges," he said. "Whatever deal Mr. Haskell was trying to make with the U.S. attorney would have been exposed in court as self-serving and dishonest. I deeply regret the death of Mr. Haskell and my fellow attorney and friend Mark Young."

He managed to escape into an elevator and brush past other media representatives on the second floor. Jimmy was already in the courtroom. "Heard about Haskell?"

"Yes, I did, Jimmy."

"Nobody's safe. These muggers are everywhere."

"I guess they are, Jimmy."

"It does kind of level the playing field though, doesn't it, Bobby?"

"Yes, I would say so."

"But I don't like a level playing field."

"I know that, Jimmy."

"Just so you know."

Bob spoke carefully. "Jimmy, someone sent my ex-wife a picture of our little girl, Robin. It was taken as she was leaving for school on Tuesday by the same person who was in a car that made a last-minute U-turn right in front of her. Robin thought he was going to come up on the sidewalk and run her over."

"They always joke about New Jersey drivers, Bobby."

"Jimmy, nothing had better happen to my daughter."

"Bobby, I don't know what you're talking about. When are they going to make your ex-wife a judge and get her out of the prosecutor's office? She shouldn't be poking around in other people's business."

Bob knew that his question had been asked and answered. One of Jimmy's people had taken the picture of Robin. He, Bob, would have to get Kerry to back off investigating the Reardon case. And he had better see to it that Jimmy was acquitted in this one.

"Good morning, Jimmy. Morning, Bob."

Bob looked up to see his father-in-law, Anthony Bartlett, slip into the chair next to Jimmy.

"Very sad about Haskell and Young," Bartlett murmured.

"Tragic," Jimmy said.

At that moment the sheriff's officer motioned to the prosecutor and Bob and Bartlett to step inside the judge's chambers. A somber Judge Benton looked up from his desk. "I assume you have all been made aware of the tragedy involving Mr. Haskell and Mr. Young." The attorneys nodded quietly.

"As difficult as it will be, I believe that, given the two months already invested in this trial, it should continue. Fortunately, the jury is sequestered and won't be exposed to this news, including the speculation that Mr. Weeks may be involved. I will simply tell them that the absence of Mr. Haskell and Mr. Young means that Mr. Haskell's case is no longer before them.

"I will instruct them not to speculate on what happened and not to let it affect their consideration of Mr. Weeks' case in any way.

"Okay—let's continue."

The jury filed in and settled in their seats. Bob could see the quizzical looks on their faces as they looked over to Haskell's and Young's empty chairs. As the judge instructed them not to speculate on what had happened, Bob knew damn well that that was exactly what they were doing. They think he pled guilty, Bob thought. That's not going to help us.

As Bob pondered how badly this would hurt Weeks, his eyes rested on juror number 10, Lillian Wagner. He knew that Wagner, prominent in the community, so proud of her Ivy League husband and sons, so aware of her position and social status, was a problem. There had to be a reason Jimmy demanded he accept her.

What Bob did not know was that an "associate" of Jimmy Weeks had quietly approached Alfred Wight, juror number 2, just before the jury had been sequestered. Weeks had learned that Wight had a terminally ill wife and was nearly bankrupt from the medical expenses. The desperate Mr. Wight had agreed to accept $100,000 in exchange for a guarantee that his vote would be Not Guilty.

64

Kerry looked with dismay at the stack of files on the worktable beside her desk. She knew she had to get to them soon; it was time to assign new cases. In addition, there were some plea bargains she had to discuss with Frank or Carmen, the first assistant. There was so much to be done there, and she should be focusing her attention.

Instead she asked her secretary to try to reach Dr. Craig Riker, the psychiatrist she sometimes used as a prosecution witness in murder trials. Riker was an experienced, no-nonsense doctor whose philosophy she shared. He believed that, while life does deal some pretty tough blows, a person just has to lick his wounds and then get on with it. Most important, he had a way of defusing the obfuscating psychiatric jargon spouted by the shrinks the defense attorneys lined up.

She especially loved him when, asked if he considered a defendant insane, he answered, "I think he's nuts, but not insane. He knew exactly what he was doing when he went into his aunt's home and killed her. He'd read the will."

"Dr. Riker is with a patient," Kerry's secretary reported. "He'll call you back at ten of eleven."

And true to his word, at exactly ten of eleven Janet called in that Dr. Riker was on the phone. "What's up, Kerry?"

She told him about Dr. Smith giving other women his daughter's face. "He denied in so many words that he did any work on Suzanne," she explained, "which could be true. He may have referred her to a colleague. But is making other women look like Suzanne a form of grieving?"

"It's a pretty sick form of grieving," Riker told her. "You say he hadn't seen her from the time she was a baby?"

"That's right."

"And then she appeared in his office?"

"Yes."

"What kind of guy is this Smith?"

"Rather formidable."

"A loner?"

"I wouldn't be surprised."

"Kerry, I need to know more and I'd certainly like to know whether or not he operated on his daughter, asked a colleague to do the job, or if she had the surgery before she went to him."

"I hadn't thought about the last possibility."

"But if, and I stress the word, *if,* he met Suzanne after all those years, saw a plain or even a palpably homely young woman, operated on her, created a beauty and then was enchanted by what he'd done, I think we've got to look for erotomania."

"What is that?" Kerry asked.

"It covers a lot of territory. But if a doctor who is a loner meets his daughter after all those years, transforms her into a beauty and then has the sense of having done something magnificent, we could argue that it falls into that category. He's possessive of her, even in love with her. It's a delusional disorder that often applies to stalkers, for example."

Kerry thought of Deidre Reardon telling her how Dr. Smith treated Suzanne as an object. She told Dr. Riker about Smith patting away a smudge on Suzanne's cheek and then lecturing her on preserving beauty. She also told him of Kate Carpenter's conversation with Barbara Tompkins, and of the latter's fear that Smith was stalking her.

There was a pause. "Kerry, I've got my next patient coming in. Keep me posted, won't you? This is a case I'd love to follow."

65

Kerry had intended to leave the office early so she could be at Dr. Smith's office just after his last appointment. She had changed her mind, however, realizing that it would be better to wait until she had a better perspective on Dr. Smith's relationship with his daughter. She also wanted to be home with Robin.

Mrs. Reardon believed that Smith's attitude toward Suzanne was "unhealthy," she thought.

And Frank Green had remarked on how Smith had been totally unemotional on the stand.

Skip Reardon had said his father-in-law wasn't around their house much, that when Suzanne saw him, they usually met alone.

I need to talk to someone who knew these people and who has no axe to grind, Kerry thought. I'd also like to talk to Mrs. Reardon again, more calmly. But what can I say to her? That a mobster who happens to be on trial right now was known to call Suzanne Sweetheart when he played golf with her? That a golf caddie sensed that there might be something going on between them?

Those disclosures might only nail Skip Reardon's coffin a little more tightly shut, she reasoned. As a prosecutor I could argue that even if Skip wanted a divorce so he could get back together with Beth, it would have infuriated him if he had learned that Suzanne was running around with a multimillionaire while charging three-thousand-dollar Saint Laurent suits to him.

She was just leaving the office at five o'clock when Bob phoned. She caught the tension in his voice. "Kerry, I need to stop by for a few minutes. Will you be home in an hour or so?"

"Yes."

"I'll see you then," he said, and hung up.

What was bringing Bob to the house? she wondered. Concern about the picture of Robin she'd received? Or had he had an unexpectedly tough day in court? That was certainly possible, she told herself, remembering how Frank Green had commented that even without Haskell's testimony the government would be able to convict Jimmy Weeks. She reached for her coat and slung her shoulder bag over her arm, remembering wryly how for the year and a half of her marriage, she had joyfully rushed home from work to spend the evening with Bob Kinellen.

When she arrived home, Robin looked at her accusingly. "Mom, why did Alison pick me up at school and drive me home? She wouldn't give me a reason, and I felt like a jerk."

Kerry looked at the sitter. "I won't hold you up, Alison. Thanks."

When they were alone, she looked into Robin's indignant face. "That car that frightened you the other day . . . ," she began.

When she was finished, Robin sat very still. "It's kind of scary, isn't it, Mom?"

"Yes, it is."

"That's why when you came home last night you looked all tired and beat up?"

"I hadn't realized I looked quite that bad, but yes, I was pretty heartsick."

"And that's why Geoff came running up?"

"Yes, it is."

"I wish you'd told me last night."

"I didn't know how to tell you, Rob. I was too uptight myself."

"So what do we do now?"

"Take a lot of precautions that may be a nuisance until we find out who was across the street last Tuesday and why he was there."

"Do you think if he comes back, he'll run me over next time?"

Kerry wanted to shout, "No, I don't." Instead she moved over to the couch where Robin was sitting and put an arm around her.

Robin dropped her head on her mother's shoulder. "In other words, if the car comes at me again, duck."

"That's why the car isn't going to get the chance, Rob."

"Does Daddy know about this?"

"I called him last night. He's coming up in a little while."

Robin sat upright. "Because he's worried about me?"

She's pleased, Kerry thought, as though Bob has done her a favor. "Of course, he's worried about you."

"Cool. Mom, can I tell Cassie about this?"

"No, not now. You've got to promise, Robin. Until we know who's pulling this—"

"And have cuffed him," Robin interjected.

"Exactly. Once that's done, then you can talk about it."

"Okay. What are we going to do tonight?"

"Just crash. We'll send out for pizza. I stopped on the way home and rented a couple of movies."

The mischievous look Kerry loved came into Robin's face. "R-rated, I hope."

She's trying to make me feel better, Kerry thought. She's not going to let me know how scared she is.

At ten of six, Bob arrived. Kerry watched as, with a whoop of joy, Robin ran into his arms. "What do you think about me being in danger?" she asked.

"I'm going to let you two visit while I get changed," Kerry announced.

Bob released Robin. "Don't be long, Kerry," he said hurriedly. "I can only stay a few minutes."

Kerry saw the instant pain on Robin's face and wanted to throttle Kinellen. Toss her a little TLC for a change, she thought angrily. Struggling to keep her tone of voice even, she responded, "Down in a minute."

She changed quickly into slacks and a sweater, but deliberately waited upstairs for ten minutes. Then, as she was about to come down, there was a knock at her door and Robin called, "Mom."

"Come in." Kerry started to say, "I'm ready," when she saw the look on Robin's face. "What's wrong?"

"Nothing. Dad asked me to wait up here while he talks to you."

"I see."

Bob was standing in the middle of the study, obviously uncomfortable, obviously anxious to be gone.

He hasn't bothered to take off his coat, Kerry thought. And what did he do to upset Robin? Probably spent the whole time telling her how rushed he was.

He turned when he heard her footsteps. "Kerry, I've got to get back to the office. There's a lot of work I have to do for tomorrow's session. But there's something very important I have to tell you."

He pulled a small sheet of paper out of his pocket. "You heard what happened to Barney Haskell and Mark Young?"

"Obviously."

"Kerry, Jimmy Weeks has a way of getting information. I'm not sure how, but he does. For example, he knows that you went to see Reardon in prison Saturday."

"Does he?" Kerry stared at her ex-husband. "What difference would that make to him?"

"Kerry, don't play games. I'm worried. Jimmy is desperate. I just told you that he has a way of finding out things. Look at this."

Kinellen handed her what seemed to be a copy of a note written on a six-by-nine-inch sheet torn from a pad. On it were six musical notes in the key of C, and underneath were the words, "I'm in love with you." It was signed "J."

"What's this supposed to be?" Kerry asked, even as she mentally hummed the notes she was reading. Then, before Bob had a chance to answer, she understood, and her blood ran cold. They were the opening notes to the song "Let Me Call You Sweetheart."

"Where did you get this and what does it mean?" she snapped.

"They found the original in Mark Young's breast pocket when they went through his clothes at the morgue. It was Haskell's writing, and on a sheet of paper torn from the pad next to Young's phone. The secretary remembers putting a fresh pad there last night, so Haskell had to have jotted it down sometime between seven and seven-thirty this morning."

"A few minutes before he died?"

"Exactly. Kerry, I'm certain it's connected to the plea bargain Haskell was trying to make."

"The plea bargain? You mean the homicide he was hinting he could connect to Jimmy Weeks was the Sweetheart Murder Case?" Kerry could not believe what she was hearing. "Jimmy *was* involved with Suzanne Reardon, wasn't he? Bob, are you telling me that whoever took Robin's picture and came within an inch of running her over works for Jimmy Weeks, and this is his way of scaring me off?"

"Kerry, I'm not saying anything except leave it alone. For Robin's sake, *leave it alone.*"

"Does Weeks know you're here?"

"He knows that, for Robin's sake, I'd warn you."

"Wait a minute." Kerry looked at her former husband with disbelief. "Let me get this straight. You're here to warn me off because your client, the thug and murderer you represent, has given you a threat, veiled or otherwise, to convey to me. My God, Bob, how low you have gone."

"Kerry, I'm trying to save my child's life."

"Your child? All of a sudden she's so important to you? Do you know how many times you've devastated her when you didn't show up to see her? It's insulting. Now get out."

As he turned, she snatched the paper from his hand. "But I'll take this."

"Give that to me." Kinellen grabbed her hand, forcing her fingers open and pulling the paper from her.

"Dad, let go of Mom!"

They both whirled to see Robin standing in the doorway, the fading scars bright once more against the ashen pallor of her face.

66

D r. Smith had left the office at 4:20, only a minute or so after his last patient—a post–tummy-tuck checkup—had departed.

Kate Carpenter was glad to see him go. She found it disturbing just to be around him lately. She had noticed the tremor in his hand again today when he removed the skull stitches from Mrs. Pryce, who had had an eyebrow lift procedure. The nurse's concern went beyond the physical, however; she was sure that mentally there was something radically wrong with the doctor as well.

The most frustrating thing for Kate, though, was that she didn't know where to turn. Charles Smith was—or at least had been—a brilliant surgeon. She didn't want to see him discredited, or drummed out of the profession. If circumstances were different, she would have talked to his wife or best friend. But in Dr. Smith's case, she couldn't do that—his wife was long gone, and he seemed to have no friends at all.

Kate's sister Jean was a social worker. Jean probably would understand the problem and be able to advise her on where to turn to get Dr. Smith the help he obviously needed. But Jean was on vacation in Arizona, and Kate didn't know how to reach her even if she wanted to.

At four-thirty Barbara Tompkins phoned. "Mrs. Carpenter, I've had it. Last night, Dr. Smith called and practically demanded that I have dinner with him. But then he kept calling me Suzanne. And he wants me to call him Charles. He asked if I had a serious boyfriend. I'm sorry, I know I owe him a lot, but I think he is really creepy, and this is getting to me. I find that even at work I'm looking over my shoulder, expecting to see him lurking somewhere. I can't stand it. This can't go on."

Kate Carpenter knew she couldn't stall any longer. The one possible person who came to her mind in whom she might confide was Robin Kinellen's mother, Kerry McGrath.

Kate knew she was a lawyer, an assistant prosecutor in New Jersey, but she was also a mother who was very grateful that Dr. Smith had treated her daughter in an emergency. She also realized that Kerry McGrath knew more about Dr. Smith's personal background than did she or anyone else on his staff. She wasn't sure why Kerry had been checking on the doctor, but Kate didn't feel that it was for any harmful purpose. Kerry had shared with her the information that Smith had been not only divorced but also was the father of a woman who was murdered.

Feeling like Judas Iscariot, Mrs. Kate Carpenter gave Barbara

67

For a long time after Bob Kinellen left, Kerry and Robin sat on the sofa, not talking, shoulders touching, legs up on the coffee table.

Then, choosing her words carefully, Kerry said, "Whatever I said, or whatever the scene you just witnessed might have implied, Dad loves you very much, Robin. His worry is for you. I don't admire the fixes he gets himself into, but I respect his feeling for you even when I get so angry I throw him out."

"You got mad at him when he said he was worried about me."

"Oh, come on, those were just words. He makes me so angry sometimes. Anyhow, I know that you're not going to grow up to be the kind of person who lets herself drift into problems that are obvious to everyone else, then pleads situational ethics—meaning 'this may be wrong but it's necessary.'"

"That's what Dad's doing?"

"*I* think so."

"Does he know who took my picture?"

"He *suspects* he knows. It has to do with a case Geoff Dorso has been working on and that he's tried to get me to help him with. He's trying to get a man out of prison that he's convinced is innocent."

"Are you helping him with it?"

"Actually, I'd pretty well decided that by getting involved I was stirring up a hornet's nest for no reason. Now I'm beginning to think I may have been wrong, that there are a couple of very good reasons to think that Geoff's client indeed may have been unfairly convicted. But on the other hand, I'm certainly not going to put you in any danger to prove it. I promise you that."

Robin stared ahead for a moment and then turned to her mother. "Mom, that doesn't make sense. That's totally unfair. You're putting Dad down for something, and then you're doing the same thing. Isn't *not* helping Geoff if you think his client shouldn't be in prison 'situational ethics'?"

"Robin!"

"I mean it. Think about it. Now can we order the pizza? I'm hungry."

Shocked, Kerry watched as her daughter stood up and reached for the bag with the video movies they were planning to watch. Robin examined the titles, chose one and put it in the VCR. Just before she turned it on, she said, "Mom, I really think that guy in the car the other day was just trying to scare me. I don't think he really would have run me over. I don't mind if you drop me off at school and Alison picks me up. What's the dif?"

Kerry stared at her daughter for a moment, then shook her head. "The dif is that I'm proud of you and ashamed of myself." She hugged Robin quickly, then released her and went into the kitchen.

A few minutes later, as she was getting out plates for the pizza, the phone rang and a hesitant voice said, "Ms. McGrath, I'm Barbara Tompkins. I apologize for bothering you, but Mrs. Carpenter, in Dr. Charles Smith's office, suggested that I call you."

As she listened, Kerry grabbed a pen and began jotting notes on the message pad. *Dr. Smith was consulted by Barbara . . . He showed her a picture . . . Asked her if she wanted to look like this woman . . . Operated on her . . . Began counseling her . . . Helped her select an apartment . . . Sent her to a personal shopper . . . Now is calling her "Suzanne" and stalking her . . .*

Finally Tompkins said, "Ms. McGrath, I'm so grateful to Dr. Smith. He's turned my life around. I don't want to report him to the police and ask for a restraining order. I don't want to hurt him in any way. But I can't let this go on."

"Have you ever felt you were in physical danger from him?" Kerry asked.

There was a brief hesitation before Tompkins answered slowly, "No, not really. I mean he's never tried to force himself on me physically. He's actually been quite solicitous, treating me as though I were fragile somehow—like a china doll. But I also get a sense occasionally of terrible, restrained anger in him, and that it could easily be unleashed, maybe on me. For example, when he showed up to take me out to dinner last night, I could tell he wasn't happy that I was ready to immediately get out of my apartment. And for a moment I thought he might lash out. It's just that I didn't want to be alone with him. And now I feel as if I outright *refused* to see him, he could get very, very angry. But as I told you, he's been so good to me. And I know a restraining order could seriously damage his reputation."

"Barbara, I'm going in to see Dr. Smith on Monday. He doesn't know it, but I am. I think from what you tell me, and particularly from the fact that he calls you Suzanne, that he's suffering from some sort of breakdown. I hope he might be persuaded to seek help. But I can't advise you not to speak to the New York police if you're frightened. In fact, I think you should."

"Not yet. There's a business trip I was going to make next month, but I can rearrange my schedule and take it next week. I'd like to talk to you again when I come back; then I'll decide what I should do."

. . .

When she hung up, Kerry sank into a kitchen chair, the notes of the conversation in front of her. The situation was getting much more complicated. Dr. Smith had been stalking Barbara Tompkins. Had he also been stalking his own daughter? If so, it was very likely that it was *his* Mercedes Dolly Bowles and little Michael had seen parked in front of the Reardon house the night of the murder.

She remembered the partial license numbers Bowles claimed to have seen. Had Joe Palumbo had a chance to check them against Smith's car?

But if Dr. Smith had turned on Suzanne the way Barbara Tompkins feared he might turn on her, if he was the one responsible for her death, then why was Jimmy Weeks so afraid of being connected to Suzanne Reardon's murder?

I need to know more about Smith's relationship with Suzanne before I see him, before I know which questions to ask him, Kerry thought. That antique dealer, Jason Arnott—he might be the one to speak to. According to the notes she had found in the file, he had been just a friend but went into New York frequently with Suzanne to auctions and whatever. Perhaps Dr. Smith met them sometimes.

She placed a call to Arnott, leaving a message requesting him to call her back. Kerry then debated about making one more call.

It would be to Geoff, asking him to set up a second meeting at the prison with Skip Reardon.

Only this time she would want to have both his mother and his girlfriend, Beth Taylor, there as well.

68

Jason Arnott had planned to stay quietly at home on Friday night and prepare a simple dinner for himself. With that in mind he had sent his twice-weekly cleaning woman shopping, and she had returned with the filet of sole, watercress, pea pods and crisp French bread he had requested. But when Amanda Coble phoned at five o'clock to invite him to dinner at the Ridgewood Country Club with Richard and her, he had accepted gladly.

The Cobles were his kind of people—superrich but marvelously unpretentious; amusing; very, very smart. Richard was an international banker and Amanda an interior designer. Jason successfully handled his own portfolio and keenly enjoyed talking with Richard about futures and foreign markets. He knew that Richard respected his judgment and Amanda appreciated his expertise in antiques.

He decided they would be a welcome diversion after the disquieting time he had spent in New York yesterday with Vera Todd. And in addition, he had met a number of interesting people through the Cobles. In fact, their introduction had led to a most successful forage in Palm Springs three years ago.

He drove up to the front door of the club just as the Cobles surrendered their car to the parking valet. He was a moment behind them going through the front entrance, then waited as they greeted a distinguished-looking couple who were just leaving. He recognized the man immediately. Senator Jonathan Hoover. He'd been at a couple of political dinners where Hoover put in an appearance but they'd never met face to face.

The woman was in a wheelchair but still managed to look regal in a deep blue dinner suit with a skirt that came to the tips of high-laced shoes. He had heard that Mrs. Hoover was disabled, but had never seen her before. With an eye that instantly absorbed the smallest detail, he noted the position of her hands, clasped together, partially concealing the swollen joints of her fingers.

She must have been a knockout when she was young, and before all this happened, he thought as he studied the still-stunning features dominated by sapphire blue eyes.

Amanda Coble glanced up and saw him. "Jason, you're here." She waved him over and made the introductions. "We're talking about those terrible murders in Summit this morning. Both Senator Hoover and Richard knew the lawyer, Mark Young."

"It's pretty clear that it was a mob hit," Richard Coble said angrily.

"I agree," Jonathan Hoover said. "And so does the governor. We all know how he's cracked down on crime these eight years, and now we need Frank Green to keep up the good work. I can tell you this: If Weeks were being tried in a state court, you can bet the attorney general would have completed the plea bargain and gotten Haskell's testimony, and these murders never would have happened. And now Royce, the man who bungled this whole operation, wants to be governor. Well, not if I can help it!"

"Jonathan," Grace Hoover murmured reprovingly. "You can tell it's an election year, can't you, Amanda?" As they all smiled, she added, "Now we mustn't keep you any longer."

"My wife has been keeping me in line since we met as college freshmen," Jonathan Hoover explained to Jason. "Good seeing you again, Mr. Arnott."

"Mr. Arnott, haven't we met before as well?" Grace Hoover asked suddenly.

Jason felt his internal alarm system kick in. It was sending out a strong warning. "I don't think so," he answered slowly. I'm sure I'd have remembered, he thought. *So what makes her think we've met?*

"I don't know why, but I feel as though I know you. Well, I'm sure I'm wrong. Good-bye."

Even though the Cobles were their usual interesting selves and the dinner was delicious, Jason spent the evening heartily wishing he had stayed home alone and cooked the filet of sole.

When he got back to his house at ten-thirty, his day was further ruined by listening to the one message on his answering machine. It was from Kerry McGrath, who introduced herself as a Bergen County assistant prosecutor, gave her phone number, asked him to call her at home till eleven tonight or first thing in the morning. She explained that she wanted to talk to him unofficially about his late neighbor and friend, the murder victim, Suzanne Reardon.

On Friday evening, Geoff Dorso went to dinner at his parents' home in Essex Fells. It was a command performance. Unexpectedly, his sister Marian, her husband, Don, and their two-year-old twins had come in from

Boston for the weekend. His mother immediately tried to gather together her four other children, their spouses and offspring, to welcome the visitors. Friday was the only night all the others could make it at once, so Friday it would have to be.

"So you will postpone any other plans, won't you, Geoff?" his mother had half pleaded, half ordered when she had called him that afternoon.

Geoff had no plans, but in the hopes of building up credit against another demand invitation, he hedged: "I'm not sure, Mom. I'll have to rearrange something, but . . ."

Immediately he was sorry for having chosen that tack. His mother's voice changed to a tone of lively interest as she interrupted, "Oh, you've got a date, Geoff! Have you met someone nice? Don't cancel it. Bring her along. I'd love to meet her!"

Geoff groaned inwardly. "Actually, Mom, I was just kidding. I don't have a date. I'll see you around six."

"All right, dear." It was clear his mother's pleasure in his acceptance was tempered by the fact that she wasn't about to be introduced to a potential daughter-in-law.

As he got off the phone, Geoff admitted to himself that if this were tomorrow night, he would be tempted to suggest to Kerry that she and Robin might enjoy dinner at his parents' home. She'd probably run for the hills, he thought.

He found it suddenly disquieting to realize that several times during the day the thought had run through his mind that his mother would like Kerry very, very much.

At six o'clock he drove up to the handsome, rambling Tudor house that his parents had bought twenty-seven years ago for one-tenth of its present value. It was an ideal family home when we were growing up, he thought, and it's an ideal family home now with all the grandchildren. He parked in front of the old carriage house that now was the residence of his youngest and still-single sister. They'd all had their turn at using the carriage house apartment after college or graduate school. He'd stayed there when he was at Columbia Law School, then for two years after that.

We've had it great, he acknowledged as he breathed in the cold November air and anticipated the warmth of the inviting, brightly lighted house. His thoughts turned toward Kerry. I'm glad I'm not an only child, he said to himself. I'm grateful Dad didn't die when I was in college and Mother didn't remarry and settle a couple of thousand miles away. It couldn't have been easy for Kerry.

I should have called her today, he thought. Why didn't I? I know she doesn't want anyone hovering over her, but, on the other hand, she doesn't really have anyone to share her worries with. She can't protect Robin the way this family could protect one of our kids if there were a threat.

He went up the walk and let himself into the noisy warmth, so typical when three generations of the Dorso clan gathered.

After effusive greetings to the Boston branch and a casual hello to the siblings whom he saw regularly, Geoff managed to escape into the study with his father.

Lined with law books and signed first editions, it was the one room off limits to exploring youngsters. Edward Dorso poured a scotch for his son and himself. Seventy years old, he was a retired attorney who had specialized in business and corporate law and once numbered among his clients several Fortune 500 companies.

Edward had known and liked Mark Young and was anxious to hear any behind-the-scenes information about his murder that Geoff might have picked up in court.

"I can't tell you much, Dad," Geoff said. "It's hard to believe the coincidence that a mugger or muggers just happened to botch a robbery and kill Young, just when his fellow victim, Haskell, was about to plea bargain in return for testifying against Jimmy Weeks."

"I agree. Speaking of which, I had lunch in Trenton today with Sumner French. Something that would interest you came up. There is a planning board official in Philadelphia they're positive gave Weeks inside information ten years ago, about a new highway being built between Philly and Lancaster. Weeks picked up some valuable property and made a huge profit selling it to developers when the plans for the highway were made public."

"Nothing new about inside tips," Geoff observed. "It's a fact of life and almost impossible to police. And frequently difficult to prove, I might add."

"I brought this case up for a reason. I gather that Weeks bought some of these properties for next to nothing because the guy who had the options on them was desperate for cash."

"Anyone I know?"

"Your favorite client, Skip Reardon."

Geoff shrugged. "We travel in close circles, Dad, you know that. It's just one more way Skip Reardon was pushed down the tube. I remember Tim Farrell talking at the time about how Skip was liquidating everything for his defense. On paper, Skip's financial picture looked great, but he had a lot of optioned land, a heavy construction mortgage on an extravagant house and a wife who seemed to think she was married to King Midas. If Skip hadn't gone to prison, he'd be a rich man today, because he was a good businessman. But my recollection is that he sold off all the options for fair market value."

"Not fair market if the purchaser has privileged information," his father said tartly. "One of the rumors I heard is that Haskell, who was Weeks' accountant even then, was aware of that transaction too. Anyhow it's one of those pieces of information that may be useful some way, some day."

Before Geoff could comment, a chorus of voices from outside the study shouted, "Grandpa, Uncle Geoff, dinner's ready."

"And it has come, the summons, kind . . . ," Edward Dorso quoted as he stood and stretched.

"Go ahead, Dad, I'll be right behind you. I want to check my messages." When he heard Kerry's husky, low voice on the answering machine tape, he pressed the receiver to his ear.

Was Kerry actually saying that she wanted to go to the prison and see Skip again? That she wanted to have his mother and Beth Taylor there? "Hallelujah!" he said aloud.

Grabbing Justin, his nephew who had been sent to get him, Geoff scrambled to the dining room, where he knew his mother was impatiently waiting for everyone to sit down so that grace could be offered.

When his father had concluded the blessing, his mother added, "And we're so grateful to have Marian and Don and the twins with us."

"Mother, it's not as though we live at the North Pole," Marian protested, winking at Geoff. "Boston is about three and a half hours away."

"If your mother had her way, there'd be a family compound," his father commented with an amused smile. "And you'd all be right here, under her watchful eye."

"You can all laugh at me," his mother said, "but I love seeing my whole family together. It's wonderful to have three of you girls settled, and Vickey with a steady boyfriend as nice as Kevin."

Geoff watched as she beamed at that couple.

"Now if I could just get our only son to find the right girl . . ." Her voice trailed off as everyone turned to smile indulgently at Geoff.

Geoff grimaced, then smiled back, reminding himself that when his mother wasn't riding this horse, she was a very interesting woman who had taught medieval literature at Drew University for twenty years. In fact, he had been named Geoffrey because of her great admiration for Chaucer.

Between courses, Geoff slipped back into the den and phoned Kerry. He was thrilled to realize that she sounded glad to hear from him.

"Kerry, can you go down and see Skip tomorrow? I know his mother and Beth will drop everything to be there when you come."

"I want to, Geoff, but I don't know if I can. I'd be a wreck leaving Robin, even at Cassie's house. The kids are always outside, and it's right on an exposed corner."

Geoff didn't know he had the solution until he heard himself say, "Then I've got a better idea. I'll pick you both up, and we can leave Robin here with my folks while we're away. My sister and her husband and their kids are here. And because of them, the other grandchildren will be dropping by. Robin will have plenty of company, and if that isn't enough, my brother-in-law is a captain in the Massachusetts State Police. Believe me, she'll be safe."

70

Jason Arnott lay sleepless most of the night, wrestling with trying to decide how to treat the call from Assistant Prosecutor Kerry McGrath, even, as she so delicately put it, in an "unofficial" capacity.

By 7:00 A.M. he'd made up his mind. He would return her call and, in a courteous, civil, but distant tone, inform her that he would be delighted to meet with her, provided it would not take too long. His excuse would be that he was about to leave on a business trip.

To the Catskills, Jason promised himself. I'll hide out at the house. Nobody will find me there. In the meantime, this will all blow over. But I can't look as though I have anything to be concerned about.

The decision made, he finally fell into a sound sleep, the kind of sleep he enjoyed after he had successfully completed a mission and knew he was home free.

He called Kerry McGrath first thing when he woke up at nine-thirty. She picked up on the first ring. He was relieved to hear what seemed to be genuine gratitude in her tone.

"Mr. Arnott, I really appreciate your calling, and I assure you this is unofficial," she said. "Your name came up as having been a friend and antiques expert for Suzanne Reardon, years ago. Something has developed about that case, and I'd very much appreciate an opportunity to talk to you about the relationship you saw between Suzanne and her father, Dr. Charles Smith. I promise, I'll only take a few minutes of your time."

She meant it. Jason could spot a phony, had made a career of it, and she wasn't a phony. It wouldn't be hard to talk about Suzanne, he told himself. He frequently had shopped with her the way he shopped with Vera Shelby Todd yesterday. She had been at many of his parties, but so had dozens of other people. No one could make anything of that.

Jason was totally amenable to Kerry's explanation that she had a firm commitment to be picked up at one and would so much appreciate visiting him within the hour.

Kerry decided to bring Robin with her when she drove to Jason Arnott's house. She knew that it had upset Robin to see her struggling with Bob the night before over the copy of the Haskell note, and she reasoned that the drive to

Alpine would give them a half hour each way to chat. She blamed herself for the scene with Bob. She should have realized that there was no way he would let her have the note. Anyhow, she knew what it said. She had jotted it down just as she had seen it so she could show it to Geoff later.

It was a sunny, crisp day, the kind, she thought, that renews the spirit. Now that she knew she had to look seriously into the Reardon case and really see it through, she was determined to do it quickly.

Robin willingly had agreed to come along for the ride, although she pointed out that she wanted to be back by noon. She wanted to invite Cassie over for lunch.

Kerry then told her about the plan for her to visit Geoff's family while she went to Trenton on business.

"Because you're worried about me," Robin said matter-of-factly.

"Yes," Kerry admitted. "I want you where I know you'll be okay, and I know you'll be fine with the Dorsos. Monday, after I drop you off at school, I'll have a talk with Frank Green about all this. Now, Rob, when we get to Mr. Arnott's house, you come in with me, but you do know I have to talk privately to him. You brought a book?"

"Uh-huh. I wonder how many of Geoff's nieces and nephews will be there today. Let's see, he has four sisters. The youngest isn't married. The one next to Geoff has three kids, a boy who's nine—he's the one closest to my age—and a girl who's seven and a boy who's four. Geoff's second sister has four kids, but they're kind of little—I think the oldest is six. Then there's the one with the two-year-old twins."

"Rob, for heaven sake, when did you learn all this?" Kerry asked.

"The other night at dinner. Geoff was talking about them. You were kind of out of it, I guess. I mean, I could tell you weren't listening. Anyhow I think it will be cool to go down there. He says his mother's a good cook."

As they were leaving Closter and entering Alpine, Kerry glanced down at her directions. "It's not far now."

Five minutes later they drove up a winding road to Jason Arnott's European-style mansion. The bright sun played on the structure, a breathtaking combination of stone, stucco, brick and wood, with towering leaded-pane windows.

"Wow!" Robin said.

"Sort of makes you realize how modestly *we* live," Kerry agreed, as she parked in the semicircular driveway.

Jason Arnott opened the door for them before they could find the buzzer. His greeting was cordial. "Ms. McGrath, and is this your assistant?"

"I said it would be an unofficial visit, Mr. Arnott," Kerry said, as she introduced Robin. "Perhaps she could wait here while we talk." She indicated a chair near a life-size bronze sculpture of two knights in combat.

"Oh, no. She'll be much more comfortable in the little study." Arnott indicated a room to the left of the entrance hall. "You and I can go into the library. It's just past the study."

This place is like a museum, Kerry thought as she followed Arnott. She would have loved to have had the chance to stop and study the exquisite wall coverings, the fine furniture, the paintings, the total harmony of the interior. Keep your mind on what you're doing, she warned herself. You promised him you'd only be half an hour.

When she and Arnott were seated opposite each other on handsome morocco armchairs, she said, "Mr. Arnott, Robin suffered some facial injuries in a car accident several weeks ago and was treated by Dr. Charles Smith."

Arnott raised his eyebrows. "The Dr. Charles Smith who was Suzanne Reardon's father?"

"Exactly. On each of two follow-up visits, I saw a patient in his office who bore a startling resemblance to Suzanne Reardon."

Arnott stared at her. "By coincidence, I hope. Surely you're not saying that he is deliberately re-creating Suzanne?"

"An interesting choice of words, Mr. Arnott. I'm here because, as I told you on the phone, I need to know Suzanne better. I need to know what her relationship with her father really was, and so far as you knew it, with her husband."

Arnott leaned back, looked up at the ceiling and clasped his hands under his chin.

That's so posed, Kerry thought. He's doing it to impress me. Why?

"Let me start with meeting Suzanne. It would be about twelve years ago now. One day she simply rang the bell. I must tell you she was an extraordinarily beautiful girl. She introduced herself and explained that she and her husband were in the process of building a house in the neighborhood, that she wanted to furnish it with antiques and that she'd heard that I went with good friends to assist them in their bidding at auctions.

"I told her that that was true, but I did not consider myself an interior designer, nor did I intend to be considered a full-time advisor."

"Do you charge for your services?"

"In the beginning I did not. But then, as I realized I was having a very good time accompanying pleasant people on these jaunts, warning them off bad bargains, helping them to get fine objects at excellent prices, I set a fair commission rate. At first I was not interested in becoming involved with Suzanne. She was rather smothering, you see."

"But you did become involved?"

Arnott shrugged. "Ms. McGrath, when Suzanne wanted something, she got it. Actually, when she realized that flirting outrageously with me was only annoying me, she turned on the charm in a different way. She could be most amusing. Eventually we became very good friends; in fact, I still miss her very much. She added a great deal to my parties."

"Did Skip come with her?"

"Seldom. He was bored, and frankly my guests did not find him simpatico. Now don't misunderstand me. He was a well-mannered and intelligent young man, but he was different from most of the people I know. He was the kind of man who got up early, worked hard and had no interest in idle chatter—as he publicly told Suzanne one night when he left her here and went home."

"Did she have her own car that evening?"

Arnott smiled. "Suzanne never had a problem getting a ride."

"How would you judge the relationship between Suzanne and Skip?"

"Unraveling. I knew them for the last two years of their marriage. At first they seemed to be very fond of each other, but eventually it became clear that she was bored with him. Toward the end they did very little together."

"Dr. Smith said that Skip was wildly jealous of Suzanne and that he threatened her."

"If he did, Suzanne did not confide that to me."

"How well did you know Dr. Smith?"

"As well as any of her friends did, I suppose. If I went into New York with Suzanne on days when his office was closed, he often managed to show up and join us. Finally, though, his attention seemed to annoy her. She'd say things like, 'Serves me right for telling him that we were coming here today.' "

"Did she show him she was annoyed?"

"Just as she was quite public in displaying her indifference to Skip, she made no effort to hide her impatience with Dr. Smith."

"You knew that she had been raised by her mother and a stepfather?"

"Yes. She told me her growing-up years were miserable. Her stepsisters were jealous of her looks. She once said, 'Talk about Cinderella—in some ways I lived her life.' "

That answers my next question, Kerry thought. Obviously Suzanne had not confided to Arnott that she had grown up as the plain sister named Susie.

A sudden question occurred to her. "What did she call Dr. Smith?"

Arnott paused. "Either Doctor or Charles," he said after a moment.

"Not Dad."

"Never. At least not that I recall." Arnott looked pointedly at his watch.

"I know I promised not to take up too much of your time, but there's one more thing I need to know. Was Suzanne involved with another man? Specifically, was she seeing Jimmy Weeks?"

Arnott seemed to consider before answering. "I introduced her to Jimmy Weeks in this very room. It was the one and only time he was ever here. They were quite taken with each other. As you may know, there has always been a formidable feeling of power about Weeks, and that instantly attracted Suzanne. And, of course, Jimmy always had an eye for a beautiful woman. Suzanne bragged that after they met, he started appearing frequently at the Palisades Country Club, where she spent a lot of her time. And I think Jimmy was already a member there as well."

Kerry thought about the caddie's statement as she asked, "Was she happy about that?"

"Oh, very. Although I don't think she let Jimmy know it. She was aware that he had a number of girlfriends, and she enjoyed making him jealous. Do you remember one of the early scenes in *Gone With the Wind*, the one where Scarlett collects everyone else's beaux?"

"Yes, I do."

"That was our Suzanne. One would think she'd have outgrown that. After all, it's quite an adolescent trick, isn't it? But there wasn't a man Suzanne didn't try to dazzle. It didn't make her very popular with women."

"And Dr. Smith's reaction to her flirting?"

"Outraged, I would say. I think that if it had been possible, Smith would have built a guardrail around her to keep others away from her, pretty much the way museums put guardrails around their most precious objects."

You don't know how close you are to the mark, Kerry

thought. She recalled what Deidre Reardon had said about Dr. Smith's relationship to Suzanne, that he treated her as an object. "If your theory is correct, Mr. Arnott, wouldn't that be a reason for Dr. Smith to resent Skip Reardon?"

"Resent him? I think it went deeper than that. I think he hated him."

"Mr. Arnott, did you have any reason to think that Suzanne was given jewelry by any man other than her husband and father?"

"If she was, I wasn't privy to it. Suzanne had some very fine pieces, that I *do* know. Skip bought her a number of things every year for her birthday, and again for Christmas, always after she pointed out exactly what she wanted. She also had several one-of-a-kind older Cartier pieces that I believe her father gave her."

Or so he said, Kerry thought. She got up. "Mr. Arnott, do you think Skip Reardon killed Suzanne?"

He rose to his feet. "Ms. McGrath, I consider myself very knowledgeable about antique art and furnishings. I'm less good at judging people. But isn't it true that love and money are the two greatest reasons to kill? I'm sorry to say that in this case both of these reasons seem to apply to Skip. Don't you agree?"

From a window, Jason watched Kerry's car disappear down the driveway. Thinking over their brief exchange, he felt he had been sufficiently detailed to seem helpful, sufficiently vague so that she, like both the prosecution and defense ten years ago, would decide there was no purpose in questioning him further.

Do I think Skip Reardon killed Suzanne? No, I don't, Ms. McGrath, he thought. I think that, like far too many men, Skip might have been *capable* of murdering his wife. Only that night someone else beat him to it.

72

S kip Reardon had endured what was arguably one of the worst weeks of his life. Seeing the skepticism in Assistant Prosecutor Kerry McGrath's eyes when she had come to visit him had completed the job that the news about possibly no more appeals had begun.

It was as though a Greek chorus were chanting the words endlessly inside his head: *"Twenty more years before even the possibility of parole."* Over and over again. All week, instead of reading or watching television at night, Skip had stared at the framed pictures on the walls of his cell.

Beth and his mother were in most of them. Some of the pictures went back to seventeen years ago, when he was twenty-three years old and had just begun dating Beth. She had just started her first teaching job, and he had just launched Reardon Construction Company.

In these ten years he had been incarcerated, Skip had spent many hours looking at those pictures and wondering how everything had gone so wrong. If he hadn't met Suzanne that night, by now he and Beth would have been married fourteen or fifteen years. They probably would have two or three kids. What would it be like to have a son or a daughter? he wondered.

He would have built Beth a home they would have planned together—not that crazy, modern, vast figment of an architect's imagination that Suzanne had demanded and that he had come to detest.

All these years in prison he had been sustained by the knowledge of his innocence, his trust in the American justice system and the belief that someday the nightmare would go away. In his fantasies, the appeals court would agree that Dr. Smith was a liar, and Geoff would come down to the prison and say, "Let's go, Skip. You're a free man."

By prison rules, Skip was allowed two collect phone calls a day. Usually he called both his mother and Beth twice a week. At least one of them came down to see him on Saturday or Sunday.

This week Skip had not phoned either one of them. He had made up his mind. He would not let Beth visit him anymore. She had to get on with her life. She'd be forty her next birthday, he reasoned. She should meet someone else, get married, have kids. She loved children. That was why she had chosen teaching and then counseling as a career.

And there was something else that Skip decided: He wasn't going to waste any more time designing rooms and houses with the dream that someday he would get to build them. By the time he got out of prison—if he ever did get out—he would be in his sixties. It would be too late to get started again. Besides, there would be no one left to care.

That was why on Saturday morning, when Skip was told his lawyer was phoning him, he took the call with the firm intention of telling Geoff to forget about him as well. He too should get on to other things. The news that Kerry McGrath was coming down to see him as well as his mother and Beth angered him.

"What does McGrath want to do, Geoff?" he asked "Show Mom and Beth exactly *why* they're wasting their time trying to get me out of here? Show them how every argument *for* me is an argument *against* me? Tell McGrath I don't need to listen to that again. The court's done a great job of convincing me."

"Shut up, Skip," Geoff's firm voice snapped. "Kerry's interest in you and this murder case is causing her a hell of a lot of trouble, including a threat that something could happen to her ten-year-old daughter if she doesn't pull out."

"A threat? Who?" Skip looked at the receiver he was holding as though it had suddenly become an alien object. It was impossible to comprehend that Kerry McGrath's daughter had been threatened because of him.

"Not only *who?* but *why?* We're sure Jimmy Weeks is the 'who.' The 'why' is that for some reason he's afraid to have the investigation reopened. Now listen, Kerry wants to go over every inch of this case with you, and with your mother and Beth. She has a bunch of questions for all of you. She also has a lot to tell you about Dr. Smith. I don't have to remind you what his testimony did to you. We'll be there for the last visiting period, so plan to be cooperative. This is the best chance we have had of getting you out. It may also be the last."

Skip heard the click in his ear. A guard took him back to his cell. He sat down on the bunk and buried his face in his hands. He didn't want to let it happen, but in spite of himself, the flicker of hope that he thought he had successfully extinguished had jumped back to life and now was flaming throughout his being.

73

Geoff picked up Kerry and Robin at one o'clock. When they reached Essex Fells, Geoff brought Kerry and Robin into the house and introduced them around. At the end of the family dinner the night before, he had briefly explained to the adults the circumstances of his bringing Robin for a visit.

Immediately his mother's instincts had zeroed in on the fact that this woman Geoff insisted on calling "Robin's mother" might have special significance for her son.

"Of course, bring Robin over for the afternoon," she had said. "Poor child, that anyone could even think of harming her. And Geoff, after you and her mother—Kerry, did you say her name was?—come back from Trenton, you must stay and have dinner with us."

Geoff knew his vague "We'll see" cut no ice. Chances are, unless something untoward happens, we will eat at my mother's table tonight, he said to himself.

Instantly he detected the approval in his mother's eyes as she took in Kerry's appearance. Kerry was wearing a belted camel's hair coat over matching slacks. A hunter green turtleneck sweater accentuated the green tones in her hazel eyes. Her hair was brushed loosely over her collar. Her only makeup other than lip blush seemed to be a touch of eye shadow.

Next he could see that his mother was pleased by Kerry's sincere, but not effusive, gratitude for letting Robin visit. Mom had always stressed that voices should be well modulated, he thought.

Robin was delighted to hear that all nine grandchildren were somewhere in the house. "Don is taking you and the two oldest to Sports World," Mrs. Dorso told her.

Kerry shook her head and murmured, "I don't know . . ."

"Don is the brother-in-law who's the captain in the Massachusetts State Police," Geoff told her quietly. "He'll stick by the kids like glue."

It was clear that Robin expected to have a good time. She watched as the two-year-old twins, chased by their four-year-old cousin, pell-melled past them. "Sort of like baby rush hour around here," she observed happily. "See you later, Mom."

In the car, Kerry leaned back against the seat and sighed deeply.

"You're not worried, are you?" Geoff asked quickly.

"No, not at all. That was an expression of relief. And now let me fill you in on what I didn't tell you before."

"Like what?"

"Like Suzanne's years growing up, and what she saw when she looked in the mirror in those days. Like what Dr. Smith is up to with one of the patients whom he has given Suzanne's face. And like what I learned from Jason Arnott this morning."

Deidre Reardon and Beth Taylor were already in the visitors' reception room in the prison. After Geoff and Kerry registered with the clerk, they joined them, and Geoff introduced Kerry to Beth.

While they waited to be called, Kerry deliberately kept the conversation impersonal. She knew what she wanted to talk about when they were with Skip, but she wanted to save it until then. She did not want to lose the spontaneity of having the three of them trigger each other's memories as she raised the different points. Understanding Mrs. Reardon's restrained greeting, she concentrated on chatting with Beth Taylor, whom she liked immediately.

Promptly at three o'clock they were led to the area where family members and friends were allowed contact visits with the prisoners. It was more crowded today than it had been when Kerry visited last week. Dismayed, Kerry realized that it might have been better to have officially asked for one of the private conference rooms that were available when both prosecutor and defense attorney requested a joint visit. But that would have meant going on record as a Bergen County assistant prosecutor paying a visit to a convicted murderer, something she still was not quite ready to do.

They did manage to get a corner table, whose location filtered out some of the background noise. When Skip was escorted in, Deidre Reardon and Beth both jumped up. After the guard removed Skip's handcuffs, Beth held back while Deidre hugged her son.

Then Kerry watched as Beth and Skip looked at each other. The expressions on their faces and the very restraint of their kiss told more of what was between them than would have the most ardent, demonstrative embraces. In that moment Kerry vividly relived the memory of that day in court when she had seen the agony on Skip Reardon's face as he was sentenced to a minimum of thirty years' imprisonment, and had listened to his heartrending protest that Dr. Smith was a liar. Thinking back on it, she realized that, knowing very little about the case at the time, she still had felt she heard the ring of truth in Skip Reardon's voice that day.

She had brought a yellow pad on which she had written a series of questions, leaving room under each to make notes of their answers. Briefly she told them everything that had impelled her to make this second visit: Dolly Bowles' story about the presence of the Mercedes the night Suzanne died; the fact that Suzanne had been extremely plain growing up; Dr. Smith's bizarre re-creation of her face when operating on current patients; Smith's attraction to Barbara Tompkins; the fact that Jimmy Weeks' name had come up in the investigation; and, finally, the threat to Robin.

Kerry felt that it was a credit to the three of them that after their initial shock over hearing the disclosures, they did not waste time reacting among themselves. Beth Taylor reached for Skip's hand as she asked, "What can we do now?"

"First, let's clear the air by saying I now have grave doubts whether Skip is guilty, and if we uncover the kinds of things I expect to find, I'll do my best to help Geoff get the verdict reversed. This is how I see it," Kerry told them. "A week ago, Skip, you surmised after we talked, that I didn't believe you. That really isn't accurate. What I felt, and what I thought, was that there was nothing I had heard that couldn't be interpreted in two ways—for you or against you. Certainly there was nothing I heard that would provide grounds for a new appeal. Isn't that right, Geoff?"

Geoff nodded.

"Dr. Smith's testimony is the main reason that you were convicted, Skip. The one great hope is to discredit that testimony. And the only way I can see to do that is to back him into a corner by exposing some of his lies and confronting him with them."

She did not wait for any of them to speak. "I already have the answer to the first question I intended to ask—Suzanne never told you that she'd had plastic surgery. And incidentally, let's cut the formalities. My name is Kerry."

For the remaining hour and fifteen minutes of the visit she fired questions at them. "First of all, Skip, did Suzanne ever mention Jimmy Weeks?"

"Only casually," he said. "I knew he was a member of the club and that she sometimes played in a foursome with him. She used to brag about her golf scores all the time. But when she knew I was getting suspicious that she was involved with some-one, she began to mention only the names of the women she played with."

"Isn't Weeks the man on trial for income tax evasion?" Deidre Reardon asked.

Kerry nodded.

"That's incredible. I thought it was terrible that the govern-ment is harassing him. Last year I was a volunteer on the cancer drive, and he let us hold it on the grounds of his estate in Pea-pack. He underwrote the whole thing and then made a huge donation. And you are saying that he was involved with Suzanne and that he's threatening your little girl!"

"Jimmy Weeks has made sure his public image as basic good guy has been carefully nurtured," Kerry told her. "You're not the only one who thinks he's a victim of government harassment. But trust me—nothing could be further from the truth." She turned to Skip. "I want you to describe the jewelry that you believe Suzanne had received from another man."

"One piece was a gold bracelet with zodiac figures engraved in silver, except for the Capricorn symbol. That was the center-piece, and all encrusted with diamonds. Suzanne was a Capri-corn. It was obviously a very expensive piece. When I asked about it, she told me her father had given it to her. The next time I saw him, I thanked him for his generosity to her, and, just as I expected, he didn't know what I was talking about."

"That's the kind of item we might be able to trace. We can put out a flyer to jewelers in New Jersey and Manhattan for open-ers," Kerry said. "It's surprising how many of them can either identify a piece they've sold years before, or recognize someone's style when it's a one-of-a-kind design."

Skip told her about an emerald-and-diamond ring that looked like a wedding band. The diamonds alternated with the emeralds and were set in a delicate pink-gold band.

"Another one she claimed her father gave her?"

"Yes. Her story was that he was making up for the years he hadn't given her anything. She said that some of the pieces were family jewelry from his mother. That was easier to believe. She also had a flower-shaped pin that was obviously very old."

"I remember that one," Deidre Reardon said. "It had a smaller bud-shaped pin attached to it by a silver chain. I still have a picture I cut out of one of the local papers showing Suzanne wearing it at some sort of fund-raiser. Another heirloom-type piece was the diamond bracelet Suzanne was wearing when she died, Skip."

"Where was Suzanne's jewelry that night?" Kerry asked.

"Except for what she was wearing, in her jewelry case on top of her dressing table," Skip said. "She was supposed to put it in the lockbox in her dressing room, but she usually didn't bother."

"Skip, according to your testimony at the trial several items were missing from your bedroom that night."

"There were two things missing that I'm positive of. One was the flower pin. The problem is that I can't swear it was in the jewelry box that day. But I can swear that a miniature frame that was on the night table was gone."

"Describe it to me," Kerry said.

"Let me, Skip," Deidre Reardon interrupted. "You see, Kerry, that little frame was exquisite. It was reputed to have been made by an assistant to the jeweler Fabergé. My husband was in the army of occupation after the war and bought it in Germany. It was a blue enamel oval with a gold border that was encrusted with pearls. It was my wedding present to Skip and Suzanne."

"Suzanne put a picture of herself in it," Skip explained.

Kerry saw the guard at the door look at the wall clock. "We've only got a few minutes," she said hurriedly. "When did you last see that frame, Skip?"

"It was there that last morning when I got dressed. I remember particularly, because I looked at it when I was changing the stuff in my pockets to the suit I'd just put on. That night, when the detectives told me they were taking me in for questioning, one of them came up to the bedroom with me while I got a sweater. The frame was gone."

"If Suzanne was involved with someone else, is it possible she gave that picture of herself to someone that day?"

"No. It was one of her best pictures, and she liked looking at it. And I don't think even she would have had the guts to give my mother's wedding present away."

"And it never showed up?" Kerry asked.

"Never. But when I tried to say it might have been stolen, the prosecutor argued that if a thief had been there, all that jewelry would have been gone."

The bell signaled the end of visiting hours. This time when Skip got up, he put one arm around his mother, the other around Beth, and drew them to him. Over their heads, he looked at Kerry and Geoff. His smile made him seem ten years younger. "Kerry, you find a way to get me out of this place and I'll build a house for you that you'll never want to leave for the rest of your life." Then he suddenly laughed. "My God," he said, "In this place, I can't believe I said that."

Across the room, convict Will Toth was sitting with his girl-friend, but he gave most of his attention to the group with Skip Reardon. He had seen Skip's mother, the lawyer and the girl-friend here any number of times. Then last week he had recognized Kerry McGrath when she visited Skip. He would know her anywhere—McGrath was the reason he would spend the next fifteen years in this hellhole. She had been the prosecutor at his trial. It was clear that today she was being very cozy with Reardon; he had noticed that she spent the whole time writing down what he was telling her.

Will and his girlfriend stood up when the signal came that visiting hours were over. As he kissed her good-bye, he whispered, "Call your brother as soon as you get home and tell him to pass the word that McGrath was down here again today and taking lots and lots of notes."

74

S i Morgan, senior FBI agent in charge of investigating the Hamilton theft, was in his office at Quantico on Saturday afternoon, going over computer printouts concerning that case and the others believed to be related.

They had asked the Hamiltons, along with burglary victims in similar cases, to furnish names of all guests who attended any gathering or party at their homes during the several months before they were victimized. The computer had created a master file and then a separate list of the names that appeared frequently.

The trouble, Si thought, is that so many of these people travel in the same circles that it's not uncommon to see certain people included regularly, especially at the·big functions.

Nevertheless there were about a dozen names that turned up consistently. Si studied that alphabetized list.

The first one was Arnott, Jason.

Nothing there, Si thought. Arnott had been quietly investigated a couple of years ago and passed as clean. He had a healthy stock portfolio, and his personal accounts didn't show the sudden infusions of cash associated with burglary. His interest income was also consistent with his lifestyle. His income tax statement accurately reflected his stock market transactions. He was well respected as an art and antiques expert. He entertained frequently and was well liked.

If there was a red flag in his profile, it was that Arnott was perhaps a little too perfect. That and the fact that his in-depth knowledge of antiques and fine art was consistent with the selective first-rate-only approach the thief took to the victims' possessions. Maybe it wouldn't hurt to run a check on him again if nothing else shows up, Si thought. But he was much more interested in another name on the frequent list, Sheldon Landi, a man who had his own public relations firm.

Landi certainly seems to rub shoulders with the beautiful people, Si mused. He doesn't make much money, yet he lives high. Landi also fit the general profile of the man the computer told them to look for: middle-aged; unmarried; college educated; self-employed.

They had sent out six hundred flyers with the security-camera photo to the names culled from the guest lists. So far they had received thirty tips. One of them came from a woman who had phoned to say she thought the culprit might be her ex-husband. "He robbed me blind the whole time we were married and lied his way into a big settlement when we were divorced, and he has that kind of pointy chin I see in the picture," she'd explained eagerly. "I'd check on him if I were you."

Now, as he leaned back in his desk chair, Si thought about that call and smiled. The ex-husband the woman was talking about was a United States senator.

75

Jonathan and Grace Hoover were expecting Kerry and Robin around one o'clock. They both believed that a leisurely Sunday afternoon meal was a civilized and restful custom.

Unfortunately, the brightness of Saturday had not lasted. Sunday had dawned gray and chilly, but by noon the house was pleasantly filled with the succulent aroma of roasting lamb. The fire was blazing in their favorite room, the library, and they were contentedly settled there as they awaited their guests.

Grace was absorbed in the *Times* crossword puzzle, and Jonathan was deep in the paper's "Arts and Leisure" section. He looked up when he heard Grace murmur in annoyance and saw that the pen had slipped from her fingers onto the carpet. He watched her laboriously begin the process of bending over to retrieve it.

"Grace," he said reprovingly, as he sprang up to get it for her.

She sighed as she accepted the pen from him. "Honestly, Jonathan, what would I ever do without you?"

"You'll never have to try, dear. And may I say that the sentiment is mutual."

For a moment she held his hand to her face. "I know it is, dear. And believe me, it is one of the things that gives me the strength to carry on."

On the way over to the Hoovers', Kerry and Robin talked about the previous evening. "It was much more fun staying at the Dorsos' house for dinner than going to a restaurant," Robin exulted. "Mom, I like them."

"I do too," Kerry admitted without reluctance.

"Mrs. Dorso told me that it isn't that hard to be a good cook."

"I agree. I'm afraid I let you down."

"Oh, Mom." Robin's tone was reproachful. She folded her arms and stared straight ahead at the narrowing road that indicated they were approaching Riverdale. "You make good pasta," she said defensively.

"I do, but that's about it."

Robin changed the subject. "Mom, Geoff's mother thinks he likes you. So do I. We talked about it."

"You what?"

"Mrs. Dorso said that Geoff never, ever brings a date home. She told me you're the first since his prom days. She said that it was because his little sisters used to play tricks on his dates and that now he's gun shy."

"Probably," Kerry said offhandedly. She turned her mind from the realization that coming back from the prison, she had been so weary that she had closed her eyes for just a minute and awakened later, resting against Geoff's shoulder. And that it had felt so natural, so right.

The visit with Grace and Jonathan Hoover was, as expected, thoroughly agreeable. Kerry did know that at some point they would get around to discussing the Reardon case, but it wouldn't be before coffee was served. That was when Robin was free to leave the table to read or try one of the new computer games Jonathan always had waiting for her.

As they ate, Jonathan entertained them with talk about the legislative sessions and the budget the governor was trying to get through. "You see, Robin," he explained, "politics is like a football game. The governor is the coach who sends in the plays, and the leaders of his party in the senate and the assembly are the quarterbacks."

"That's you, isn't it?" Robin interrupted.

"In the senate, yes, I guess you could call me that," Jonathan agreed. "The rest of our team protects whoever is carrying the ball."

"And the others?"

"Those from the other team do their damnedest to break up the game."

"Jonathan," Grace said quietly.

"Sorry, my dear. But there have been more attempts at pork-barreling this week than I've seen in many years."

"What's that?" Robin asked.

"Pork-barreling is an ancient but not necessarily honorable custom wherein legislators add unnecessary expenses to the budget in order to win favor with the voters in their district. Some people carry it to a fine art."

Kerry smiled. "Robin, I hope you realize how lucky you are to be learning the workings of government from someone like Uncle Jonathan."

"All very selfish," Jonathan assured them. "By the time Kerry is sworn in for the Supreme Court in Washington, we'll be getting Robin elected to the legislature and have her on her way too."

Here it comes, Kerry thought. "Rob, if you're finished, you can see what's up with the computer."

"There's something there you'll like, Robin," Jonathan told her. "I guarantee it."

The housekeeper was going around with the coffeepot. Kerry was sure she would need the second cup. From here on it's all going downhill, she thought.

She did not wait for Jonathan to ask about the Reardon case. Instead she presented everything to him and Grace exactly as she knew it, and concluded by saying, "It's clear Dr. Smith was lying. The question is how much was he lying? It's also clear that Jimmy Weeks has some very important reason not to want that case reopened. Otherwise why would he or his people be involving Robin?"

"Kinellen actually threatened that something could happen to Robin?" Grace's tone was icy with contempt.

"Warned is the better word, I think." Kerry turned, appealing to Jonathan. "Look, you must understand that I don't want to upset anything for Frank Green. He would make a good governor, and I know you were talking to me as well as explaining to Robin what goes on in the legislature. He would carry out Governor Marshall's policies. And Jonathan, dammit, I want to be a judge. I know I can be a good one. I know I can be fair without being a pushover or a bleeding heart. But what kind of judge would I make if, as a prosecutor, I turned my back on something that more and more appears to be a flagrant miscarriage of justice?"

She realized her voice had gone up slightly. "Sorry," she said. "I'm getting carried away."

"I suppose we do what we must," Grace said quietly.

"My thought is that I'm not trying to ride a horse down Main Street and wave to the crowd. If something is wrong I'd like to find out what it is and then let Geoff Dorso carry the ball. I'm going to see Dr. Smith tomorrow afternoon. The key is to discredit his testimony. I frankly think he's on the verge of a breakdown. Stalking someone is a crime. If I can push him enough to get him to break down and admit that he lied on the stand, that he didn't give Suzanne that jewelry, that someone else may well have been involved, then we've got a new ball game. Geoff Dorso could take over and file a motion for a new trial. It will take a few months for it to be properly filed and heard. By then Frank could be governor."

"But you, my dear, may not be a member of the judiciary." Jonathan shook his head. "You're very persuasive, Kerry, and I admire you even while I worry about what this may cost you. First and foremost, though, is Robin. The threat may be just that, a threat, but you must take it seriously."

"I do take it seriously, Jonathan. Except when she was with Geoff Dorso's family, she hasn't been out of my sight all weekend. She won't be left alone for a minute."

"Kerry, anytime you feel your house isn't safe, leave her here," Grace urged. "Our security is excellent, and we'll keep the outside gate closed. It's alarmed, so we'll know if anyone tries to come in. We'll find a retired cop to drive her back and forth from school."

Kerry put her hand over Grace's fingers and gave them a hint of a squeeze. "I love you two," she said simply. "Jonathan, please don't be disappointed that I have to do this."

"I'm proud of you, I guess," Jonathan said. "I'll do my best to keep your name in for the appointment but . . ."

"But don't count on it. I know," Kerry said slowly. "Goodness, choices can be pretty tough, can't they?"

"I think we'd better change the subject," Jonathan said briskly. "But keep me posted, Kerry."

"Of course."

"On a happier note, Grace felt well enough to go out to dinner the other night," he said.

"Oh, Grace, I'm so glad," Kerry said sincerely.

"We met someone there who's been on my mind ever since, purely because I can't remember where I've met him before," Grace said. "A Jason Arnott."

Kerry had not thought it necessary to talk about Jason Arnott.

For the moment she decided to say nothing except, "Why do you think you know him?"

"I don't know," Grace said. "But I'm sure that either I've met him before, or I've seen his picture in the paper." She shrugged. "It will come to me eventually. It always does."

76

The sequestered jury in the Jimmy Weeks trial did not know about the assassination of Barney Haskell and Mark Young, but the media were making sure that everyone else did. Over the weekend many newspaper columns had been dedicated to the investigation, and every television news program featured seemingly endless scene-of-the-crime coverage.

A frightened witness, whose identity was not revealed, had finally phoned the police. He had been on his way to withdraw cash from an ATM and had seen a dark blue Toyota pull into the parking lot of the small building that housed Mark Young's law office. That was at ten after seven. The front right tire of the witness's car had felt wobbly, and he had pulled over to the curb to examine it. He was crouched beside it when he saw the door of the office building open again and a man in his thirties run back to the Toyota. His face was obscured, but he was carrying what appeared to be an oversized gun.

The witness got part of the Toyota's out-of-state license number. Good police work tracked the car down and identified it as one that had been stolen Thursday night in Philadelphia. Late Friday, its burned-out frame was found in Newark.

Even the slight possibility that Haskell and Young had been the victims of a random mugging disappeared in light of that evidence. It was obviously a mob hit, and there was no doubt it had been ordered by Jimmy Weeks. But the police were unsure as to how to prove it. The witness would not be able to identify the gunman. The car was gone. The bullets that had killed the victims were undoubtedly from an unlicensed gun that was now at the bottom of a river, or would be exchanged for a toy at Christmas with no questions asked.

On Monday, Geoff Dorso once again spent a few hours at the Jimmy Weeks trial. The government was building its case brick by brick, with solid, seemingly irrefutable evidence. Royce, the U.S. attorney who seemed intent on being the candidate for governor opposite Frank Green, was resisting the impulse to grandstand. A scholarly-looking man with thinning hair and steel-framed glasses, his strategy was to be utterly plausible, to close off any alternate explanations for the outrageously complicated business affairs and money transfers of Weeks Enterprises.

He had charts that he referred to with the help of a long pointer, the kind Geoff remembered the nuns using when he was in grammar school. Geoff decided that Royce was a master at making Weeks' affairs easy for the jurors to grasp. One did not have to be a mathematical whiz or a CPA to follow his explanations.

Royce got the pilot of Jimmy Weeks' private plane on the stand and hammered at him. "How often did you fill out the appropriate paperwork for the corporate jet? . . . How often did Mr. Weeks use it solely for his private parties? . . . How often did he lend it to friends for their private entertainment? . . . Wasn't it billed to the company every single time the engines were turned on in that jet? . . . All those tax deductions he took for so-called business expenses were really for his personal joyrides, weren't they?"

When it was Bob Kinellen's turn to cross-examine, Geoff saw that he turned on all his charm, trying to make the pilot trip himself up, trying to confuse him on dates, on the purpose of the trips. Once again, Geoff thought that Kinellen was good, but probably not good enough. He knew that there was no way of being sure what was going on in the jurors' minds, but Geoff didn't think they were buying it.

He studied the impassive face of Jimmy Weeks. He always came to the courtroom dressed in a conservative business suit, white shirt and tie. He looked the part he was trying to play—a fifty-year-old businessman-entrepreneur with a variety of enterprises, who was the victim of a tax-collecting witch-hunt.

Today Geoff was observing him from the viewpoint of the connection he had had with Suzanne Reardon. What was it? he wondered. How serious had it been? Was Weeks the one who had given her the jewelry? He had heard about the paper found on Haskell's lawyer that might have been the wording on the note that accompanied the roses given to Suzanne Reardon the day she died, but with Haskell dead and the actual note still missing, it would be impossible to prove any connection to Weeks.

The jewelry might provide an interesting angle, though, Geoff realized, and one worth investigating. I wonder if he goes to any one place to buy baubles for his girlfriends? he asked himself. Who did I date a couple of years ago who told me she'd been out with Weeks? he wondered. The name wouldn't come, but he would go through his daily reminders of two and three years ago. He was sure he had marked it down somewhere.

When the judge called a recess, Geoff slipped quickly out of the courtroom. He was halfway down the corridor when from behind him he heard someone call his name. It was Bob Kinellen. He waited for him to catch up. "Aren't you taking a lot of interest in my client?" Kinellen asked quietly.

"General interest at this point," Geoff replied.

"Is that why you're seeing Kerry?"

"Bob, I don't think you have even the faintest right to ask that question. Nevertheless I'll answer it. I was glad to be there for her after you dropped the bombshell that your illustrious client is threatening her child. Has anyone nominated you for Father of the Year yet? If not, don't waste your time waiting for the phone to ring. Somehow I don't think you'll make it."

77

On Monday morning, Grace Hoover stayed in bed longer than usual. Even though the house was comfortably warm, the winter cold seemed to somehow find its way into her bones and joints. Her hands and fingers and legs and knees and ankles ached fiercely. After the legislature completed the present session, she and Jonathan would go to their home in New Mexico. She reminded herself that it would be better there, that the hot, dry climate always helped her condition.

Years ago, at the onset of her illness, Grace had decided that she would never succumb to self-pity. To her, that was the dreariest of all emotions. Even so, on her darkest days she admitted to herself that besides the constantly increasing pain, it had been devastating to have to constantly lessen her activities.

She had been one of the few wives who actually enjoyed going to the many affairs that a politician such as Jonathan had to attend. God knows it wasn't that she wanted to spend hours at them, but she relished the adulation Jonathan received. She was so proud of him. He should have been governor. She knew that.

Then, after Jonathan made the obligatory appearances at these functions, they would enjoy a quiet late dinner, or on the spur of the moment decide to escape somewhere for the weekend. Grace smiled to herself, remembering how twenty years after they were married, someone they chatted with at an Arizona resort remarked that they had the look of honeymooners.

Now the nuisance of the wheelchair, and the necessity of bringing along a nurse's aide to help her bathe and dress, made a hotel stay a nightmare for Grace. She would not let Jonathan give her that kind of assistance and was better off at home, where a practical nurse came in daily.

She had enjoyed going to the club for dinner the other night. It was the first time in many weeks that she had been out. But that Jason Arnott—isn't it funny that I can't get him out of my mind? she thought as she restlessly tried to flex her fingers. She had asked Jonathan about him again, but he could reason only that possibly she had been with him at some fund-raiser Arnott may have attended.

It had been a dozen years since Grace went to any of those big events. By then she had been on two canes, and disliked jostling crowds. No, she knew it was something else that triggered her memory of him. Oh well, she said to herself, it will come in time.

The housekeeper, Carrie, came into the bedroom with a tray. "I thought you'd be ready for a second cup of tea around now," she said cheerfully.

"I am, Carrie. Thanks."

Carrie laid down the tray and propped up the pillows. "There. That's better." She reached in her pocket and pulled out a folded sheet of paper. "Oh, Mrs. Hoover, this was in the wastebasket in the senator's study. I know the senator was throwing it away, but I still want to ask if it's all right if I take it. All my grandson

Billy talks about is being an FBI agent someday. He'd get such kick out of seeing a genuine flyer they sent out." She unfolded it and handed it to Grace.

Grace glanced at it and started to hand it back, then stopped. Jonathan had shown this to her on Friday afternoon, joking, "Anyone you know?" The covering letter explained that the flyer was being sent to anyone who had been a guest at gatherings in homes that were burglarized shortly afterwards.

The grainy, almost indistinguishable picture was of a felon in the process of committing a robbery. He was believed to be responsible for many similar break-ins, almost all of them following a party or social function of some kind. One theory was that he might have been a guest.

The covering letter concluded with the promise that any information would be kept confidential.

"I know the Peales' Washington home was broken into a few years ago," Jonathan had said. "Terrible business. I had been there to Jock's victory party. Two weeks later his mother came home early from a family vacation and must have walked in on the thief. She was found at the bottom of the staircase with a broken neck, and the John White Alexander painting was missing."

Maybe it was because I know the Peales that I paid so much attention to this picture, Grace thought as she gripped the flyer. The camera must have been below him, the way his face is angled.

She studied the blurry image, the narrow neck, sharp-tipped nose, pursed lips. It wasn't what you'd notice when you look directly at someone's face, she thought. But when you're looking up at him from a wheelchair, you see him from this angle.

I would swear this looks like that man I met at the club the other night, Jason Arnott, Grace thought. Was it possible?

"Carrie, hand me the phone, please." A moment later Grace was speaking to Amanda Coble, who had introduced her to Jason Arnott at the club. After the usual greetings, she brough the conversation around to him. She confessed that she was still plagued by the impression that she had met him before. Where did he live? she asked. What did he do?

When she hung up, Grace sipped the now cooling tea and studied the picture again. According to Amanda, Arnott was an art and antiques expert, and he traveled in the best social circles from Washington to Newport.

Grace called Jonathan in his Trenton office. He was out at the time, but when he got back to her at three-thirty that afternoon, she told him what she believed she had figured out, that Jason Arnott was the burglar the FBI was looking for.

"That's quite an accusation, dear," Jonathan said cautiously.

"I've got good eyes, Jonathan. You know that."

"Yes, I do," he agreed quietly. "And frankly, if it were anyone other than you, I would hesitate to pass the name along to the FBI. I don't want to put anything in writing, but give me the confidential number on that flyer. I'll make a phone call."

"No," Grace said. "As long as you agree that it's all right to speak to the FBI, I'll make the call. If I'm dead wrong, you're not connected to it. If I'm right, I at least get to feel that at last I've done something useful again. I very much liked Jock Peale's mother when I met her years ago. I'd love to be the one who found her killer. No one should be allowed to get away with murder."

78

D r. Charles Smith was in a very bad mood. He had spent a solitary weekend made more frustratingly lonely by the fact that he could not reach Barbara Tompkins. Saturday had been such a beautiful day, he thought she might enjoy a drive up through Westchester, with a stop for an early lunch at one of the little inns along the Hudson.

He got her answering machine, however, and if she was home, she did not return his call.

Sunday was no better. Usually on Sunday Smith forced himself to look in the "Arts and Leisure" section of the *Times* to find an off-Broadway play or a recital or a Lincoln Center event to attend. But he had no heart for any of it that day. Most of Sunday was passed lying on top of his bed, fully dressed, studying the picture of Suzanne on the wall.

What I achieved was so incredible, he said to himself. That painfully plain, bad-tempered offspring of two handsome parents had been given back her birthright—and so much more. He had given her beauty so natural, so breathtaking, that it inspired awe in those who encountered it.

On Monday morning he tried Barbara at the office and was told that she was on a business trip to California, that she would not be back for two weeks. Now he really was upset. He knew that was a lie. In the course of conversation at dinner on Thursday night, Barbara had mentioned something about looking forward to a business lunch at La Grenouille this Wednesday. He remembered because she said she had never been to that restaurant and was especially looking forward to it.

For the rest of Monday, Smith found it difficult to concentrate on his patients. Not that his schedule was very busy. He seemed to have fewer and fewer patients, and those who came in for initial consultation seldom came back. Not that he really cared —so few of them had the potential for genuine beauty.

And once again he felt Carpenter's eyes following him. She was very efficient, but he had decided it might be time to let her go. He had noticed that the other day, during the rhinoplasty, she had watched him like an anxious mother, hoping her child will perform his part in the school play without stumbling.

When his three-thirty appointment canceled, Smith decided to go home early. He would get the car and drive up to Barbara's office and park across the street. She usually left a few minutes after five, but he wanted to be there early just in case. The thought that she might be deliberately evading him was intolerable. If he learned that was true . . .

He was just stepping from the building lobby onto Fifth Avenue when he saw Kerry McGrath approaching. He looked around quickly for some way to avoid her, but it was impossible. She was blocking his path.

"Dr. Smith, I'm glad I caught you," Kerry said. "It's very important that I speak to you."

"Ms. McGrath, Mrs. Carpenter and the receptionist are still in the office. Any assistance you require can be handled by them." He turned and tried to walk past her.

She fell into step beside him. "Dr. Smith, Mrs. Carpenter and the receptionist can't discuss your daughter with me, and neither one of them is responsible for putting an innocent man in prison."

Charles Smith reacted as though she had thrown hot tar on him. "How dare you?" He stopped and grabbed her arm.

Kerry realized suddenly that he was about to strike her. His face was contorted with fury, his mouth twisted in a narrow snarl. She felt the trembling of his hand as his fingers pinched her wrist.

A man passing by looked at them curiously and stopped. "Are you all right, miss?" he asked.

"Am I all right, Doctor?" Kerry asked, her voice calm.

Smith released her arm. "Of course. Of course." He started to walk quickly down Fifth Avenue.

Kerry kept stride with him. "Dr. Smith, you know you will have to talk to me eventually. And I think it would be a much better idea to hear me out before things get out of hand and some very unpleasant situation occurs."

He did not respond.

She stayed next to him. She realized his breathing was rapid. "Dr. Smith, I don't care how fast you walk. I can outrun you. Shall we go back to your office, or is there some place around here where we could get a cup of coffee? We have got to talk. Otherwise I'm afraid you're going to be arrested and charged with being a stalker."

"Charged . . . with . . . what?" Again Smith whirled to face her.

"You have frightened Barbara Tompkins with your attention. Did you frighten Suzanne as well, Doctor? You were there the night she died, weren't you? Two people, a woman and a little boy, saw a black Mercedes in front of the house. The woman remembered part of the license plate, a 3 and an L. Today I learned that your license plate has an 8 and an L. Close enough to make it possible, I would say. Now, where shall we talk?"

He continued to stare at her for several moments, anger still flaring in his eyes. She watched as resignation gradually took its place, as his whole body seemed to go slack.

"I live down this street," he said, no longer looking at her. They were near the corner, and he pointed to the left.

Kerry took the words as an invitation. Am I making a mistake going inside with him? she wondered. He seems to be at the breaking point. Is there a housekeeper there?

But she decided whether she was alone with Smith or not, she might not get this chance again. The shock value of what she had said to him might have cracked something in his psyche. Dr. Smith, she was sure, did not mind seeing another man in prison but would not relish the prospect of facing the court in any way as a defendant.

They were at number 28 Washington Mews. Smith reached for his key and with a precise gesture inserted it in the lock, turned it and pushed the door open. "Come in if you insist, Ms. McGrath," he said.

79

The tips continued to filter in to the FBI from people who had been guests at one or more of the various burglarized homes. They now had twelve potential leads, but Si Morgan thought he had struck gold when on Monday afternoon his chief suspect, Sheldon Landi, admitted that his public relations firm was a coverup for his real activity.

Landi had been invited in for questioning, and for a brief moment Si thought he was about to hear a confession. Then Landi, perspiration on his brow, his hands twisting together whispered, "Have you ever read *Tell All*?"

"That's a supermarket tabloid, isn't it?" Si asked.

"Yes. One of the biggest. Four million circulation a week." For an instant there was a bragging note in Landi's tone. Then his voice dropped almost to the point of being inaudible as he said, "This must not go beyond this room, but I'm *Tell All*'s chief writer. If it ever gets out, I'll be dropped by all my friends."

So much for that, Si thought, after Landi left. That little sneak is just a gossipmonger; he wouldn't have the guts to pull off any of those jobs.

At quarter of four, one of his investigators came in. "Si, there's someone on the Hamilton case confidential line I think you should talk to. Her name is Grace Hoover. Her husband is New Jersey State Senator Hoover, and she thinks she saw the guy we're looking for the other night. It's one of the birds whose name has come up before, Jason Arnott."

"Arnott!" Si grabbed the phone. "Mrs. Hoover, I'm Si Morgan. Thank you for calling."

As he listened, he decided that Grace Hoover was the kind of witness lawmen pray to find. She was logical in her reasoning, clear in her presentation and articulate in explaining how, looking up from her wheelchair, her eyes were probably at the same angle as the lens of the surveillance camera in the Hamilton house.

"Looking straight at Mr. Arnott you would think his face was fuller than it appears when you're looking up at him," she explained. "Also when I asked him if we knew each other, his lips pursed together very tightly. I think it may be a habit he has when he's concentrating. Notice how they're scrunched in your picture. My feeling is that when the camera caught him, he was concentrating very much on that statuette. I would guess he was deciding whether or not it was genuine. My friend tells me he's quite an expert on antiques."

"Yes, he is." Si Morgan was excited. At last he had struck gold! "Mrs. Hoover, I can't tell you how much I appreciate this call. You do know that if this leads to a conviction, there's a substantial reward, over one hundred thousand dollars."

"Oh, I don't care about that," Grace Hoover said. "I'll simply send it on to a charity."

When Si hung up he thought of the tuition bills that were sitting on his desk at home for the spring semester at his sons' colleges. Shaking his head he turned on the intercom and sent for the three investigators who were working on the Hamilton case.

He told them that he wanted Arnott followed round the clock. Judging from the investigation they had made of him two years ago, if he was the thief, he had done an excellent job of concealing his tracks. It would be better to trail him for a while. He might just lead them to where he was keeping stolen property.

"If this isn't another red herring, and we can get proof he's committed the burglaries," Si said, "our next job will be to nail the Peale murder on him. The boss wants that one solved big time. The president's mother used to play bridge with Mrs. Peale."

80

Dr. Smith's study was clean, but Kerry noticed that it had the shabby look of a room that had endured years of neglect. The ivory silk lamp shades, the kind she remembered from her grandmother's house, were darkened with age. One of them had at some point been scorched, and the silk around the burn mark was split. The overstuffed velour chairs were too low and felt scratchy.

It was a high-ceilinged room that could have been beautiful, but to Kerry it seemed frozen in time, as though it were the setting for a scene in a black-and-white movie made in the forties.

She had slipped off her raincoat, but Dr. Smith did not attempt to take it from her. The lack of even the gesture of courtesy seemed to suggest that she would not be staying long enough for him to bother. She folded the coat and draped it on the arm of the chair in which she was sitting.

Smith sat rigidly erect in a high-backed chair that she was sure he never would have chosen if he were alone.

"What do you want, Ms. McGrath?" The rimless glasses enlarged eyes that chilled with their hostile probing.

"I want the truth," Kerry said evenly. "I want to know why you claimed that it was you who gave Suzanne jewelry, when, in fact, it was given to her by another man. I want to know why you lied about Skip Reardon. He never threatened Suzanne. He may have lost patience with her; he may have gotten angry at her. But he never threatened her, did he? What possible reason would you have for swearing that he did?"

"Skip Reardon killed my daughter. He strangled her. He strangled her so viciously that her eyes hemorrhaged, so violently that blood vessels in her neck broke, her tongue hung out of her mouth like a dumb animal's . . ." His voice trailed off. What had started as an angry outburst ended almost as a sob.

"I realize how painful it must have been for you to examine those pictures, Dr. Smith." Kerry spoke softly. Her eyes narrowed as she saw that Smith was looking past her. "But why have you always blamed Skip for the tragedy?"

"He was her husband. He was jealous, insanely jealous. That was a fact. It was clear to everyone." He paused. "Now, Ms. McGrath, I don't want to discuss this any further. I demand to know what you mean by accusing me of stalking Barbara Tompkins."

"Wait. Let's talk about Reardon first, Doctor. You are wrong.

Skip was not insanely jealous of Suzanne. He did know she was seeing someone else." Kerry waited. "But so was he."

Smith's head jerked as though she had slapped him. "That's impossible. He was married to an exquisite woman and he worshiped her."

"*You* worshiped her, Doctor." Kerry hadn't expected to say that, but when she did, she knew it was true. "You put yourself in his position, didn't you? If you had been Suzanne's husband and had found out she was involved with another man, you'd have been capable of murder, wouldn't you?" She stared at him.

He did not blink. "How dare you! Suzanne was my daughter!" he said coldly. "Now get out of here." He stood and moved toward Kerry as though he might grab her to throw her out.

Kerry jumped up, clutching her coat, and stepped back from him. With a glance she checked to see that, if necessary, she could get around him to the front door. "No, Doctor," she said, "*Susie Stevens* was your daughter. *Suzanne* was your creation. And you felt you owned her, just as you believe you own Barbara Tompkins. Doctor, you were in Alpine the night Suzanne died. Did you kill her?"

"Kill Suzanne? Are you crazy?"

"But you were there."

"I was not!"

"Oh yes you were, and we're going to prove it. I promise you that. We're going to reopen the case and get the innocent man you condemned out of prison. You were jealous of him, Dr. Smith. You punished him because he had constant access to Suzanne and you didn't. But how you tried! In fact, you tried so hard that she became sick of your demands for her attention."

"That's not true." The words escaped through his clenched teeth.

Kerry saw that Smith's hand was trembling violently. She lowered her voice, took a more conciliatory tone. "Dr. Smith, if you didn't kill your daughter, someone else surely did. But it wasn't

Skip Reardon. I believe that you loved Suzanne in your own way. I believe that you wanted her murderer to be punished. But do you know what you've done? You've given Suzanne's killer a free ride. He's out there laughing at you, singing your praises for covering up for him. If we had the jewelry Skip is sure you didn't give Suzanne, we could try to trace it. We might be able to find out who did give it to her. Skip is certain that at least one piece is missing and may have been taken that night."

"He's lying."

"No, he isn't. It's what he's been saying from the beginning. And something else was stolen that night—a picture of Suzanne in a miniature frame. It had been on her night table. Did you take it?"

"I was not in that house the night Suzanne died!"

"Then who borrowed your Mercedes that night?"

Smith's "Get out!" was a guttural howl.

Kerry knew she had better not stay any longer. She circled around him but at the door turned to him again. "Dr. Smith, Barbara Tompkins spoke to me. She is alarmed. She moved up a business trip solely to get away from you. When she returns in ten days, I'm going to personally escort her to the New York police to lodge a complaint against you."

She opened the door to the old carriage house, and a blast of cold air swept into the foyer. "Unless," she added, "you come to terms with the fact that you need both physical and psychological help. And unless you satisfy me that you have told the full truth about what happened the night Suzanne died. And unless you give me the jewelry you suspect may have been given to her by a man other than you or her husband."

When Kerry bundled up her collar and thrust her hands in her pockets for the three-block walk to her car, she was aware neither of Smith's probing eyes studying her from behind the grille in the study window, nor of the stranger parked on Fifth Avenue who picked up his cellular phone and called in a report of her visit in Washington Mews.

81

The U.S. attorney, in cooperation with the Middlesex and Ocean County prosecutor's offices, obtained a search warrant for both the permanent residence and the summer home of the late Barney Haskell. Living apart from his wife most of the time, Barney resided in a pleasant split-level house on a quiet street in Edison, an attractive middle-income town. His neighbors there told the media that Barney had never bothered with any of them but was always polite if they met face to face.

His other home, a modern two-story structure overlooking the ocean on Long Beach Island, was where his wife resided year round. Neighbors there told the investigators that during the summer Barney was around a lot, had always spent a good amount of time fishing on his twenty-three-foot Chris-Craft, and that his other hobby was carpentry. His workshop was in his garage.

A couple of neighbors said his wife had invited them in to show off the massive white-oak hutch Barney had made to house their entertainment center last year. It seemed to be his pride and joy.

The investigators knew that Barney had to have had solid

evidence against Jimmy Weeks to back up his attempted plea bargain. They also knew that if they didn't find it quickly, Jimmy Weeks' people would ferret it out and destroy it.

Despite the screeching protests of his widow, who cried that Barney was a victim, and that this was her home even if poor Barney's name was on it, and that they had no right to destroy it, they took apart everything, including the oak hutch that was nailed to the wall of the television room.

When they had ripped the wood from the plaster, they found themselves looking at a safe large enough to house the records of a small office.

As the media gathered outside, television cameras recorded the arrival on the scene of a retired safecracker now on the payroll of the United States government. Fifteen minutes later the safe was opened, and shortly afterwards, at 4:15 P.M. that afternoon, U.S. Attorney Royce received a phone call from Les Howard.

A second set of books for Weeks Enterprises had been found, as well as day-at-a-glance date books going back fifteen years, in which Barney had chronicled Jimmy's appointments along with his own notations about the purpose of the meetings and what was discussed.

A delighted Royce was told that there were also shoe boxes with copies of receipts for high-tag items, including furs and jewelry and cars for Jimmy's various girlfriends, which Barney had flagged "No sales tax paid."

"It's a bonanza, a treasure trove," Howard assured Royce. "Barney sure must have heard that old adage, 'Treat your friend as though he may become your enemy.' He has to have been preparing since day one to barter his way out of prison by throwing Jimmy to us if they ever got indicted."

The judge had adjourned the trial until the next morning rather than start with a new witness at four o'clock. Another break, Royce thought. After he hung up the phone, a smile continued to linger on his lips as he savored the splendid news. He said aloud, "Thanks, Barney, I always knew you'd come through." Then he sat in silence while he considered his next move.

Martha Luce, Jimmy's personal bookkeeper, was scheduled to be a defense witness. They already had her sworn statement that the records she had kept were totally accurate and the only set that existed. Given the choice of turning government witness in exchange for immunity from a long prison sentence, Royce decided that it shouldn't be too hard to convince Ms. Luce where her best interests lay.

82

Jason Arnott had awakened late on Sunday morning with flulike symptoms and decided not to go to the Catskill house as planned. Instead he spent the day in bed, getting up only long enough to prepare some light food for himself. It was at times such as this that he regretted not having a live-in housekeeper.

On the other hand, he thoroughly enjoyed the privacy of having the house to himself without someone underfoot. He brought books and newspapers to his room and spent the day reading, in between sipping orange juice and dozing.

Every few hours, however, he compulsively pulled out the FBI flyer to reassure himself that no one could possibly tie him to that grainy caricature of a picture.

By Monday evening he was feeling much better and had completely convinced himself that the flyer was not a threat. He reminded himself that even if an FBI agent showed up at the door to subject him to routine questioning because he had been one of the guests at a Hamilton party, they would never be able to connect him to the theft.

Not with that picture. Not with his phone records. Not with a single antique or painting in this house. Not with the most scrupulous financial check. Not even with the reservation at the hotel in Washington the weekend of the robbery at the Hamilton home, since he had used one of his fake identities when he checked in.

There was no question. He was safe. He promised himself that tomorrow, or certainly by Wednesday, he would drive up to the Catskills and spend a few days enjoying his treasures.

Jason could not know that the FBI agents had already obtained a court order allowing them to tap his phone and were now quietly surveying his house. He could not know that from now on he wouldn't make a single move without being observed and without being followed.

83

Driving north out of Manhattan's Greenwich Village, Kerry was caught in the first surge of rush hour traffic. It was twenty of five when she pulled her car out of the garage on Twelfth Street. It was five past six when she turned into her driveway and saw Geoff's Volvo parked in front of the other door of the two-car garage.

She had called home from the car phone as she was leaving the garage, and had been only partially reassured to talk to both Robin and Alison, the sitter. She had warned them both not to go out under any circumstances and not to open the door for anyone until she got home.

Seeing Geoff's car made her realize that Alison's car was gone. Had Geoff come because of a problem? Kerry turned off the engine and lights, scrambled from her car, slammed the door behind her and ran toward the house.

Robin had obviously been watching for her. The front door opened as she raced up the steps.

"Rob, is anything wrong?"

"No, Mom, we're fine. When Geoff got here he told Alison it was all right to go ahead home, that he'd wait for you." Robin's face became worried. "That was okay, wasn't it? I mean letting Geoff in."

"Of course." Kerry hugged Robin. "Where is he?"

"In here," Geoff said as he appeared at the door of the kitchen. "I thought that having had one Dorso home-cooked meal on Saturday night, you might be game for another tonight. Very simple menu. Lamb chops, a green salad and baked potato."

Kerry realized she was both tense and hungry. "Sounds wonderful," she sighed as she unbuttoned her coat.

Geoff quickly moved to take it from her. It seemed natural that as he put it over one arm, he slid the other arm around her and kissed her cheek. "Hard day at the factory?"

For a brief moment she let her face rest in the warm spot beneath his neck. "There have been easier ones."

Robin said, "Mom, I'm going upstairs to finish my homework, but I do think since I'm the one in danger, I should know exactly what's going on. What did Dr. Smith say when you saw him?"

"Finish your homework and let me unwind for a few minutes. I promise a full report later."

"Okay."

Geoff had turned on the gas fire in the family room. He had brought in sherry and had glasses ready alongside the bottle on the coffee table there. "I hope I'm not making myself too much at home," he apologized.

Kerry sank onto the couch and kicked off her shoes. She shook her head and smiled. "No, you're not."

"I've got news for you, but you go first. Tell me about Smith."

"I'd better tell you about Frank Green first. I told him I was leaving the office early this afternoon, and I told him why."

"What did he say?"

"It's what he *didn't* say that hung in the air. But in fairness to him, even though I think he was choking on the words, he told me that he hoped I didn't think he would rather see an innocent man in prison than be politically embarrassed himself." She shrugged. "The problem is, I wish I could believe him."

"Maybe you can. How about Smith?"

"I got to him, Geoff. I know I did. The guy is cracking up. If he doesn't start telling the truth, my next move is to get Barbara Tompkins to file a stalking complaint against him. The prospect of that shocked him right down to his toes, I could tell. But I think rather than risk having it happen, he'll come through and we'll get some answers."

She stared into the fire, watching the flames lick at the artificial logs. Then she added slowly, "Geoff, I told Smith that we had two witnesses who saw his car that night. I threw at him that maybe the reason he was so anxious to see Skip convicted was because he was the one who killed Suzanne. Geoff, I think he was in love with her, not as a daughter, maybe not even just as a woman, but as his *creation*."

She turned to him. "Think about this scenario. Suzanne is sick of having her father around her so much, of having him show up wherever she goes. Jason Arnott told me that much, and I believe him. So on the evening of the murder, Dr. Smith drives out to see her. Skip has come and gone, just as he claimed. Suzanne is in the foyer, arranging flowers from another man. Don't forget, the card was never found. Smith is angry, hurt and jealous. It isn't just Skip he has to contend with; now it's Jimmy Weeks as well. In a fit of rage he strangles Suzanne, and because he's always hated Skip, he takes the card, makes up the story of Suzanne being afraid of Skip and becomes the prosecution's principal witness.

"This way Skip, his rival for Suzanne's attention, is not only punished by spending at least thirty years in prison, but the police don't look elsewhere for a suspect."

"It makes sense," Geoff said slowly. "But then why would Jimmy Weeks be so worried about your reopening the case?"

"I've thought about that too. And, in fact, you could make an equally good argument that he was involved with Suzanne. That they quarreled that night, and he murdered her. Another scenario is that Suzanne told him about the land in Pennsylvania that Skip had optioned. Could Jimmy have inadvertently told her about the highway going through and then have killed her to keep her from telling Skip? He picked up those options for next to nothing, I gather."

"You've done a lot of thinking today, lady," Geoff said. "And you've made a damn good case for either scenario. Did you happen to listen to the news on the way home?"

"My brain needed a rest. I listened to the station with the golden oldies. Otherwise I'd have gone mad in that traffic."

"You made a better choice. But if you had listened to a news station, you'd know that the stuff Barney Haskell was planning to swap for a plea bargain is now in the U.S. attorney's hands. Apparently Barney kept records like nobody else ever kept records. Tomorrow, if Frank Green is smart, instead of resisting your investigation he'll request access to any records they can find of jewelry Weeks bought in the months before Suzanne's murder. If we can tie him to stuff like the zodiac bracelet, we've got proof Smith was a liar." He stood up. "I would say, Kerry McGrath, that you have sung for your supper. Wait here. I'll let you know when it's ready."

Kerry curled up on the couch and sipped the sherry, but even with the fire the room felt somehow less than comfortable. A moment later she got up and walked into the kitchen. "Okay if I watch you play chef? It's warmer in here."

Geoff left at nine o'clock. When the door closed behind him, Robin said, "Mom, I've got to ask you. This guy Dad is defending? From what you tell me, Dad's not going to win the case. Is that right?"

"Not if all the evidence we believe has been found is what it's cracked up to be."

"Will that be bad for him?"

"No one likes to lose a case, but no, Robin, I think the best thing that could ever happen to your father is to see Jimmy Weeks convicted."

"You're sure Weeks is the one who's trying to scare me?"

"Yes, I'm about as sure as I can get. That's why the sooner we can find out his connection to Suzanne Reardon, the sooner he won't have any reasons to try to scare us off."

"Geoff's a defense attorney, isn't he?"

"Yes, he is."

"Would Geoff ever defend a guy like Jimmy Weeks?"

"No, Robin. I'm pretty sure he wouldn't."

"I don't think he would either."

At nine-thirty, Kerry remembered that she'd promised to report to Jonathan and Grace about her meeting with Dr. Smith. "You think he may break down and admit he lied?" Jonathan asked when she reached him.

"I think so."

Grace was on the other extension. "Let's tell Kerry my news,

Jonathan. Kerry, today I've either been a good detective or made an awful fool of myself."

Kerry had not thought it important to bring up Arnott's name on Sunday when she told Jonathan and Grace about Dr. Smith and Jimmy Weeks. When she heard what Grace had to say about him, she was glad that neither one of them could see the expression on her face.

Jason Arnott. The friend who was constantly with Suzanne Reardon. Who, despite his seeming frankness, had struck Kerry as being too posed to be true. If he was a thief, if, according to the FBI flyer Grace described, he was also a murder suspect, where did he fit in the conundrum surrounding the Sweetheart Murder Case?

84

D r. Charles Smith sat for long hours after he forced Kerry to leave. "Stalker!" "Murderer!" "Liar!" The accusations she had thrown at him made him shudder with revulsion. It was the same revulsion he felt when he looked at a maimed or scarred or ugly face. He could feel his very being tremble with the need to change it, to redeem it, to make things right. To find for it the beauty that his skilled hands could wrest from bone and muscle and flesh.

In those instances the wrath he felt had been directed against the fire or the accident or the unfair blending of genes that had caused the aberration. Now his wrath was directed at the young woman who had sat here in judgment of him.

"Stalker!" To call him a stalker because a brief glimpse of the near perfection he had created gave him pleasure! He wished he could have looked into the future and known that this was the way Barbara Tompkins would express her thanks. He would have given her a face all right—a face with skin that collapsed into wrinkles, eyes that drooped, nostrils that flared.

Suppose McGrath took Tompkins to the police to file that complaint. She had said she would, and Smith knew she meant it.

She had called him a murderer. *Murderer!* Did she really think that he could have done that to Suzanne? Burning misery raced through him as he lived again the moment when he had rung the bell, over and over, then turned the handle and found the door unlocked.

And Suzanne there, in the foyer, almost at his feet. Suzanne—but not Suzanne. That distorted creature with bulging, hemorrhaged eyes, and gaping mouth and protruding tongue—that was not the exquisite creature he had created.

Even her body appeared awkward and unlovely, crumpled as it was, the left leg twisted under the right one, the heel of her left shoe jabbing her right calf, those fresh red roses scattered over her, a mocking tribute to death.

Smith remembered how he had stood over her, his only thought an incongruous one—that this is how Michelangelo would have felt had he seen his *Pietà* broken and defaced as it had been by the lunatic who attacked it years ago in St. Peter's.

He remembered how he had cursed Suzanne, cursed her because she had not heeded his warnings. She had married Reardon against his wishes. "Wait," he had urged her. "He's not good enough for you."

"In your eyes, no one will ever be good enough for me," she had shouted back.

He had endured the way they looked at each other, the way their hands clasped across the table, the way they sat together, side by side on the couch, or with Suzanne on Reardon's lap in the big, deep chair, as he had seen them when he had looked through the window at night.

To have to endure all that had been bad enough, but it was too much when Suzanne became restless and began seeing other men, none of them worthy of her, and then came to him, asking for favors, saying "Charles, you must let Skip think you bought me this . . . and this . . . and this . . ."

Or she would say, "Doctor, why are you so upset? You told me I should have all the good times I've missed. Well, I'm having them. Skip works too hard. He isn't fun. You take risks when you operate. I'm just like you. I take risks too. Now remember, Doctor Charles, you're a generous daddy." Her impudent kiss, flirting with him, sure of her power, of his tolerance.

Murderer? No, Skip was the murderer. As he stood over Suzanne's body, Smith had known exactly what had happened. Her loutish husband had come home to find Suzanne with flowers from another man, and he had exploded. Just as *I* would, Smith had thought when his eye fell on the card half hidden by Suzanne's body.

And then, standing there over her, a whole scenario had played itself out in his mind. Skip, the jealous husband—a jury might be lenient with a man who killed his wife in a moment of passion. He might get off with a light sentence. Or maybe even no sentence at all.

I won't let that happen, he had vowed. Smith remembered how he had closed his eyes, blotting out the ugly, distorted face in front of him and, instead, seeing Suzanne in all her beauty. *Suzanne, I promise you that!*

It had not been hard to keep the promise. All he had to do was take the card that had come with the flowers, then go home and wait for the inevitable call that would tell him that Suzanne, his daughter, was dead.

When the police had questioned him, he had told them that Skip was insanely jealous, that Suzanne feared for her life, and, obeying the last request she made of him, he claimed he had given her all the pieces of jewelry that Skip had questioned.

No, let Ms. McGrath say all she might want. The murderer was in jail. And he would stay there.

It was almost ten o'clock when Charles Smith got up. It was all over. He couldn't operate anymore. He no longer wanted to see Barbara Tompkins. She disgusted him. He went into the bedroom, opened the small safe in the closet and took out a gun.

It would be so easy. Where would he go? he wondered. He did believe that the spirit moves on. Reincarnation? Maybe. Maybe this time he would be born Suzanne's peer. Maybe they would fall in love. A smile played on his lips.

But then, as he was about to close the safe, he looked at Suzanne's jewelry case.

Suppose McGrath was right. Suppose it hadn't been Skip but another person who had taken Suzanne's life. McGrath had said that person was laughing now, mockingly grateful for the testimony that had condemned Skip.

There was a way to rectify that. If Reardon was not the killer, then McGrath would have all that she needed to find the man who had murdered Suzanne.

Smith reached for the jewelry case, laid the gun on top of it and carried both to his desk in the study. Then with precise movements he took out a sheet of stationery and unscrewed the top from his pen.

When he was finished writing, he wrapped the jewelry case and the note together and managed to force them into one of the several Federal Express mailers that he kept at home for convenience. He addressed the package to Assistant Prosecutor Kerry McGrath at the Bergen County Prosecutor's Office, Hackensack, New Jersey. It was an address he remembered well.

He put on his coat and muffler and walked eight blocks to the Federal Express drop that he had used on occasion.

It was just eleven o'clock when he returned home. He took off his coat, picked up the gun, went back into the bedroom and stretched out on the bed, still fully dressed. He turned off all the lights except the one that illuminated Suzanne's picture.

He would end this day with her and begin the new life at the stroke of midnight. The decision made, he felt calm, even happy.

At eleven-thirty the doorbell began to ring. Who? he wondered. Angrily he tried to ignore it, but a persistent finger was pressed against it. He was sure he knew what it was. Once there had been an accident on the corner, and a neighbor had run to him for help. After all, he was a doctor. If there had been an accident, just this one more time his skill might be put to use.

Dr. Charles Smith unlocked and opened his door, then slumped against it as a bullet found its mark between his eyes.

Tuesday, November 7th

85

On Tuesday morning, Deidre Reardon and Beth Taylor were already in the reception room of Geoff Dorso's law office when he arrived at nine o'clock.

Beth apologized for both of them. "Geoff, I'm so sorry to come without calling first," she said, "but Deidre has to go into the hospital for the angioplasty tomorrow morning. I know it will rest her mind if she has a chance to talk to you for a few minutes and give you that picture of Suzanne we talked about the other day."

Deidre Reardon was looking at him anxiously. "Oh, come on, Deidre," Geoff said heartily, "you know you don't have to make excuses for seeing me. Aren't you the mother of my star client?"

"Sure. It's all those billing hours you're logging," Deidre Reardon murmured with a relieved smile, as Geoff took her hands in his. "It's just that I'm so embarrassed at the way I barged into that lovely Kerry McGrath's office last week and treated her like dirt. And then to realize her own child has been threatened because Kerry's trying to help my son."

"Kerry absolutely understood how you felt that day. Come back to my office. I'm sure the coffeepot's on."

"We will only stay five minutes," Beth promised as Geoff placed a coffee mug in front of her. "And we won't waste your time saying it's been a glimpse of heaven to think that finally there's real, genuine hope for Skip. You know how we feel, and you know how grateful we are for everything you are doing."

"Kerry saw Dr. Smith late yesterday afternoon," Geoff said. "She thinks she got to him. But there are other developments as well." He told them about Barney Haskell's records. "We may at last have a chance to track the source of the jewelry we think Weeks gave Suzanne."

"That's one of the reasons we're here," Deidre Reardon told him. "Remember I said I had a picture that showed Suzanne wearing the missing set of antique diamond pins? As soon as I got home from the prison Saturday night I went to get it out of the file and couldn't find it. I spent all Sunday and yesterday ransacking the apartment, looking for it. Of course it wasn't there. Stupidly, I had forgotten that at some point I'd covered it with one of those plastic protectors and put it with my own personal papers. Anyway, I finally found it. With all the talk about the jewelry the other day, I felt it important for you to have it."

She handed him a legal-size manila envelope. From it, he extracted a folded page from *Palisades Community Life*, a tabloid-sized weekly paper. As he opened it Geoff noticed the date, April 24th, nearly eleven years ago and barely a month before Suzanne Reardon died.

The group picture from the Palisades Country Club took up the space of four columns of print. Geoff recognized Suzanne Reardon immediately. Her outstanding beauty leaped from the page. She was standing at a slight angle, and the camera had clearly caught the sparkling diamonds on the lapel of her jacket.

"This is the double pin that disappeared," Deidre explained, pointing to it. "But Skip doesn't know when he last saw it on Suzanne."

"I'm glad to have this," Geoff said. "When we can get a copy of some of those records Haskell kept, we may be able to trace the pin."

It almost hurt to see the eager hope on both their faces. Don't let me fail them, he prayed as he walked them back to the reception room. At the door he hugged Deidre. "Now remember, you get this angioplasty over and start feeling better. We can't have you sick when they unlock the door for Skip."

"Geoff, I haven't walked barefoot through hell this long to check out now."

After having taken care of a number of client calls and queries, Geoff decided to call Kerry. Maybe she would want to have a fax of the picture Deidre had brought in. Or maybe I just want to talk to her, he admitted to himself.

When her secretary put her through, Kerry's frightened voice sent chills through Geoff. "I just opened a Federal Express package that Dr. Smith sent me. Inside was a note and Suzanne's jewelry case and the card that must have come with the sweetheart roses. Geoff, he admits he lied about Skip and the jewelry. He told me that by the time I read this he'll have committed suicide."

"My God, Kerry, did—"

"No, it's not that. You see, he *didn't*. Geoff, Mrs. Carpenter from his office just called me. When Dr. Smith didn't come in for an early appointment, and didn't answer the phone, she went to his house. His door was open a crack and she went in. She found his body lying in the foyer. He'd been shot, and the house ransacked. Geoff, was it because someone didn't want Dr. Smith to change his testimony and was looking for the jewelry? Geoff, who is doing this? Will Robin be next?"

86

At nine-thirty that morning, Jason Arnott looked out the window, saw the cloudy, overcast sky and felt vaguely depressed. Other than some residual achiness in his legs and back, he was over the bug or virus that had laid him low over the weekend. But he could not overcome the uneasy sense that something was wrong.

It was that damn FBI flyer, of course. But he had felt the same way after that night in Congressman Peale's house. A few of the downstairs lamps that were on an automatic switch had been on when he got there, but the upstairs rooms were all dark. He had been coming down the hallway, carrying the painting and the lockbox that he had pried from the wall, when he heard footsteps coming up the stairs. He had barely had time to hold the painting in front of his face when light flooded the hallway.

Then he had heard the quavering gasp, "Oh, dear God," and knew it was the congressman's mother. He hadn't intended to hurt her. Instinctively he had rushed toward her, holding the painting as a shield, intending only to knock her down and grab her glasses so he could make his getaway. He had spent a long time talking with her at Peale's inaugural party, and he knew she was blind as a bat without them.

But the heavy portrait frame had caught the side of her head harder than he intended, and she had toppled backwards down he stairs. He knew from that final gurgle that she made before she went still that she was dead. For months afterward he had looked over his shoulder, expecting to see someone coming toward him with handcuffs.

Now, no matter how hard he tried to convince himself otherwise, the FBI flyer was giving him that same case of the jitters.

After the Peale case, his only solace had been to feast his eyes on the John White Alexander masterpiece *At Rest,* which he had taken that night. He kept it in the master bedroom of the Catskill house just as Peale had kept it in his master bedroom. It was so amusing to know that thousands of people trooped through the Metropolitan Museum of Art to gaze on its companion piece, *Repose.* Of the two, he preferred *At Rest.* The reclining figure of a beautiful woman had the same long sinuous lines as *Repose,* but the closed eyes, the look on the sensual face reminded him now of Suzanne.

The miniature frame with her portrait was on his night table, and it amused him to have both in his room, even though the imitation Fabergé frame was unworthy of the glorious company it kept. The night table was gilt and marble, an exquisite example of Gothic Revival, and had been obtained in the grand haul when he had hired a van and practically emptied the Merriman house.

He would call ahead. He enjoyed arriving there to find the heat on and the refrigerator stocked. Instead of using his home phone, however, he would call his housekeeper on a cellular phone that was registered to one of his aliases.

Inside what seemed to be a repair van of Public Service Gas and Electric the signal came that Arnott was making a call. As the agents listened, they smiled triumphantly at each other. "I think we are about to trace the foxy Mr. Arnott to his lair," the senior agent on the job observed. They listened as Jason concluded the conversation by saying, "Thank you, Maddie. I'll leave here in an hour and should be there by one."

Maddie's heavy monotone reply was, "I'll have everything ready for you. You can count on me."

87

Frank Green was trying a case, and it was noon before Kerry was able to inform him of Smith's murder and the Federal Express packet she had received from him late that morning. She was fully composed now and wondered why she had allowed herself to lose control when Geoff had phoned. But her emotions were something that she would explore later. For now, the knowledge that Joe Palumbo was parked outside Robin's school, waiting to escort her home and then stand watch at the house until Kerry got home, was enough to help relieve her immediate fears.

Green went carefully through the contents of the jewelry box, comparing each piece with those Smith had mentioned in the letter he had included in the package to Kerry. "Zodiac bracelet," he read. "That's right here. Watch with gold numerals, ivory face, diamond and gold band. Okay. Here it is. Emerald and diamond ring set in pink gold. That's right here. Antique diamond bracelet. Three bands of diamonds attached by diamond clasps." He held it up. "That's a beauty."

"Yes. You may remember Suzanne was wearing that bracelet when she was murdered. There was one more piece, an antique diamond pin or double pin, that Skip Reardon had described

Dr. Smith doesn't mention it, and apparently he didn't have it, but Geoff just faxed me a picture from a local newspaper showing Suzanne wearing that pin only a few weeks before she died. It never showed up in the items found at the house. You can see that it's very much like the bracelet and obviously an antique. The other pieces are beautiful, but very modern in design."

Kerry looked closely at the blurred reproduction and understood why Deidre Reardon had described it as evoking a mother-and-child image. As she'd explained, the pin appeared to be in two parts, the larger being a flower, the smaller a bud. They were attached by a chain. She studied it for a moment, perplexed because it looked oddly familiar.

"We'll watch out for this pin to see if it is mentioned in Haskell's receipts," Green promised. "Now let's get this straight. As far as you know, everything the doctor mentioned, excluding this particular pin, is the total of the jewelry Suzanne asked the doctor to tell Skip he gave her?"

"According to what Smith wrote in his letter, and it does coincide with what Skip Reardon told me Saturday."

Green put down Smith's letter. "Kerry, do you think you might have been followed when you went to see Smith yesterday?"

"I think now I probably was. That's why I'm so concerned about Robin's safety."

"We'll keep a squad car outside your house tonight, but I wouldn't be unhappy to have you and Robin out of there and in some more secure place with all this coming to a head. Jimmy Weeks is a cornered animal. Royce may be able to tie him to tax fraud, but with what you've uncovered, we may be able to tie him to a murder."

"You mean because of the card Jimmy sent with the sweetheart roses?" The card was already being analyzed by handwriting experts, and Kerry had reminded Green of the paper found in Haskell's lawyer's pocket after both men had been murdered.

"Exactly. No clerk in a flower shop drew those musical notes. Imagine describing an inscription like that over the phone. From what I understand, Weeks is a pretty good amateur musician. The life of the party when he sits down at the piano. That kind. With that card—and if the jewelry ties in to those receipts—the Reardon case is a whole new ball game.

"And if Skip is granted a new trial, he'll be entitled to release on bail pending that trial—or dismissal of the charges," Kerry said evenly.

"If the scenario plays out, I'll recommend that," Green agreed.

"Frank, there's one other point I have to raise," Kerry said. "We know that Jimmy Weeks is trying to scare us off this investigation. But it may be for some reason other than we think. I have learned that Weeks picked up Skip Reardon's options on valuable Pennsylvania property when Skip had to liquidate. He apparently had inside information, so there's a good chance the whole transaction was illegal. It's certainly not as major a crime as murder—and we still don't know, of course; he *may* have been Suzanne's killer—but if the IRS had that information, along with the tax evasion charges and what-have-you, Weeks could be put away for a long time as it is."

"And you think he's worried that your probing into the Reardon murder case might expose those earlier deals?" Green asked.

"Yes, it's very possible."

"But do you really think that is sufficient to make him threaten you through Robin? That seems a little extreme to me." Green shook his head.

"Frank, from what I have learned from my ex-husband, Weeks is ruthless enough and arrogant enough to go to almost any lengths to protect himself, and it would make no difference what the charge—it could be murder or it could be stealing a newspaper. But all this aside, there's still another reason why the murder scenario may not play out, even if we can tie Jimmy Weeks to Suzanne," Kerry said. Then she began to fill him in on Jason Arnott's connection to Suzanne and Grace Hoover's theory that he was a professional thief.

"Even if he is, are you tying him to Suzanne Reardon's murder?" Green asked.

"I'm not sure," Kerry said slowly. "It depends on whether or not he is involved in those thefts."

"Sit tight. We can get that flyer faxed in from the FBI right away," Green decreed as he pressed the intercom. "We'll find out who's running the investigation."

Less than five minutes later his secretary brought in the flyer. Green pointed out the confidential number. "Tell them to put me through to the top guy on this."

Sixty seconds later, Green was on the phone with Si Morgan. He turned on the phone's speaker so that Kerry could listen too.

"It's breaking now," Morgan told him. "Arnott has another place, in the Catskills. We've decided to ring the doorbell and see if the housekeeper will talk to us. We'll keep you posted."

Kerry gripped the arms of her chair and turned her head toward the detached voice coming out of the speaker phone. "Mr. Morgan, this is terribly important. If you can still contact your agent, ask him to inquire about a miniature oval picture frame. It's blue enamel with seed pearls surrounding the glass. It may or may not hold a picture of a beautiful dark-haired woman. If it's there, we'll be able to connect Jason Arnott to a murder case."

"I can still reach him. I'll have him ask about it, and I'll get back to you," he promised.

"What was that about?" Green asked as he snapped off the speaker.

"Skip Reardon has always sworn that a miniature frame that was a Fabergé copy disappeared from the master bedroom the day Suzanne died. That and the antique pin are the two things we can't account for as of now."

Kerry leaned over and picked up the diamond bracelet. "Look at this. It's from a different world from the other jewelry." She held up the picture of Suzanne wearing the antique pin. "Isn't it funny? I feel as though I've seen a pin like that before, I mean the little one joined to the big one. It may just be because it came up repeatedly in statements from Skip and his mother at the time of the investigation. I've read that file until I'm dizzy."

She laid the bracelet back in the case. "Jason Arnott spent a great deal of time with Suzanne. Maybe he wasn't the neuter he tried to make himself out to be. Think of it this way, Frank. Let's say he fell for Suzanne too. He gave her the antique pin and the bracelet. It's exactly the kind of jewelry he would select. Then he realized that she was fooling around with Jimmy Weeks. Maybe he came in that night and saw the sweetheart roses and the card we believe Jimmy sent."

"You mean he killed her and took back the pin?"

"And her picture. From what Mrs. Reardon tells me, it's a beautiful frame."

"Why not the bracelet?"

"While I was waiting for you this morning, I looked at the pictures taken of the body before it was moved. Suzanne had a gold link bracelet on her left hand. You can see it in the picture. The diamond bracelet, which was on the other arm, doesn't show. I checked the records. It was pushed up on her arm under the sleeve of her blouse so that it wasn't visible. According to the medical examiner's report it had a new and very tight security clasp. She may have shoved the bracelet out of sight because she had changed her mind about wearing it and was having trouble getting it off, or she may have been aware that her attacker had come to retrieve it, probably because it was a gift from him, and she may have been hiding it. Whatever the reason, it worked, because he didn't find it."

While they waited for Morgan to call back, Green and Kerry worked together to prepare a flyer, with pictures of the jewelry in question, that would be distributed to New Jersey jewelers.

At one point Frank observed, "Kerry, you do realize that if Mrs. Hoover's hunch works out, it means that a tip from our state senator's wife will have caught the murderer of Congress-

284

man Peale's mother. Then if Arnott is tied to the Reardon case . . ."

Frank Green, gubernatorial candidate, Kerry thought. He's already figuring how to sugarcoat having convicted an innocent man! Well, that's politics, I guess, she told herself.

88

Maddie Platt was not aware of the car that followed her when she stopped at the market and did the shopping, carefully gathering all the items she had been instructed to get. Nor did she notice it continued to follow her when she drove farther out of Ellenville, down narrow, winding roads to the rambling country house owned by the man she knew as Nigel Grey.

She let herself in and ten minutes later was startled when the doorbell rang. Nobody ever dropped in at this house. Furthermore, Mr. Grey had given her strict orders never to admit anyone. She was not about to open the door without knowing who it was.

When she peeked out the side window she saw the neatly dressed man standing on the top step. He saw her and held up a badge identifying him as an FBI agent. "FBI, ma'am. Would you please open the door so I can talk to you?"

Nervously, Maddie opened the door. Now she stood inches

from the badge showing the unmistakable FBI seal and identifying picture of the agent.

"Good afternoon, ma'am. I'm FBI agent Milton Rose. I don't
mean to startle or upset you, but it's very important that I speak
with you about Mr. Jason Arnott. You are his housekeeper,
aren't you?"

"Sir, I don't know any Mr. Arnott. This house is owned by
Mr. Nigel Grey, and I've worked for him for many years. He's
due here this afternoon, in fact he should be here shortly. And I
can tell you right now—I am under strict orders not to ever let
anyone in this house without his permission."

"Ma'am, I'm not asking to come in. I don't have a search
warrant. But I still need to talk to you. Your Mr. Grey is really
Jason Arnott, whom we suspect has been responsible for dozens
of burglaries involving fine art and other valuable items. He
might even be responsible for the murder of a congressman's
elderly mother, who may have surprised him during the burglary
of her home."

"Oh my God," Maddie gasped. Certainly Mr. Grey had always been completely a loner here, but she had just assumed that
this Catskill home was where he escaped to for privacy and
relaxation. She now realized that he might well have been "escap-
ing" here for very different reasons.

Agent Rose went on to describe to her many of the stolen
pieces of art and other items that had disappeared from homes
where Arnott had previously attended social functions. Sadly,
she confirmed that virtually all of these items were in this house.
And, yes, the miniature oval blue frame encrusted with seed
pearls, with a woman's picture in it, was on his night table.

"Ma'am, we know that he will be here soon. I must ask you
to come with us. I'm sure you didn't know what was happening,
and you're not in any trouble. But we are going to make a telephone application for a search warrant so that we can search
Mr. Arnott's home and arrest him."

Gently, Agent Rose led the bewildered Maddie to the waiting car. "I can't believe this," she cried. "I just didn't know."

At twelve-thirty, a frightened Martha Luce, who for twenty years had been bookkeeper to James Forrest Weeks, sat twisting a damp handkerchief as she cowered in the office of U.S. Attorney Brandon Royce.

The sworn statement she had given to Royce months ago had just been read back to her.

"Do you stand by what you told us that day?" Royce asked as he tapped the papers in his hand.

"I told the truth as far as I knew it to be the truth," Martha told him, her voice barely above a whisper. She cast a nervous sidelong glance at the stenotypist and then at her nephew, a young attorney, whom she had called in a panic when she learned of the successful search of Barney Haskell's home.

Royce leaned forward. "Miss Luce, I cannot emphasize strongly enough how very serious your position is. If you continue to lie under oath, you do so at your own peril. We have enough to bury Jimmy Weeks. I'll lay out my cards. Since Barney Haskell has unfortunately been so abruptly taken from us, it will be helpful to have you as a living witness"—he emphasized the word "living"—"to corroborate the accuracy of his records. If you do not, we will still convict Jimmy Weeks, but then, Miss Luce, we will turn our full attention to you. Perjury is a very serious offense. Obstructing justice is a very serious offense. Aiding and abetting income tax evasion is a very serious offense."

Martha Luce's always timid face crumbled. She began to sob. Tears that immediately reddened her pale blue eyes welled and flowed. "Mr. Weeks paid every single bill when Mama was sick for such a long time."

"That's nice," Royce said. "But he did it with taxpayers' money."

"My client has a right to remain silent," the nephew/attorney piped up.

Royce gave him a withering glance. "We've already established that, counselor. You might also advise your client that we're not crazy about putting middle-aged women with misguided loyalties in prison. We're prepared, this one—and only this one—time, to offer total immunity to your client in exchange for full cooperation. After that, she's on her own. But you remind your client" —here Royce's voice was heavy with sarcasm—"that Barney Haskell waited so long to accept a plea bargain offer that he never got to take it."

"Total immunity?" the nephew/lawyer asked.

"Total, and we'll immediately put Ms. Luce in protective custody. We don't want anything to happen to her."

"Aunt Martha . . . ," the young man began, his voice cracking.

She stopped sniffling. "I know, dear. Mr. Royce, perhaps I always suspected that Mr. Weeks . . ."

90

The news that a cache had been found in a hidden safe in Barney Haskell's summer home was, to Bob Kinellen, the death knell of any hope of getting Jimmy Weeks an acquittal. Even Kinellen's father-in-law, the usually unruffleable Anthony Bartlett, was clearly beginning to concede the inevitable.

On this Tuesday morning, U.S. Attorney Royce had requested and been granted that the lunch recess be extended an hour. Bob suspected what that maneuver meant. Martha Luce, a defense witness, and one of their most believable because of her timid, earnest demeanor, was being leaned on.

If Haskell had made a copy of the books he had kept, Luce's testimony swearing to the accuracy of Jimmy's records was probably being held as a weapon over her head.

If Martha Luce turned prosecution witness in exchange for immunity, it was all over.

Bob Kinellen sat silently looking at every possible thing in the room other than his client. He felt a terrible weariness, like a weight crushing him, and he wondered at what moment it had invaded him. Thinking back over the recent days, he suddenly knew. It was when I delivered a threat concerning my own child, he said to himself. For eleven years he had been able to keep to the letter of the law. Jimmy Weeks had the right to a defense, and his job was to keep Jimmy from getting indicted. He did it by legal means. If other means were also being used, he did not know nor did he want to know about them.

But in this trial he had become part of the process of circumventing the law. Weeks had just told him the reason he'd insisted on having Mrs. Wagner on the jury: She had a father in prison in California. Thirty years ago he had murdered an entire family of campers in Yosemite National Park. He knew he intended to hold back the information that juror Wagner had a father in prison and make that part of Weeks' appeal. He knew, too, that was unethical. Skating on thin ice was over. He had gone beyond that. The burning shame he had felt when he heard Robin's stricken cry as he struggled with Kerry still seared him. How had Kerry explained that to Robin? *Your father was passing along a threat his client made about you? Your father's client was the man who ordered some bum to terrify you last week?*

Jimmy Weeks was terrified of prison. The prospect of being locked up was unbearable to him. He would do anything to avoid it.

It was obvious that Jimmy was wildly upset. They had lunch in a private room of a restaurant a few miles from the courtroom. After the orders were taken, Jimmy said abruptly, "I don't want any talk about plea bargaining from you two. Understand?"

Bartlett and Kinellen waited without responding.

"In the jury room, I don't think we can count on the wimp with the sick wife not to buckle."

I could have told you that, Bob thought. He didn't want to discuss any of this. If his client had tampered with that juror, it was without his knowledge, he reassured himself. *And Haskell was the victim of a mugging,* an interior voice mocked.

"Bobby, my sources tell me the sheriff's officer in charge of the jury owes you a favor," Weeks said.

"What are you talking about, Jimmy?" Bob Kinellen toyed with his salad fork.

"You know what I'm talking about. You got his kid out of trouble, big trouble. He's grateful."

"And?"

"Bobby, I think the sheriff's officer has to let that prune-face, uptight Wagner dame know that her daddy, the murderer, is going to make big headlines unless she comes up with some reasonable doubt when this case goes to the jury."

Lie down with dogs and you'll get up with fleas. Kerry had told him that before Robin was born.

"Jimmy, we already have grounds for a new trial because she didn't reveal that fact. That's our ace in the hole. We don't need to take it any further." Bob shot a glance at his father-in-law. "Anthony and I are sticking our necks out by not reporting that to the court as it is. We can get away with claiming that it only came to our attention after the trial was over. Even if you're convicted you'll be out on bail, and then we delay and delay and delay."

"Not good enough, Bobby. This time you've got to put yourself on the line. Have a friendly chat with the sheriff's officer. He'll listen. He'll talk to the lady who already is in trouble for lying on her questionnaire. Then we have a hung jury, if not an acquittal. And then we delay and delay and delay while you two figure out a way to make sure we get an acquittal next time."

The waiter returned with their appetizers. Bob Kinellen had ordered the escargots, a specialty here that he thoroughly enjoyed. It was only when he finished and the waiter was removing the plate that he realized he hadn't tasted a thing. *Jimmy isn't the only one who's being backed into a corner*, he thought.

I'm right there with him.

91

Kerry went back to her office after the call from Si Morgan came through. She was now convinced that Arnott was irrevocably tied in some way to Suzanne Reardon's death. Just how, though, would have to wait until he was in FBI custody and she and Frank Green had had a chance to interrogate him.

There was a pile of messages on her desk, one of which, from Jonathan, was marked "Urgent." He had left his private number at his local office. She called him immediately.

"Thanks for calling back, Kerry. I have to come over to Hackensack and I want to talk to you. Buy you lunch?"

A few weeks ago, he had started the conversation with "Buy you lunch, Judge?"

Kerry knew the omission today was not accidental. Jonathan played it straight. If the political fallout from her investigation cost Frank Green the nomination, she would have to forget about a judgeship, no matter how justified she had been. That was politics, and besides, there were plenty of other highly qualified people panting for the job.

"Of course, Jonathan."

"Solari's at one-thirty."

She was sure she knew why he was calling. He had heard about Dr. Smith and was worried about her and Robin.

She dialed Geoff's office. He was having a sandwich at his desk.

"I'm glad I'm sitting down," he told her when she filled him in about Arnott.

"The FBI will be photographing and cataloguing everything they find in the Catskill house. Morgan said the decision hasn't been made whether to move everything into a warehouse or to just invite the people who've been robbed to come and identify their stuff right at that site. However they do it, when Green and I go up to talk to Arnott we want Mrs. Reardon along to positively identify the picture frame."

"I'll ask her to postpone going in for the angioplasty for a few days. Kerry, one of our associates was in federal court this morning. He tells me that Royce requested an extra hour for the lunch break. The word is that he may be offering immunity to Jimmy Weeks' bookkeeper. He's not going to take a chance on losing another prize witness by playing hardball."

"It's coming to a head, then?"

"Exactly."

"Have you called Skip about Smith's letter?"

"Right after I talked to you."

"What was his reaction?"

"He started to cry." Geoff's voice became husky. "I did too. He's going to get out, Kerry, and you're the reason."

"No, you're wrong. You and Robin are. I was ready to turn my back on him."

"We'll argue about that another time. Kerry, Deidre Reardon's on the other phone. I've been trying to reach her. I'll talk to you later. I don't want you and Robin alone in your place tonight."

Before Kerry left to meet Jonathan, she dialed Joe Palumbo's cellular phone. He answered on the first ring. "Palumbo."

"It's Kerry, Joe."

"Recess is over. Robin is back inside. I'm parked in front of the main entrance, which is the only unlocked door. I'll drive her

home and stay with her and the sitter." He paused. "Don'
worry, Momma. I'll take good care of your baby."

"I know you will. Thanks, Joe."

It was time to meet Jonathan. As she hurried out to the corri
dor and rushed through the just-closing elevator door, Kerry kep
thinking about the missing pin. Something about it seemed s
familiar. The two parts. The flower and the bud, like a mothe
and child. A momma and a baby . . . why did that seem to ring
bell? she wondered.

Jonathan was already seated at the table, sipping a club soda
He got up when he saw her coming. His brief, familiar hug wa
reassuring. "You look very tired, young lady," he said. "Or is
very stressed?"

Whenever he talked to her like that, Kerry felt the remembere
warmth of the days when her father was alive and felt a rush o
gratitude that Jonathan in so many ways had been a surrogat
father to her.

"It's been quite a day so far," she said as she sat down. "Di
you hear about Dr. Smith?"

"Grace called me. She heard the news when she was havin
breakfast at ten o'clock. Sounds like more of Weeks' handiworl
We're both heartsick with worry about Robin."

"So am I. But Joe Palumbo, one of our investigators, is outsid
her school. He'll stay with her till I get home."

The waiter was at the table. "Let's order," Kerry suggeste
"and then I'll fill you in."

They both decided on onion soup, which arrived almost imm
diately. While they were eating, she told him about the Feder
Express package with all the jewelry and the letter from D
Smith.

"You make me ashamed that I tried to dissuade you from you
investigation, Kerry," Jonathan said quietly. "I'll do my best, b
if the governor decides Green's nomination is in jeopardy,
would be like him to take it out on you."

"Well, at least there's hope," Kerry said. "And we can tha

Grace for the tip she gave the FBI." She told him what she had learned about Jason Arnott. "I can see where Frank Green is already planning to defuse negative publicity about Skip Reardon being unfairly prosecuted. He's dying to announce that the cat burglar who murdered Congressman Peale's mother was captured because of a tip from the wife of Senator Hoover. You're going to come out of this as his best friend, and who can blame him? God knows you're probably the most respected politician in New Jersey."

Jonathan smiled. "We can always stretch the truth and say that Grace consulted Green first and he urged her to make the call." Then the smile vanished. "Kerry, how does Arnott's possible guilt in the Reardon case affect Robin? Is there a possibility that Arnott is the one who took that picture of her and sent it to you?"

"No way. Robin's own father passed along the warning and in essence admitted that Jimmy Weeks had that picture taken."

"What's the next step?"

"Probably that Frank Green and I will bring Deidre Reardon up to the Catskills first thing tomorrow morning to positively identify that miniature frame. Arnott should be being cuffed right about now. They'll keep him in the local jail, at least for the present. Then, once they start connecting the stolen goods to specific burglaries, they'll begin arraigning him in different locations. My guess is they're itching to try him first for the murder of Congressman Peale's mother. And, of course, if he was responsible for Suzanne Reardon's death, we'll want to try him here."

"Suppose he won't talk?"

"We're sending flyers to all the jewelers in New Jersey, naturally concentrating on Bergen County since both Weeks and Arnott live here. My guess is that one of those jewelers will recognize the more contemporary jewelry and tie it to Weeks, and that the antique bracelet will turn out to be from Arnott. When it was found on Suzanne's arm it obviously had a new clasp, and the bracelet is so unusual some jeweler might remember it. The more we can find to use in confronting Arnott, the easier it should be to make him try to strike a deal."

"Then you expect to leave early in the morning for the Cats-kills?"

"Yes. I'm certainly not going to leave Robin alone in the house in the morning again, but if it turns out that Frank wants to be on the road very early, I'll see if the sitter will stay over."

"I have a better idea. Let Robin stay with us tonight. I'll drop her off at school in the morning, or, if you want, you can have that Palumbo man pick her up. Our house has state-of-the-art security. You know that. I'll be there, of course, and I don't know whether you realize that even Grace has a gun in her night table drawer. I taught her to use it years ago. Besides, I really think it would be good for Grace to have Robin visit. She's been rather down lately, and Robin is such fun to have around."

Kerry smiled. "Yes, she is." She thought for a moment. "Jonathan, that really could work. I really should get some work in on another case I'll be trying, and then I want to go through the Reardon file with a fine-toothed comb to see if there's anything more I can pick up to use when we question Arnott. I'll call Robin when I know she's home from school and tell her the plan. She'll be delighted. She's crazy about you and Grace, and she loves the pink guest room."

"It used to be yours, remember?"

"Sure. How could I forget? That's back when I was telling Grace's cousin, the landscaper, that he was a crook."

92

The extended recess over, U.S. Attorney Royce returned to court for the afternoon trial session of the United States versus James Forrest Weeks. He went secure in the knowledge that behind her timid, unassuming facade, Martha Luce had the memory of a personal computer. The damning evidence that would finally nail Jimmy Weeks was spilling from her as she responded to the gentle prodding of two of Royce's assistants.

Luce's nephew/attorney, Royce admitted to himself, had possibilities. He insisted that before Martha began singing, the bargain she was striking had to be signed and witnessed. In exchange for her honest and forthright cooperation, which she would not later rescind, any possible federal or other criminal or civil charges would not be pressed against her either now or in the future.

Martha Luce's evidence would come later, however. The prosecution case was unfolding in a straightforward way. Today's witness was a restaurateur who in exchange for having his lease renewed admitted to paying a five-thousand-dollar-a-month cash bonus to Jimmy's collector.

When it was the defense's turn to cross-examine, Royce was kept busy jumping to his feet with objections as Bob Kinellen jabbed at the witness, catching him in small errors, forcing him to admit that he had never actually seen Weeks touch the money, that he really couldn't be sure that the collector hadn't been working on his own. Kinellen is good, Royce thought, too bad he's wasting his talent on this scum.

Royce could not know that Robert Kinellen was sharing that same thought even as he grandstanded to a receptive jury.

93

Jason Arnott knew there was something terribly wrong the minute he walked in the door of his Catskill home and realized that Maddie was not there.

If Maddie's not here and she didn't leave a note, then something is happening. It's all over, he thought. How long before they would close in on him? Soon, he was sure.

Suddenly he was hungry. He rushed to the refrigerator and pulled out the smoked salmon he had asked Maddie to pick up. Then he reached for the capers and cream cheese and the package of toast points. A bottle of Pouilly-Fuissé was chilling.

He prepared a plate of salmon and poured a glass of wine. Carrying them with him, he began to walk through the house. A kind of final tour, he thought, as he assessed the riches around him. The tapestry in the dining room—exquisite. The Aubusson in the living room—a privilege to walk on such beauty. The Chaim Gross bronze sculpture of a slender figure holding a small child in the palm of her hand. Gross had loved the mother-and-child theme. Arnott remembered that Gross's mother and sister had died in the Holocaust.

He would need a lawyer, of course. A good lawyer. But who? A smile made his lips twitch. He knew just the one: Geoffrey Dorso, who for ten years had so relentlessly worked for Skip Reardon. Dorso had quite a reputation and might be willing to take on a new client, especially one who could give him evidence that would help him spring poor Reardon.

The front doorbell rang. He ignored it. It rang again, then continued persistently. Arnott chewed the last toast point, relishing the delicate flavor of the salmon, the pungent bite of the capers.

The back doorbell was chiming now. Surrounded, he thought. Ah, well. He had known it would happen someday. If he had only obeyed his instincts last week and left the country. Jason sipped the last of the wine, decided another glass would be welcome and went back to the kitchen. There were faces at all the windows now, faces with the aggressive, self-satisfied look of men who have the right to exercise might.

Arnott nodded to them and held up the glass in a mocking toast. As he sipped, he walked to the back door, opened it, then stood aside as they rushed in. "FBI, Mr. Arnott," they shouted. "We have a warrant to search your home."

"Gentlemen, gentlemen," he murmured, "I beg you to be careful. There are many beautiful, even priceless objects here. You may not be used to them, but please respect them. Are your feet muddy?"

94

Kerry called Robin at three-thirty. She and Alison were at the computer, Robin told her, playing one of the games Uncle Jonathan and Aunt Grace had given her. Kerry told her the plan: "I have to work late tonight and be on the way by seven tomorrow. Jonathan and Grace really would like to have you stay with them, and I'd feel good knowing you're there."

"Why was Mr. Palumbo parked outside our school and why did he drive me home and why is he parked outside now? Is it because I'm in really big danger?"

Kerry tried to sound matter-of-fact. "Hate to disappoint you, but it's just a precaution, Rob. The case is really coming to a head."

"Cool. I like Mr. Palumbo, and, okay, I'll stay with Aunt Grace and Uncle Jonathan. I like them too. But what about you? Will Mr. Palumbo stay in front of the house for you?"

"I won't be home till late, and when I get there, the local cops will drive by every fifteen minutes or so. That's all I need."

"Be careful, Mom." For a moment, Robin's bravado vanished, and she sounded like a frightened little girl.

"You be careful, sweetheart. Do your homework."

"I will. And I'm going to ask Aunt Grace if I can pull out her old photo albums again. I love looking at the old clothes and hairstyles, and if I remember it right, they are arranged in the order they were taken. I thought I might get some ideas, since our next assignment in camera class is to create a family album so that it really tells a story."

"Yeah, there are some great pictures there. I used to love to go through those albums when I was house-sitting," Kerry reminisced. "I used to count to see how many different servants Aunt Grace and Uncle Jonathan grew up with. I still think about them sometimes when I'm pushing the vacuum or folding the wash."

Robin giggled. "Well, hang in there. You may win the lottery someday. Love you, Mom."

At five-thirty, Geoff phoned from his car. "You'll never guess where I am." He didn't wait for an answer. "I was in court this afternoon. Jason Arnott had been trying to reach me. He left a message."

"Jason Arnott!" Kerry exclaimed.

"Yes. When I got back to him a few minutes ago, he said he has to talk to me immediately. He wants me to take his case."

"Would you represent him?"

"I couldn't because he's connected to the Reardon case, and I wouldn't if I could. I told him that, but he still insists on seeing me."

"Geoff! Don't let him tell you anything that would have lawyer-client privilege."

Geoff chuckled. "Thank you, Kerry. I never would have thought of that."

Kerry laughed with him, then explained the arrangement she had made for Robin for the night. "I'm working late right here. When I start home I'll let the Hohokus cops know I'm on the way. It's all set."

"Now be sure you do." His voice became firm. "The more I've thought about you going into Smith's house alone last night, the more I realize what a lousy idea it was. You could have been there when he was shot, just the way Mark Young was gunned down with Haskell."

Geoff signed off after promising to call and report to Kerry after he had seen Arnott.

It was eight o'clock before Kerry had finished the work she needed to do in preparing for an upcoming case. Then once again she reached for the voluminous Reardon file.

She looked closely at the pictures of the death scene. In his letter, Dr. Smith had described entering the house that night and finding Suzanne's body. Kerry closed her eyes at the awful prospect of ever finding Robin like that. Smith said he had deliberately removed the "Let Me Call You Sweetheart" card because he was so sure Skip had murdered Suzanne in a fit of jealous rage, and he didn't want him to escape maximum punishment, to get off with a reduced sentence.

She believed what Smith had written—most people don't lie when they plan to kill themselves, she reasoned. And what Dr. Smith had written also supports Skip Reardon's story. So now, Kerry thought, the murderer is the man who visited that house between the time Skip left at around six-thirty, and when the doctor arrived at around nine o'clock.

Jason Arnott? Jimmy Weeks? Which one had killed Suzanne? she wondered.

At nine-thirty Kerry closed the file. She hadn't come up with any new angles in her plan to question Arnott tomorrow. If I were in his boots, she thought, I'd claim that Suzanne gave me the picture frame that last day because she was afraid a couple of pearls were getting loose and wanted me to have it fixed. Then, when she was found dead, I didn't want to become involved in a murder investigation, so I kept the frame.

A story like that could easily hold up in court because it was entirely plausible. The jewelry, however, was a different story. It all came back to the jewelry. It she could prove that Arnott gave Suzanne those valuable antique pieces, there was no way he could get away with saying it was a gift of pure friendship.

At ten o'clock she left the now-quiet office and went into the parking lot. Realizing suddenly that she was starving, she drove to the Arena diner around the corner and had a hamburger, french fries and coffee.

Substitute a cola for the coffee, and you have Robin's favorite meal, she thought, sighing inwardly. I have to say I miss my baby.

The momma and the baby . . .

The momma and the baby . . .

Why did that singsong phrase keep echoing in her head? she wondered again. Something about it seemed wrong, so terribly wrong. But what was it?

She should have called and said good night to Robin before she left her office, she realized suddenly. Why hadn't she? Kerry ate quickly and got back in the car. It was twenty of eleven, much too late to call. She was just pulling out of the lot when the car phone rang. It was Jonathan.

"Kerry," he said, his voice low and taut, "Robin is in with Grace. She doesn't know I'm calling. She didn't want me to worry you. But after she fell asleep she had a terrible nightmare. I really think you should come over. So much has been going on. She needs you."

"I'll be right there." Kerry switched the turn signal from the right to the left one, pressed her foot on the accelerator and rushed to get to her child.

95

It was a long and miserable ride from New Jersey up the thruway to the Catskills. An icy rain began falling around Middletown, and traffic slowed to a crawl. An overturned tractor trailer that blocked all lanes caused an extra hour to be added to the already torturous trip.

It was a quarter of ten before a tired and hungry Geoff Dorso arrived at the Ellenville police headquarters, where Jason Arnott was being held. A team of FBI agents was waiting to question Arnott as soon as he had had the chance to speak to Geoff.

"You're wasting your time waiting for me," Geoff had told them. "I *can't be his lawyer*. Didn't he tell you that?"

A handcuffed Arnott was escorted into the conference room. Geoff had not seen the man in the nearly eleven years since Suzanne's death. At that time, he had been considered to have a relationship with Suzanne Reardon that combined friendship and business. No one, including Skip, ever suspected that he had any other interest in her.

Now Geoff studied the man closely. Arnott was somewhat more full-faced than Geoff remembered, but he still had that same urbane, world-weary expression. The lines around his eyes suggested deep fatigue, but the turtleneck cashmere shirt still looked fresh under his tweed jacket. Country gentleman, cultivated connoisseur, Geoff thought. Even in these circumstances, he certainly looks the part.

"It's good of you to come, Geoff," Arnott said amiably.

"I really don't know why I'm here," Geoff replied. "As I warned you on the phone, you are now connected to the Reardon case. My client is Skip Reardon. I can tell you that nothing you may say to me is a privileged communication. You've had your Miranda warning. I am not your lawyer. I will repeat anything you say to the prosecutor, because I intend to try to place you in the Reardon house the night of Suzanne's death."

"Oh, I was there. That's why I sent for you. Don't worry. That isn't privileged information. I intend to admit it. I asked you here because I can be a witness for Skip. But in exchange, once he is cleared, I want you to represent me. There won't be any conflict of interest then."

"Look, I'm not going to represent you," Geoff said flatly. "I've spent ten years of my life representing an innocent man who got sent to prison. If you either killed Suzanne, or know who did, and you let Skip rot in that cell all this time, I'd burn in hell before I would raise a finger to help you."

"You see, now that's the kind of determination I want to hire." Arnott sighed. "Very well. Let's try it this way. You're a criminal defense attorney. You know who the good ones are whether they're from New Jersey or elsewhere. You promise to find me the best attorney money can buy, and I'll tell you what I know of Suzanne Reardon's death—which, incidentally, I am not responsible for."

Geoff stared at the man for a moment, considering his offer. "Okay, but before we say another word, I want to have a signed and witnessed statement that any information you give me will not be privileged, and that I can use it in whatever way I see fit to assist Skip Reardon."

"Of course."

The FBI agents had a stenotypist with them. She took down

Arnott's brief statement. When he and a couple of witnesses had signed it, he said, "It is late and it has been a long day. Have you been thinking about what lawyer I should have?"

"Yes," Geoff said. "George Symonds, from Trenton. He's an excellent trial lawyer and a superb negotiator."

"They're going to try to convict me of deliberate murder in the death of Mrs. Peale. I swear it was an accident."

"If there's a way to get it down to felony murder, he'll find it. At least you wouldn't face the death penalty."

"Call him now."

Geoff knew that Symonds lived in Princeton, having once been invited to dinner at his home. He also remembered that the Symonds phone was listed in his wife's name. Using his cellular phone, he made the call in Arnott's presence. It was ten-thirty.

Ten minutes later, Geoff put the phone back. "All right, you've got a top-drawer lawyer. Now talk."

"I had the misfortune to be in the Reardon house at the time Suzanne died," Arnott said, his manner suddenly grave. "Suzanne was so wildly careless of her jewelry, some of which was quite beautiful, that the temptation proved too great. I knew Skip was supposed to be in Pennsylvania on business, and Suzanne had told me she had a date with Jimmy Weeks that evening. You know, odd as it may seem, she really had quite a crush on him."

"Was he in the house while you were there?"

Arnott shook his head. "No, the way they had arranged it, she was to drive to the shopping mall in Pearl River, leave her car there and join him in his limo. As I understood it, she was meeting Jimmy early that night. Obviously I was wrong. There were a few lights on downstairs when I got to Suzanne's house, but that was normal. They came on automatically. From the back I could see that the windows of the master bedroom were wide open. It was child's play to climb up, since the second-story roof of that very modern house slopes almost to the ground."

"What time was that?"

"Precisely eight o'clock. I was on my way to a dinner party in

Cresskill; one of the reasons for my long and successful career is that almost invariably I could furnish an impeccable set of witnesses as to my whereabouts on particular nights."

"You went into the house . . . ," Geoff encouraged.

"Yes. There wasn't a sound, so I assumed everyone was away as planned. I had no idea that Suzanne was still downstairs. I went through the sitting room of the suite, then into the bedroom and over to the night table. I'd only seen the picture frame in passing and had never been sure if it was a genuine Fabergé; obviously I had never wanted to seem too interested in it. I picked it up and was studying it when I heard Suzanne's voice. She was shouting at someone. It was quite disconcerting."

"What was she saying?"

"Something to the effect of 'You gave them to me and they're mine. Now get out. You bore me.' "

You gave them to me and they're mine. The jewelry, Geoff thought. "So that must mean that Jimmy Weeks had changed plans and arranged to pick Suzanne up that night," he reasoned.

"Oh, no. I heard a man shout, 'I have to have them back,' but it was much too refined a voice to have been Jimmy Weeks, and it certainly wasn't poor Skip." Arnott sighed. "At that point, I dropped the frame in my pocket, almost unconsciously. A dreadful copy as it turns out, but Suzanne's picture has been a pleasure, so I have enjoyed having it. She was so entertaining. I do miss her."

"You dropped the frame in your pocket," Geoff prodded.

"And realized suddenly that someone was coming upstairs. I was in the bedroom, you remember, so I jumped into Suzanne's closet and tried to hide behind her long gowns. I hadn't closed the door completely."

"Did you see who came?"

"No, not the face."

"What did that person do?"

"Made straight for the jewelry case, picked among Suzanne's baubles and took out something. Then, apparently not finding

307

everything he wanted, he began going through all the drawers. He seemed rather frantic. After only a few minutes he either found what he was looking for or gave up. Fortunately he didn't go through the closet. I waited as long as I could, and then, knowing that something was terribly wrong, I slipped downstairs. That's when I saw her."

"There was a lot of jewelry in that case. What did Suzanne's killer take?"

"Given what I learned during the trial, I'm sure it must have been the flower and the bud . . . the antique diamond pin, you know. It really was a beautiful piece: one of a kind."

"Did whoever it was that gave Suzanne that pin also give her the antique bracelet?"

"Oh, yes. In fact, I think he was probably trying to find the bracelet as well."

"Do you know who gave Suzanne the bracelet and the pin?"

"Of course I know. Suzanne kept few secrets from me. Now mind you, I can't swear he was the one in the house that night, but it does make sense, doesn't it? So see what I mean? My testimony will help to deliver the real murderer. That's why I should have some consideration, don't you agree?"

"Mr. Arnott, who gave Suzanne the bracelet and pin?"

Arnott's smile was amused. "You won't believe me when I tell you."

96

It took Kerry twenty-five minutes to drive to Old Tappan. Every turn of the wheel seemed interminable. Robin, brave little Robin, who always tried to hide how disappointed she was when Bob sloughed her off, who today had so successfully hidden how scared she was—it had finally become too much for her. I never should have left her with anyone else, Kerry thought. Even Jonathan and Grace.

Even Jonathan and Grace.

Jonathan had sounded so odd on the phone, Kerry thought.

From now on, *I'll* take care of my baby, Kerry vowed.

The momma and the baby—there it was again, that phrase stuck in her mind.

She was entering Old Tappan. Only a few minutes more now.

Robin had seemed so pleased at the prospect of being with Grace and Jonathan and of going through the photo albums.

The photo albums.

Kerry was driving past the last house before reaching Jonathan's. She was turning into the driveway. Almost unconsciously she realized that the sensor lights did not go on.

The photo albums.

The flower-and-bud pin.

She had seen it before.

On Grace.

Years ago, when Kerry first started to work for Jonathan.

Grace used to wear her jewelry then. Many pictures in the album showed her wearing it. Grace had joked when Kerry admired that pin. She'd called it "the momma and the baby."

Suzanne Reardon was wearing Grace's pin in that newspaper picture! That must mean . . . Jonathan? Could he have given it to her?

She remembered now that Grace had told her that she had asked Jonathan to put all her jewelry in the safe-deposit box. "I can't put it on without help, and I can't get it off without help, and I would only worry about it if it were still in the house."

I told Jonathan I was going in to see Dr. Smith, Kerry realized. Last night, after I came home, I told Jonathan I thought Smith would crack, she said to herself. Oh my God! He must have shot Smith.

Kerry stopped the car. She was in front of the handsome limestone residence. She pushed the driver's-side door open and rushed up the steps.

Robin was with a murderer.

Kerry did not hear the faint pealing of the car telephone as she pressed her finger on the doorbell.

97

Geoff tried to phone Kerry at home. When there was no answer, he tried her car phone. Where was she? he wondered frantically. He was dialing Frank Green's office when the guard led Arnott away.

"The prosecutor's office is closed. If this is an emergency, dial . . ."

Geoff swore as he dialed the emergency number. Robin was staying with the Hoovers. Where was Kerry? Finally someone answered the emergency line.

"This is Geoff Dorso. I absolutely must reach Frank Green. It concerns a breaking murder case. Give me his home number."

"I can tell you he's not there. He was called out because of a murder in Oradell, sir."

"Can you get through to him?"

"Yes. Hold on."

It was a full three minutes before Green got on the line. "Geoff, I'm in the middle of something. This had better be important."

"It is. Very important. It has to do with the Reardon case. Frank, Robin Kinellen is staying at Jonathan Hoover's home tonight."

"Kerry told me that."

"Frank, I've just learned that Jonathan Hoover gave that antique jewelry to Suzanne Reardon. He'd been having an affair with her. I think he's our killer, and Robin is with him."

There was a long pause. Then in an unemotional voice Frank Green said, "I'm in the home of an old man who specialized in repairing antique jewelry. He was murdered early this evening. There's no evidence of a robbery, but his son tells me his Rolodex with the names of his customers is missing. I'll get the local cops over to Hoover's place fast."

98

Jonathan opened the door for Kerry. The house was dimly lit and very quiet. "She's settled down," he said. "It's all right."

Kerry's fists were hidden in the pockets of her coat, clenched in fear and anger. Still she managed to smile. "Oh, Jonathan, this is such an imposition for you and Grace. I should have known Robin would be frightened. Where is she?"

"Back in her room now. Fast asleep."

Am I crazy? Kerry wondered as she followed Jonathan upstairs. Did my imagination go hog wild? He seems so normal.

They came to the door of the guest bedroom, the pink room as Robin called it, because of the soft pink walls and draperies and quilt.

Kerry pushed the door open. In the glow provided by a small night-light, she could see Robin on her side in her usual fetal position, her long brown hair scattered on the pillow. In two strides Kerry was beside the bed.

Robin's cheek was cupped in her palm. She was breathing evenly.

Kerry looked up at Jonathan. He was at the foot of the bed, staring at her. "She was so upset. After you got here, you decided to take her home," he said. "See, her bag with her school clothes and books is packed and ready. I'll carry it for you."

"Jonathan, there was no nightmare. She didn't wake up, did she?" Kerry said, her voice even.

"No," he said indifferently. "And it would be easier for her if she didn't wake up now."

In the dim glow of the night-light, Kerry saw that he was holding a gun.

"Jonathan, what are you doing? Where's Grace?"

"Grace is fast asleep, Kerry. I felt it was better that way. Sometimes I can tell that one of her more powerful sedatives is necessary to help ease the pain. I dissolve it in the hot cocoa I bring her in bed every night."

"Jonathan, what do you want?"

"I want to keep on living just as we're living now. I want to be president of the senate and friend of the governor. I want to spend my remaining years with my wife, whom I really do love, still. Sometimes men stray, Kerry. They do very foolish things. They let young, beautiful women flatter them. Perhaps I was susceptible because of Grace's problem. I knew it was foolish of me; I knew it was a mistake. Then all I wanted to do was to take back the jewelry I had so stupidly given that vulgar Reardon girl, but she wouldn't part with it."

He waved the revolver. "Either wake up Robin or pick her up. There isn't any more time."

"Jonathan, what are you going to do?"

"Only what I have to do, and then only with great regret. Kerry, Kerry, why did you feel you had to tilt at windmills? What did it matter that Reardon was in prison? What did it matter that Suzanne's father claimed as his gift the bracelet that could have so desperately harmed me? Those things were meant to be. I was supposed to continue to serve the state I love, and to live with the wife I love. It was sufficient penance to know that Grace had so easily spotted my betrayal."

Jonathan smiled. "She is quite marvelous. She showed me that picture and said, 'Doesn't that remind you of my flower-and-bud pin? It makes me want to wear it again. Please get it out of the safe-deposit box, dear.' She knew, and I knew that she knew, Kerry. And suddenly from being a middle-aged romantic fool . . . I felt soiled."

"And you killed Suzanne."

"But only because she not only refused to return my wife's gems but had the gall to tell me she had an interesting new boyfriend, Jimmy Weeks. My God, the man's a thug. A mobster. Kerry, either wake up Robin or carry her as she sleeps."

"Mom," Robin was stirring. Her eyes opened. She sat up. "Mom." She smiled. "Why are you here?"

"Get out of bed, Rob. We're leaving now." He's going to kill us, Kerry thought. He's going to say that Robin had a nightmare and I came to get her and drove off with her.

She put her arm around Robin. Sensing something was wrong, Robin shrank against her. "Mom?"

"It's all right."

"Uncle Jonathan?" Robin had seen the gun.

"Don't say anything else, Robin," Kerry said quietly. What can I do? she thought. He's crazy. He's out of control. If only Geoff hadn't gone to see Jason Arnott. Geoff would have helped. Somehow, Geoff would have helped.

As they were going down the stairs, Jonathan said quietly, "Give me your car keys, Kerry. I'll follow you out, and then you and Robin will get in the trunk."

Oh God, Kerry thought. He'll kill us and drive us somewhere and leave the car and it will look like a mob killing. It will be blamed on Weeks.

Jonathan spoke again as they crossed the foyer: "I am truly sorry, Robin. Now open the door slowly, Kerry."

Kerry bent down to kiss Robin. "Rob, when I spin around, you run," she whispered. "Run next door and keep screaming."

"The door, Kerry," he prodded.

Slowly she opened it. He had turned off the porch lights so that the only illumination was the faint glow thrown off by the torchère at the end of the driveway. "My key is in my pocket," she said. She turned slowly, then screamed, "Run, Robin!"

At the same moment she threw herself across the foyer at Jonathan. She heard the gun go off as she hurtled toward him, then felt a burning pain in the side of her head, followed immediately by waves of dizziness. The marble floor of the foyer rushed up to greet her. Around her she was aware of a cacophony of sound: Another gunshot. Robin screaming for help, her voice fading into the distance. Sirens approaching.

Then suddenly only the sirens, and Grace's broken cry, "I'm sorry, Jonathan. I'm sorry. I couldn't let you do this," she said. "Not this. Not to Kerry and Robin."

Kerry managed to pull herself up and press her hand against the side of her head. Blood was trickling down her face, but the dizziness was receding. As she looked up, she saw Grace slide from her wheelchair onto the floor, drop the pistol from her swollen fingers and gather her husband's body in her arms.

99

The courtroom was packed for the swearing-in ceremony of Assistant Prosecutor Kerry McGrath to the judiciary. The festive hum of voices subsided into silence when the door from the chambers opened and a stately procession of black-robed judges marched in to welcome a new colleague to their midst.

Kerry quietly walked from the side of the chamber and took her place to the right of the bench as the judges went to the chairs reserved for them in front of the guests.

She looked out at the assembly. Her mother and Sam had flown in for the ceremony. They were sitting with Robin, who was ramrod straight on the edge of her seat, her eyes wide with excitement. There was barely a trace of the lacerations that had brought them to that fateful meeting with Dr. Smith.

Geoff was in the next row with his mother and father. Kerry thought of how he had rushed down in the FBI helicopter to come to her in the hospital, how he had been the one to comfort a hysterical Robin and then bring her home to his family when

317

the doctor insisted Kerry stay overnight. Now she blinked back tears at what she saw in his face as he smiled at her.

Margaret, old friend, best friend, was there, fulfilling her vow to be part of this day. Kerry thought of Jonathan and Grace. They had planned to be present too.

Grace had sent a note.

I am going home to South Carolina and will live with my sister. I blame myself for everything that happened. I knew Jonathan was involved with that woman. I also knew it wouldn't last. If only I had ignored that picture in which she was wearing my pin, none of this would have happened. I didn't care about the jewelry. That was my way of warning Jonathan to give her up. I didn't want his career ruined by scandal. Please forgive me and forgive Jonathan if you can.

Can I? Kerry wondered. Grace saved my life, but Jonathan would have killed Robin and me to save himself. Grace knew Jonathan had been involved with Suzanne and might even have been her murderer, yet she let Skip Reardon rot in prison all those years.

Skip, his mother and Beth were somewhere in the crowd. Skip and Beth were getting married next week; Geoff would be best man.

It was customary for a few close friends or associates to make brief remarks before the swearing-in. Frank Green went first. "Searching my memory, I cannot imagine any person—man or woman—who is more suited to assume this high position than Kerry McGrath. Her sense of justice led her to request me to reopen a murder case. Together we faced the appalling fact that a vengeful father had condemned his daughter's husband to prison, while the real killer was enjoying freedom. We . . ."

That's my boy, Kerry thought. Lemonade from lemons. But in the end, Frank had stood by her. He had personally met with the governor and urged that her name be placed before the senate for confirmation.

Frank had been the one to clear up the Jimmy Weeks connection to Suzanne Reardon. One of his sources, a small-time hood who had been a gofer for Jimmy, supplied the answer. Suzanne indeed had been involved with Jimmy, and he had given her jewelry. He had also sent the roses to her that night and was supposed to meet her for dinner. When she didn't show up, he had become furious and in drunken anger had even said he would kill her. Since Weeks was not generally given to idle threats, a couple of his people thought he really had been the murderer. He was always afraid that if his connection to her came out, her death would be pinned on him.

Now the assignment judge, Robert McDonough, was speaking, talking about how when Kerry came into the courtroom for the first time eleven years ago as a brand-new assistant prosecutor, she had looked so young that he thought she was a college kid on a summer job.

I was a brand-new bride too, Kerry thought wryly. Bob was an assistant prosecutor then. I only hope he has the brains to stay away from Jimmy Weeks and his ilk from now on, she mused. Weeks had been convicted on all counts. Now he was facing another trial for tampering with a juror. He had tried to blame that on Bob but hadn't been able to make it stick. But Bob had narrowly missed being indicted himself. And Weeks wouldn't get anywhere if he complained about the juror whose father had been incarcerated. He knew that during the trial and could have asked then that she be replaced by an alternate. Maybe all this would scare Bob before it was too late. She hoped so.

Judge McDonough was smiling at her. "Well, Kerry, I think it's time," he said.

Robin came forward, carrying the heavy Bible. Margaret rose and walked behind her, the black robe over her arm, waiting to present it to Kerry after the oath. Kerry raised her right hand, placed her left hand on the Bible and began to repeat after Judge McDonough: "I, Kerry McGrath, do solemnly swear . . ."